Ann Arbor South '96

A Novel Based on True Events

Skot Harris

PublishAmerica
Baltimore

First printing

At the specific preference of the author, PublishAmerica allowed this work to remain exactly as the author intended, verbatim, without editorial input.

ISBN: 1-4241-1269-9
PUBLISHED BY PUBLISHAMERICA, LLLP
www.publishamerica.com
Baltimore

Printed in the United States of America

Author's Note

This book is a work of fiction. Although based in truth, names, characters, places, and events have been altered, changed, or are used fictitiously. Any resemblance to actual events, locations, or persons, living or dead, is entirely coincidental.

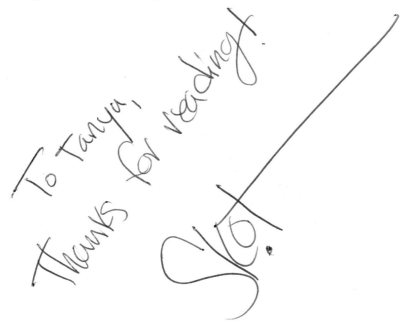

For Monica and Nikki,
who make up 2/3 of my soul.

Acknowledgments

The following people forced me to be fearless in revisiting the past and writing about its demons no matter how hard my heart refused: Kate "Cher" Hicks, Amanda Griffith, Patti LaJoye, Trish Klukowski, Cassie Bewley, Amy Kaherl, Mary Forrest, and Radhika "Shags" Anand. I could not ask to be surrounded by a better group of people.

Thanks to my father who inspired me to quit the Detroit Zoo (the only job that ever made me cry) and finish this book. He told me, "No job is ever worth your tears," and he was right.

Words will never be able to express enough gratitude to my mother…or enough love.

A very special and loving thanks to Jared Kovach for the midnight backrubs and last-minute ideas, but most of all for his never-ending patience and love.

Nikki Murray showed me the power of laughter and tears. Thank you for your honesty and understanding. So much of this book exists because of you.

And a final thank you to Monica Hughes, who lovingly taught me to appreciate yellow butterflies and the importance of wearing sunscreen.

*"The way I see it, if you want the rainbow
you gotta put up with the rain."*

Dolly Parton

Chapter One

"Justin Drake is such an asshole!" Kate Crawford screamed as her white knuckles gripped the steering wheel. The swanky blue S-10 pick-up truck ahead of her, with ultra-arrogant Justin Drake behind the wheel, braked suddenly and almost smashed into the front end of Kate's Grand Am. With only a four-cylinder engine in the two-door coupe, Kate still road the Pontiac hard and pushed it to its limits.

She rolled the window down and extended her pretty French-manicured middle finger into the crisp summer air. It was the last week of August and the Michigan sun still made an early appearance by seven as she drove to school with her best friend, Eric Anderson. The wind blew through her long, blonde hair, colored to perfection with just a hint of bronze lowlights. She never had gas money for her car, but her $110 salon bill was always paid in full.

When Kate slammed her high-heeled boot onto the gas pedal, the Grand Am jerked forward, nearly smashing the S-10's back fender. The square green air freshener, which read MY OTHER RIDE IS YOUR MOTHER, twirled on its elastic string looped around the rearview mirror. It had lost its spicy scent years ago but Kate couldn't bring herself to take it down. She blared on the horn and Justin Drake waved a hand out his window, taunting her, *daring* her to hit him.

"Don't even *think* about it!" Eric Anderson said. His fingers dug into the car's gray upholstery, trying to brace himself for possible impact.

"He cut me off!"

"Kate!"

"Come on! How great would it be if I just ran him off the road and he rolled that piece of shit truck into the ditch?"

Kate's enthusiasm made Eric nervous but he certainly wasn't surprised by it. A week earlier they had ran into Justin downtown at Avery's Coney Island and she had catapulted two chilidogs into the bed of Justin's truck from across the parking lot. Justin had been relentlessly harassing Eric, as he always did, but remained a considerable distance away. They were in no real threat of attack from Justin and his beefy cohorts. Still, Kate chucked the chili across the lot for the sheer enjoyment of seeing it splat against Justin's prized pickup.

"Slow down! I don't want to spend the first day of our senior year *dead*!" Eric snapped.

"I can't believe you!" Kate said, honking the horn once more. "He's a raging prick to you every day of your life and you want me to spare him? You're getting soft, Eric."

Eric rolled his eyes, tried not to smile, and stared out the window. As Kate curved the car around State Street, their school, Ann Arbor South, appeared a few miles in the distance. Eric's heart sank the second he saw it.

"Another year, huh?" he mumbled.

Kate saw the fear on Eric's face and she eased up on the gas. The car slowed down and Justin Drake's truck barreled away. It ate her alive to watch him win the drag race, but Kate needed to pay attention to her friend more than she needed a street racing victory. Besides, there was always tomorrow.

"Calm you heart," she said softly, always knowing the right tone to use. "It's our last year. Maybe it'll be better."

Eric looked at her, his eyes heavy with dread. "Yeah, *better*," he mocked. "With gym class first period—"

"Don't be a dick to me, mister," Kate warned, only half-joking.

"Sorry," Eric said and returned his attention to the passenger side window. Glancing through it, he caught his reflection in the side-view mirror. He had his brown hair trimmed a little before the start of school. It was still too long and fell into his eyes every now and then, but he wasn't brave enough to sport the military crew cut all the jocks were wearing. It worked better on them. Plus, it was easier to hide behind long hair. It covered his thick eyebrows and big blue eyes and long dark lashes. If anyone saw his eyes, actually *saw* them, they might see the perpetual fear.

"Don't stress already, Eric," Kate said. She drove with her left knee to free up her hands to apply a fresh coat of shimmering dark pink gloss to her full lips.

"It's hard not to stress when everyone in that school's waiting to beat up the fag," Eric said.

"You're just *shitting* sunshine today!" Kate laughed but saw it wasn't shared. She dropped the smile and lovingly squeezed Eric's leg. "I know it's hard for you. It always has been and it probably always will be."

"Thanks a lot."

"But I'm right here with you," she added softly. Her driving relaxed and was more cautious. "I'll always be here, beating the shit out of everyone for you."

Eric softened, looked back to the driver, and said, "You're five feet tall. Who're you going to beat up?" He laughed at himself.

Over the years, Eric had witnessed the vicious fury in Kate's tiny fists countless times. Usually in defense of Eric, Kate had attacked more than one homophobic peer in her day and spent enough time in after-school detention to prove it. Whether she was torching Heather Powell's hair for calling Eric a *flamer* or scratching a sample of Brad Thompson's skin under her fingernails for tripping Eric in the hall, Kate always had Eric's back. Her love for him ran deep, as his did for her.

"You've seen me in action, sweetie," Kate reminded. She turned the

Grand Am onto Owen Road. The street was the main drag in town and led to the senior parking lot, the closest area to the school available to students. Having already picked up her parking pass a few days earlier, she was ready to stake her claim on a good spot. As they began their final year of high school, Kate and Eric were excited to be upperclassmen, above all other grades. Their bottom-level status within their own class remained unchanged, but there was a small triumph in reaching senior year intact.

As Kate sharked her way through the already packed parking area, Eric was sick to his stomach watching his classmates get out of their cars. Justin Drake was already parked and hanging on his truck's tailgate with his beefy buddies Chris Golden and Jeremy Flint. The lot was crawling with them: footballers Matt Murphy with his blue Trans-Am and Wes Palmer with his fiery red Mustang had rolled in while basketball star Ryan Roberts and fellow athlete Chad Kelly crawled out of the backseat of David Johnson's yellow Camaro.

"Breathe, baby," Kate said to Eric. "Remember to breathe. I don't want to do CPR on your ass this early in the morning. It'll smear my make-up."

Eric rolled his eyes again and said, "I'll be fine." It was a lie and he took a huge breath to calm his racing heart. "I always am." Another lie.

Kate drove past Justin Drake and his cronies and parked in one of the last spots, only a few cars away from Justin's S-10. "Great, I was hoping we'd have to park by this asshole," she groaned and turned the engine off. She dropped her keys into her oversized purse, which held the necessities for her everyday living inside, and unlocked the car doors. She paused and looked at Eric, who was frozen in the passenger seat. "You'll be okay," she promised.

Eric slowly turned his head to look at her. His eyes were watery and the tears embarrassed him. "It hasn't even started yet," he said, laughing nervously. He pulled the visor down and looked into the mirror. His face was tanned from so much time at the beach, which he liked since it dried out the few pimples plaguing his face and made them retreat at least for a few weeks. But mostly what he saw, other than a pair of thick lips and bushy eyebrows, was a boy terrified to step out of the car. He wiped his eyes dry and flipped the visor closed.

"We can hang out here until they go inside," Kate offered and gave Eric's shoulder a comforting pinch.

"No. We have to do it sooner or later to get it over with," Eric said, grabbing his book bag from the backseat. He touched the door handle and took another look into the parking lot. Justin Drake and his gang of friends were only three cars away, laughing loudly. Eric looked at Justin, trying not to stare but found it hard not to, as always. The worst part about hating him was loving to look at him.

Because Justin Drake was certainly not unattractive. He was beefy and beautiful, with tight muscles curving through the creases of his clothes. Short black hair—messy and standing on end—and a square jaw framed his dark eyes, thick brows and a strong, straight nose. Justin's crooked mouth usually cracked a smartass grin or troublesome smirk, but when it gave way to an actual smile of happiness, his bright white teeth brought his face to life and he ruled the world. And he knew it. His deep, dashing good looks gave him an unofficial license to be barbarically brutal to anyone outside his admired inner circle, unaffectionately known as The Innards, a name christened to the popular kids by those less fortunate.

But after so many years, even those in the Innards group embraced the title bestowed upon them by the lower life forms, the less-liked students at the bottom of the high school hierarchy. They were in turn known as The Outties, which included a wide variety of students, from the computer and chemistry geeks to the Goth kids over to the overeaters and stopping at the socially blacklisted gay kids, including Eric Anderson.

Eric stood alone on that list, having been branded the class queer since sixth grade, when four of the city's elementary schools merged into one building and growing libidos and cliques overtook everyone's life. It was survival of the fittest, a time to stake one's claim on the social hierarchy. Eric didn't have an overgrown testosterone level like the excessively macho Justin Drake or Justin's athletic buddies so Eric plummeted to the bottom of the popularity ladder, only to become the daily punching bag for the powerhouses above him.

It wasn't all bad, though. At the bottom of the ladder he found his best friend Kate Crawford, the beautiful girl who perfected the art of using cleavage to her advantage. She always picked Eric up, dusted him off, and held his hand through every abusive round. Kate had all the right qualifications to be an Innard. Pretty, confident, and curvaceous in all the right places with a great academic record to get into any college sorority. She was popular in the sense that her big breasts and bitchiness kept her in the gossip columns and on everyone's shit lists, but Kate Crawford was not an Innard. The foul mouth and tendency to pick fistfights and throw desk chairs across the room if someone looked at her cross-eyed, kept her an outcast. She fought against stupidity in her peers and encouraged individuality, but in a school where beauty and popularity ruled the throne, Kate's way of thinking was not embraced. So she screamed louder and fought harder.

In the parking lot, Eric forced himself to turn his head away from the tailgating Justin and company. His hand shook on the car's door handle. "Nice parking spot, Kate," he said. His nervous laughter returned. "Could you *be* any closer to them?"

"Relax. I got this," Kate said and swung her door open. Eric quickly followed, hoping to go undetected by the bloodthirsty jock squad.

No such luck. The instant the Grand Am doors slammed shut, Justin and the others were on Eric like flies on shit.

"Anderson!" Justin cheered. "What's up, fag?!"

Eric ignored him and circled around the back end of Kate's car. "Let's go," he told her.

The urgency in Eric's voice was desperate, but Kate wasn't alarmed. She stepped in front of him and moved toward the S-10 pick-up. Justin hopped off the tailgate and stood tall. His firm chest enlarged with a deep breath and his biceps flexed as he swaggered toward the tiny blonde girl.

"Hey, baby," Justin said. His deep voice dripped with a smooth arrogance that somehow worked for him.

"You're an asshole," Kate said matter-of-factly and flipped a chunk of her shiny hair over her shoulder.

Justin rolled his eyes. "So it's going to be like that *again* this year?"

he said, uninterested. His eyes focused on the low neckline of her shirt more than her pretty round face.

"It wouldn't have to be if you weren't such a prick," Kate snapped.

Justin and his back-up buddies enjoyed a good laugh at her expense. Instinctively, Kate's hands curled into small pulse-pounding fists. Before she could bury them deep into Justin's eye sockets, Nick Murphy approached.

"Hi guys!" Nick said cheerfully but his attention was on Kate's shaking hands.

Eric looked to him. "Hi, Nick," he said. "She's at it again."

Seeing Nick put Eric at ease. Nick was Eric and Kate's best friend, the third member of their Musketeer trio but an unlikely addition. Butch and a car lover, Nick was overly quiet, compared to Kate's boisterous behavior and the foul mouth she shared with Eric. Nick was the voice of reason and he did an excellent job of keeping them controlled, especially Kate.

Dressed in his signature Polo shirt and loose jeans, Nick Murphy stood an inch taller than Eric and was huskier, but not chubby. Nick's calm blue eyes watched every inch of his surroundings with close attention but his small mouth never commented on them. Nick rarely involved himself in anyone's business. He never gossiped unless asked a direct question and he never badmouthed anyone unless someone said something first. Only in rare moments did Nick get involved and only for a very good reason. Usually, the reason was Eric.

Nick went to Kate's fierce hands and held them in his own. He pulled her away from Justin and the others. The catcalls and howls from the pick-up truck continued as Nick ushered Kate and Eric away from an impending fight.

"You know you better behave yourself. Spear is out for your blood this year," Nick reminded Kate. "So let it go."

William Spear was Ann Arbor South's seasoned principal, having been with the school for nearly 40 years. He was a hard man, sixty-five, with aged skin sagging in all the wrong places and a thin comb-over unsuccessfully hiding a shiny baldhead. It seemed that in the three short years since Kate Crawford had been in the halls of his school, Spear aged an additional ten years. His hair went from a peppery black and gray to pure white in the course of one semester in 1994, the year Kate set Heather Powell's ponytail on fire with a Biology Bunsen burner. Even a threat of expulsion didn't faze Kate. She did her time in detention and bought Heather a professional haircut. Still, it was an endless struggle for Spear to keep Kate under control. The hardest part of disciplining her was that although she acted up and talked a good game, Kate's superior grades proved she could truly put her money where her mouth was.

To complicate things further, Spear was not receptive to Eric's pleas. The principal listened to Eric's countless complaints over the years of the Innards torture, the brutal verbal and physical abuse he endured every day, but Spear never took the accusations seriously. While Eric was on the bottom of the food chain and an all-right student, the accused Innards were Ann Arbor South's athletic champions, leading the school to yearly victories in football, baseball, and basketball. Spear took the popular route and dismissed Eric's claims, no matter how many tears Eric shed or bruises he showed, as exaggerated. Eric's voice remained silenced.

"Spear can kiss my ass," Kate snapped and readjusted her purse strap. She looked at Eric and saw pure misery on his face. He was aching to escape. She smiled to comfort him. "But you're right, Nick," she added. "Let's get the hell out of here."

Together, they turned their backs on Justin Drake and headed for the row of six glass doors, the main entrance of Ann Arbor South.

***

Once inside the front foyer of the building, Eric looked to his right and dramatically groaned at the sight of the double wooden doors leading to the gymnasium. Nick patted him on the back, trying to boost Eric's confidence.

"C'mon, man, think happy thoughts about gym class," Nick said and looked at Kate.

"Yeah, like pulling a blowtorch from your bag and boiling their buggy eyeballs out!" Kate offered with an ear-to-ear grin.

Eric rolled his eyes and laughed loudly. He took the lead of the threesome and led the way passed the glass-walled cafeteria, the prized sports trophy cases, and a long hall, which led out to the baseball diamond and football field.

"Ugh! There's that damn drinking fountain!" Kate snapped on their way toward the Art hallway.

"Stop!" Nick quickly snapped back. "I don't want to hear how you almost got a bad case of Tetanus from the drinking fountain freshman year. That never happened."

"It could have. You don't know!" Kate protested. "Have you *seen* the rust in that water?"

"Can we just get to our lockers so I can ditch you two?" Eric teased.

Squeezing through the hall, crowded with so many students, Eric and his friends turned down the Art hall after passing Principal Spear's office and the Math and Science wing. The hallway was lined with lockers freshly painted bright red and smoky gray, Ann Arbor South's school colors.

Eric and his friends separated to organize their lockers. On the way to his storage space, Eric spotted Justin Drake making his way toward him. Justin's face was cute and overly smug as usual and he strutted with a perfected arrogance fitting for such a cocky young man. When he reached Eric, Justin had a smile wide, proud, and ready to torment.

"What's up, *Erica*?" Justin said. Eric tried to bypass him, but Justin's stance blocked his locker, preventing Eric from getting inside.

Eric folded his arms across his chest and waited for Justin's next move. The longer Eric stood there, faking boredom, the more restless Justin became. It was a typical reaction. Ignoring the Innards infuriated them, so Eric refused to let them see him sweat.

"Move me, fag!" Justin's chuckling turned to growling. "COME ON!"

Eric sidestepped Justin to leave, but Justin matched him step for step in a wicked dance.

"MOVE!" Eric finally screamed and immediately regretted it.

Justin's face lit up like the headlights on a deer hunter's pick-up truck. Eric had fed the beast and the worst was yet to come. Justin's rock-solid arm and fist cocked into position. Reflexively, Eric turned his head to the right since punches to his left cheek didn't hurt as much.

"Justin, get the hell out of here!" a sweet but fierce familiar voice called into the tense air. Eric opened his tightly clenched eyes and looked past Justin. It was Kate to the rescue, *again*.

Justin looked over his broad shoulders and rolled his eyes. "Why're you always around?" he moaned. "You sure know how to kill a guy's good time."

"I'm so sorry to hear that," Kate said and shoved Justin hard with both of her tiny hands to his chest. He was too smug to budge and refused to be moved. Kate walked around him and wrapped her arm around Eric. As she escorted him away, Kate glanced back to Justin and said, "I'm not in the mood for your shit this year. Lay off."

Proudly, Justin replied, "The best is yet to come, baby!"

The loud ring of the school bell echoed through the hallways, signaling two minutes before the start of first period. Nick Murphy rejoined his friends on their way out of the Art hall at the sound of the bell.

Eric groaned and said, "Here I go."

"Good luck in gym, honey," Kate said as carefully as she could.

"Yeah, hang in there, man," was all Nick could say.

Kate quickly added, "And remember, although it's a dirty card to play, kick those bastards in the balls and run like hell if you have to."

Eric stared at her, fighting off laughter as best he could, but his teeth peeked through his lips and gave way to a wide smile. He kissed Kate's cheek, smiled at Nick, and playfully said, "I hate you both."

Eric took a deep breath and headed for the gymnasium.

Chapter Two

The instant Eric walked into the gymnasium, he smelled it, the familiar suffocating stench of testosterone-driven anger and flexing muscles, ready to dribble a ball or beat some ass. It choked Eric's throat as he slowly crept in through the back door. The gym was enormous, with two full basketball courts, a large stage to house the band and choir concerts and graduation ceremony. Lining the walls around the entire room were folded wooden bleachers that popped out for the same events and games. On either side of the room were separate entrances for the boys' and girls' locker rooms. Ann Arbor South had no co-ed physical education classes and they were scheduled at different times of the day so the boys and girls never interacted while in gym shorts.

Aside from the gagging scent of sweat and wood varnish, the gym looked the same as the previous year. Eric's eyes, always aware and surveying his surroundings, scanned it for differences. The only obvious change was the members of his class. Junior year he at least had his friend Nick beside him. As Eric stared at the fifteen senior boys, though, he saw no friends. Only enemies. Every enemy he had ever had.

Together.

In one room.

Wrestlers Nate Dover, Jason Frost, and Chad Kelley were there, standing under the basketball hoop, seeing who could jump the highest and finger the net first. Eric noticed their necks had thickened even more over the summer, leaving no visible jaw line. Their earlobes and mouths just blended into thick, muscular tree trunks.

They were all there: Matt Murphy and his crooked nose, having been broke one too many times during rough games of street hockey; David Johnson, who was voted Prettiest Eyes for his blue-green peepers three years in a row; Jeremy Flint, the first boy to sprout hair on his chest two years back and the deep voice and growth spurt suited him well; and Wes Palmer, a dark haired boy almost as unfairly attractive as Justin Drake, with his rippling basketball captain physique and a supremely smug attitude that the others emulated.

The rest of Ann Arbor South's popular athletes were there too, leaning against the wooden bleachers closest to the boys' locker room. Ahead of them, of course, was Justin Drake, spewing his endless supply of dirty jokes and offensive gestures to entertain his friends.

They all grew up over the summer into even more handsome, buff young men, ready to play sports and kick the shit out of something. When their sights locked on Eric, their mouths salivated with hunger.

"Hey, fag!" Wes Palmer cheered.

The others joined in unison, "FAG!"

With a deep breath, Eric took his place against the bleachers with the others and waited for the gym instructor to arrive and begin class. When the final bell rang, Leon Dickson appeared at the locker room door.

"MEN!" he said proudly, his voice bursting with excitement upon seeing most of the same boys he had been coaching in one sport or another for years.

Dickson was an ex-Army drill sergeant and damn proud of it. His nickname—Dick—fit well because he really was a supreme *dick*. In his mid-sixties, short, with thick snow-white hair and blurry green tattoos on both forearms, Dick was hard and his face showed it. His tight, spotty skin stretched across his bones and his piercing blue eyes were not beautiful, but terrifying in their vicious take-no-prisoners stare. He ran his class like he had run his boot camp, pushing the young men to their absolute limits and accepting nothing less.

So when Dick made his way up and down the single-filed line of young men in his early morning class, he nodded approvingly at the Justins, Ryans, Nates, and Jeremys. When his scathing gaze landed on Eric, his proud smile slithered into a cold, vindictive scowl.

"Anderson," Dick said, his voice raspy from too many cigarettes.

"Yes, sir?" Eric groaned.

The boys laughed at Eric's attempt at a deeper voice. Dick gladly laughed with them. Staring at Eric closely, Dick's steely stare never flinched. Eric held his own, as best he could, and stared back, but his eyes occasionally wandered to the floor and back.

"All right, men!" Dick yelled into the chilling silence. "We're starting swimming tomorrow. So bring your suits! You know the drill. I'm not going to baby you about the rules of the class this year. You know what I expect and I know you won't disappoint. So use today as a freebie, play ball, but it's down to business tomorrow."

Without further instruction or any questions, the boys fanned out in the gym, grabbed a basketball, and began a game. Eric didn't move, though. He stayed against the bleachers, where Dick had him cornered.

"Come to my office, Anderson," Dick ordered.

Eric had to nearly run to keep up with Dick's fast pace. Eric followed without a sound into the dark, smelly locker room, around the right hand corner and into Dick's office. The room was small, with a large wooden door opened to a metal desk cluttered with a telephone, papers and empty gym bags. A rickety old chair on wheels and a freestanding first aid cabinet filled the rest of the room. Over the desk was a huge glass window looking out into the locker room. With both sides lined with dented blue-green lockers, wooden benches, and a moldy tiled floor, the room was more like a dungeon. At least, that's how it felt to Eric as it chilled his bones and haunted his dreams.

"Get in here!" Dick barked.

Eric dragged his feet further into Dick's office. Standing at the edge of the desk furthest from Dick and without anything but dread in his voice, Eric said, "What?"

Sitting in the old chair with his feet propped on the desktop, Dick's smile was just a little too proud as he asked, "Ready for another year?"

"I'm beside myself with joy." Eric's deadpan straight face didn't flinch. He folded his arms against his chest, bored.

"Come on, Anderson. I bet you like being around all these sweaty men."

Eric's head cocked to the side and he belted, "What's that supposed to mean?"

Dick laughed heartily and stood to his feet. "You are some chicken shit, huh?" He was beside himself with laughter.

"Excuse me?!" Eric was fuming.

Before Eric could back away or conjure up a smartass punch-to-the-gut remark, Dick jumped to his feet and moved close to get Eric's undivided attention and leaned in until their faces were only inches apart. Eric backed away but his spine hit the doorframe and blocked him in. Dick's breath sizzled with the stale remnants of coffee and Marlboro reds.

"You better grow some stronger balls," Dick suggested, his voice restrained but ready to strike. "If you've got any down there—"

Eric immediately protested. "What the—!"

"There's no escaping my class," Dick said, dominating the conversation. "It's required for graduation so you're going to have to start playing like a man if you want to survive."

"You've *got* to be kidding me."

"I'm just giving you fair warning, Anderson," Dick added. "You know what these men are like. They're going to eat you for breakfast every day for the rest of the year."

"But—!"

Before Eric could protest, Dick gave him one good shove to the chest. The blow knocked Eric out of the doorway and back into the lion's den locker room. Dick slammed the door shut and returned to his desk. Eric spun on his heel, leaving his back to the office.

"It's good to be back," he mumbled.

***

Mark Morgan's English Composition classroom was packed with thirty some beat-up old metal desks. Most of them were filled with students as Eric rushed inside the room prior to second period. There were only a few moments to spare before the bell rang to begin class. Fearing he'd be late, Eric ran from the gym after his unpleasant pep talk with Leon Dickson to make it in time.

The dozens of students stuffed into the hot, tiny room irritated Eric. They were loud and rowdy as he searched to find his friends and sit down. The instructor's desk was at the head of the room near the door and faced the many rows of desks. Morgan sat at the desk, rifling through papers. He was relaxed, in his late-thirties and very tall. He carried his hefty weight well, but his midsection occasionally got away from him and filled out a little more than the rest. A thick head of brown hair that curled at the ends made a zany accent to his inviting, carefree face. He was a school favorite among the students since he was known to turn a blind eye to cheat sheets during tests and accepted bad excuses for missing class. Ten years earlier, he had married one of his ex-students, a girl he had started dating while she was still an Ann Arbor South senior. They married a year after she graduated. He used this as a way to relate to his students and although married, he was still a flirt with the girls.

Eric passed Morgan at the desk, smiled at him, and scanned the room. Almost instinctively, Eric found Kate and Nick in the back row, saving him a seat. Eric wound his way through the maze of desks, backpacks, and noisy peers to reach them. He plopped into the empty chair, out of breath and tired.

"Hi, guys," he said, stuffing his bag under his seat.

"How was gym?" Nick asked and his face scrunched, waiting for the response.

"It was *great*," Eric said, the words dripping with venom. "Especially when Dick told me I better tone down the homo and crank up the testosterone or the guys are going to eat me alive."

"What?!" Kate snapped. "He's there to teach everyone, not just the jocks."

"He was the same way last year when I had his class," Eric recalled. "But this time I have him the whole year and not just a semester."

"What're you going to do?" Nick asked, sensing there was a plan brewing.

Eric looked at Kate and said, "Will you go to the counselor's office with me before lunch?"

"To change your schedule?" she asked, already knowing the answer.

"I won't last another day in that class."

"They're going to give you shit about switching," Nick said as carefully as he could.

"I have to try something. Maybe I can get into another hour of gym or something. I just can't be in there with all those guys. They're going to kill me."

"All right, we'll give it a go," Kate said confidently and patted Eric's arm. "I'll meet you there at lunchtime." Kate glanced over Eric's shoulder and groaned, "Don't look now, but your day just got worse."

Eric spun in his seat and as the final bell rang to begin class, Justin Drake slid through the classroom door. Immediately, Eric scanned the room for empty seats. There were only three left, two near the front of the room and one in the back, directly in front of him.

Justin's grin was wide and excited when he spotted the pained look in Eric's eyes as he strolled to the rear of the class, sticking out his chest and strutting his perfected stroll on the way. He gladly slid into the desk ahead of Eric and didn't face the front of the room. He turned around, his elbows on Eric's desktop.

"Hey, fag!" Justin said, giddy. "Isn't this great? We've got two hours together in a row!"

"At least you can count," Eric said. "Well, to *two* anyway."

"Watch it, queer!" Justin slapped his hands on Eric's desk.

At his desk, Mark Morgan was taking attendance and talking to the pretty brunette cheerleader with legs for days, Christy Chapman. He was oblivious to Justin's slapping hands or the increasing tension between Justin and Eric.

26

"Hey, asshole," Kate butted in. Justin looked at her. He stuck his tongue out and pervertedly wiggled it around. Without skipping a beat, Kate said, "Yeah, that's what your mom did to me last night."

"Screw you!" Justin snapped.

"Look, I don't want to have to tell you this more than once so listen closely," she said calmly, laying the sarcastic sweetness on thick. "Turn your dumbass around in that seat and leave us alone!"

"But, baby—"

"Whoa!" Kate held her hand up to stop him. "Save it for someone who gives a shit. That person's not me so turn around!"

Justin rolled his eyes and looked back to Eric. "Catch ya later, fag," he said and winked before turning to face the front of the classroom.

Eric glanced over his shoulder. "Thanks," he said to his best friend.

Kate shrugged and said, "Keeping him in check is what I do best."

***

At the beginning of lunch period, Eric and Kate approached the door to Lillian Hatcher's office door. She was the school counselor in charge of scheduling classes and helping students with a wide variety of issues, including emotional instability, although she certainly did not present herself in an inviting or helpful way. Eric had spoken to her numerous times, pleading for help from the endless Innards' torment. Like Principal Spear, though, Hatcher dismissed Eric's claims as overly dramatic.

Standing in the hall, dreading Hatcher but anxious to get it over with, Eric gripped the door handle. Before turning it, he stared at Kate with a raised eyebrow.

"What?" Kate asked innocently but recognized Eric's look of warning.

"I know you're hungry and want to go to lunch, but I really need to change my schedule. I want to be in and out," Eric explained. "So try no to complicate this."

"Oh, come on, give me a little credit." Kate's attempt to sound hurt backfired. The girlish grin on her face gave herself away. She never agreed to *not* complicate anything.

Eric rolled his eyes and opened the office door. They walked in together and received a less than warm welcome from Elizabeth Tilly, the secretary. A chubby woman, nearly as wide as she was tall with red dyed hair desperately trying to cover gray, Tilly balance bifocals off the end of her fifty-something nose. Her mouth rarely smiled, which went well with her sour, unfriendly fed-up attitude, the product of too many years with bratty students. As Eric and Kate strolled into the office, Tilly made no exception on their behalf to greet them sweetly. Instead, she gave more attention to the paperwork cluttering her desk.

"Can I help you?" Tilly asked with zero interest.

Eric and Kate exchanged annoyed glances before he said, "I need to change my schedule."

Tilly's head cocked to the right and nearly lost her balanced glasses. "Why?" she asked. She was impatient and made no effort to hide it.

"I need to switch my first period gym class."

"Why?"

"I have my reasons." Eric stayed firm although the evil eyes staring coldly over the rim of Tilly's glasses buckled his knees. "Can I talk to Mrs. Hatcher?"

"She's very busy," Tilly said.

"We can wait!" Kate said sharply. She sat in the empty chair closest to Tilly's desk and cracked her gum, exaggerating her smile to the secretary. "We'll just shoot the shit with you."

"Watch your mouth, Miss Crawford," Tilly warned and hoisted her big behind from the straining chair. "Just one moment." She left the front office and walked down the hallway to the right, leading to Hatcher's office.

Eric looked to Kate, who was smiling brightly. "Only you could motivate people to do what you want just by threatening to hang around," Eric said, shaking his head.

"I do what I can," Kate said, popping another bubble.

Tilly returned quickly. "You can go in," she told Eric and squeezed back into her chair.

Without a word, Eric went to Hatcher's office. Kate stayed behind in the chair beside Tilly. She put her left arm on Tilly's desktop and tapped her manicured nails, bored.

"How is your first day back, Kate?" Tilly asked with no real concern. She never looked up from the cluttering papers but did scoot Kate's arm off her desk. "Any scheduling problems of your own? Perhaps you and Eric would like us to give you both study hall all day or off campus passes so you wouldn't have to deal with this trivial, pointless system that's so obviously bothering you both."

Kate laughed at Tilly's blatant cruelty. "Are you trying to flirt with me by saying such sweet things?" she gushed. "And since you asked so politely, my day's going grrrreat!" Kate made no effort to hide the fiery venom sizzling off her tongue. "But Eric's day is going pretty shitty, so there's obviously a problem with your system."

Immediately raising her head, Tilly heaved a loud, irritated sigh. She folded her arms onto her desktop and leaned toward Kate. "I see you still have that filthy mouth on you," she snapped. "Don't you remember all the trouble it got you in last year and the year before that?"

Kate crossed her smooth, defined legs and flipped her over her shoulder with a sweet smile. "What can I say? The principal's office is like a home away from home," she said. "I'm thinking this year I'll bring in my own family photos for the desk and maybe my own chair too. What do you think?" She flashed her pearly white teeth and winked at the secretary. "Because if I'm here anyway, I might as well be comfortable, right?"

"I don't appreciate your attitude, Miss Crawford." Sighing heavily, Tilly sat back in her seat and returned to her papers. "You need to leave."

"I'll leave when Eric's ready." Kate's gum cracked and she smiled sweetly, one eyebrow meticulously arched.

***

Lillian Hatcher had been the Ann Arbor South guidance counselor for nearly thirty years. A bony, bored and bitchy woman, Hatcher's sunken eyes and long, aerodynamic nose made her goofy looking but fitting for her demeanor.

When Eric appeared in the doorway to her office, Hatcher was leaning back in the chair behind her desk, her arms against her chest, her skeletal face already annoyed and firm.

"I'm very busy, Mr. Anderson," she said and did not invite him inside.

"I really need to switch my gym class," Eric said, trying hard to avoid whining.

"What's wrong with the class you already have?" Hatcher had no interest in the response.

"They won't leave me alone."

"Who?"

"The guys and Mr. Dick. They're attacking me and saying all kinds of shit—"

"Watch your mouth, young man," Hatcher snapped.

"*Please*," Eric begged, embarrassed by his desperation. "They're going to kill me."

"Always one for the dramatics." Her laugh was brief but bursting at the seems with a condescending tone.

"What?" Eric was frustrated and confused. "I can't take it—"

"You'll have to," Hatcher said, somewhat pleased in breaking the bad news. "You see, Eric, you can't just switch classes like switching shoes. You should be glad you have a full schedule because many of your fellow peers don't. So you'll just have to buckle down and stick with what you've got."

Eric stared at her like she had just kicked him in the gut. He tried to protest, "But—"

Hatcher cut him off. "I'm very busy," she said firmly and pointed a steady finger away.

"Way to do your job!" was all Eric could blurt out before leaving her office. He heard Hatcher laughing as he headed back toward the front entrance.

Frustrated and staring at the gray carpet as he returned to the reception area, Eric looked up, expecting to see Kate sitting pretty and Tilly rifling through papers, no doubt flustered with Kate's acidic tongue. To Eric's surprise and secret delight, though, there was another student gracing the room with his presence, Ann Arbor South's star athlete, Andy McCain.

The mere sight of him took Eric's breath away.

Andy stood next to Tilly with his elbows on the desktop. He was talking to Kate, half-turned toward her, leaving just enough of his right side in view of Eric's excited sight. Andy did not see Eric on the edge of the room and as Andy chatted quietly and waited patiently for Tilly's attention, he absentmindedly scratched his stomach under his red T-shirt, exposing a flash of tight, smooth skin. The simple gesture paralyzed Eric's motor functions. He stood, gawking, yearning, and admiring the heavenly sight.

Andy stood tall, a few inches above Eric, his shoulders wide and neck thick. His light brown hair tapered into a borderline buzz cut, with the bangs only slightly longer than the rest. His head hid nicely into a billed cap, which he managed to get away with in school since he was a celebrity, having won many a ball game in his devoted time to the Ann Arbor South sports teams. His chiseled face was smooth and clear, as if never embarrassed by an unsightly blemish. Small brown eyebrows and firm cheekbones framed a pair of beautiful, excited blue eyes and his square jaw brought attention to thick lips. When those full lips gave way to a smile, dimples with the power to stop beating hearts appeared on either side of his vibrantly white teeth, which gleamed with a proud grace no one could question or challenge.

Eric had spent many days and dreamy nights examining Andy's appeal and never tired of exploring the bodily terrain. Andy's strong hands, tipped with bitten fingernails, were a workingman's hands, a ball player's hands, callused from yard work and a loved baseball bat. His baseball biceps burst through the stitching of the tight short shirtsleeves, showcasing a hard-earned muscular frame. His shirt always seemed tight, the bottom of which fell right to the waist of his jeans so any strong movement made it rise a few inches or so and exposed his smooth, tight stomach or lower back, giving way to a pleasant view from every angle.

And then there was the ass. The baseball bubble butt popped out of

31

his arched back like a round pot of gold at the end of a spinal rainbow. Eric loved sneaking glances at the way it moved when Andy walked and the way it fittingly filled Andy's tight sports jerseys.

The most mesmerizing thing about Andy McCain, though, was his powerful, overwhelming, heart-stopping presence. He flowed with a grace unknown to him. The fluidity of his walk, the arch of his eyebrow, and the flexing of his arms all came with an innocence that exuded confidence but did not threaten. Everyone wanted a piece of him. Just to be on the receiving end of one of his vibrant, pulse-pounding smiles was on the wish list of one and all.

Glancing over Andy's shoulder, Kate spotted her frozen-in-time best friend staring at Andy's ass, his mouth gapping open like a hungry Venus Fly Trap. She left Andy and went to Eric. "Hello!" she whispered and pinched his ribcage.

"Shit!" Eric screeched, jerking away from her touch.

Tilly glanced up from her mound of paperwork and glared at him over her glasses. Andy turned to face the commotion. When he saw Eric, Andy smiled and in a deep voice said, "Hey."

"Uh…hi," Eric said, panicking at the embarrassment Kate had caused.

Kate giggled and clutched her hands onto Eric's arm. "Are you ready to go?" she asked, digging into the flesh of his forearm. "I'm starving."

"Uh—"

She dug deeper.

"Yes!" he cried. "Yes. I'm ready. Let's go eat."

Kate grabbed her bulky, oversized purse from a nearby chair and slung it over her shoulder. When she reached the door, she realized Eric wasn't with her. He hadn't moved from the same spot and his gaze hadn't left Andy's face. Rolling her eyes, Kate returned to Eric's side and held his hand, almost slicing her fingernails into his skin.

Eric winced with pain and finally moved toward the door.

"See you later, Andy," Kate said sweetly, pushing Eric out of the counseling office door.

"Later," Andy said. He smiled again at her and looked at Eric briefly before returning his attention to Tilly's desk.

"What the hell's wrong with you?" Kate snapped once the door shut behind them. They headed toward the cafeteria in the suffocating rowdiness of the student-filled hallway.

"What?" Eric asked innocently, ashamed his comeback was so weak.

"Oh, come on! Your hard-on almost knocked the pencils off Tilly's desk!"

"Shut up!" Eric shrieked. His face reddened. "You are such a...*hooker*!"

They laughed loudly and turned left at the hallway intersection. Eric and Kate fought their way through the bustling students on their way toward the lunchroom.

"What were you talking to Andy about?" Eric asked, failing at attempted nonchalance.

"He was only there a few seconds before your drooling ass came walking in so we didn't talk about much," Kate said. "You should really try to control yourself around him—"

"Anyway!" Eric barked.

"He said something about having an incomplete schedule or switching a class or something," she rambled. "I don't remember."

"Way to relay a story," Eric groaned.

"Sorry, I know I'm supposed to pump your foxy boyfriend for information," she teased. "But it's early and I'm not in my full nosey-neighbor mode just yet. Give me time!"

"You're a crotch!" he playfully snapped.

"So what did Snatcher say?" Kate giggled, proud of the nickname she christened onto the counselor. "Is she going to switch your class?"

"What do you think?"

Kate rolled her eyes. "Was she a raging bitch about it?"

"Yep!"

"Well, I might have some good news that'll cheer you up," Kate said anxiously.

Eric stared at her, his face blank. He wasn't in the mood. So Kate kept quiet and they took the last turn toward the cafeteria. It was filled with hungry students and lined with dozens of dusty glass trophy cases stuffed with decades of tarnished sport and marching band awards. Pre-homecoming football posters plastered the walls promoting the home game celebration only a few weeks away. Kate pointed to one and groaned.

"Do you think your man's going to take that skank to homecoming this year?" she asked.

"He's not my man," Eric firmly corrected. "Besides, him and *Tara* aren't seeing each other anymore, are they?"

Tara Sanderson was also a senior and Andy McCain's ex-girlfriend. She wore too much make-up and squeezed into skimpy tank top shirts that barely fit over her breasts. Her shoulder-length hair was bottle blonde and poker straight, but she crawled out of bed every morning two hours before school just to curl her artificial locks into perfect symmetrical ringlets. Although over the top, Tara somehow made it work for her because she was beautiful. The painted eyes, the flawless skin, the toned body, the edgy Shirley Temple hairdo all came together and *worked*.

She was to the female division of the Innards what Justin Drake or Wes Palmer was to the male members, the unofficial holier-than-thou leader. Tara was ruthless to anyone below her, which left only a handful of girls safe from her wrath. If Margot Deluca's shirt was the wrong color or Francesca Patterson breathed her air or Stephanie Miller even *looked* at her, Tara Sanderson made sure to correct their behavior. Tara ruled the female food chain and like many of the underdog boys admiring the young men on the Innards' side, Tara and her small gang of perfect princesses were admired and envied by all as well.

Well, almost all.

Upon hearing Tara's name, Kate dramatically spit on the floor and snapped, "Bitch!"

"Calm down, Cujo," Eric said, laughing.

"Just looking at her pretty little Maybelline face makes me want to jab pencils in her eye sockets."

"Careful, Kate, with sweet-talk like that, everyone's going to think you've got a crush on her."

"Oh, please!" Kate gagged. "And no, her and your man aren't dating anymore. It didn't last very long. Only, like, a couple of weeks—"

"Direct from the files of the National Enquirer," Eric teased.

"Do you want to hear my good news or not?" She asked.

They reached the cafeteria doors and were already annoyed by the loud, restless energy festering inside. Eric stood close to the door but didn't open it. He looked to his best friend and saw the absolute torture Kate was suffering by not spilling her guts.

Eric laughed, amused by her weak thirst for gossip, and said, "What's the news?"

"I heard your man—"

"Don't call him that."

"Fine! I heard *Andy* tell Tilly he finally has a complete schedule," Kate said in a rush.

"That's your big news? Big deal. So he's set for the semester—"

"Think about it, fool!" Kate was impatient. "He didn't have a full schedule and no first period until today."

Still, Eric was lost, staring at her with narrow eyes.

"You might be happy to know he now has gym class first thing in the morning." Kate's raised eyebrows and puckered lips screamed victory.

With a dropped jaw, Eric looked hard at Kate, trying to uncover a practical joke but he saw only dead honest truth. "Are you sure?" he asked in a low voice.

"If I'm lying, I'm dying," Kate replied. Her smirk changed to a wide grin. "Now you'll get to see your man's hot ass in all its sweaty glory."

Eric blushed and became momentarily quiet. Kate saw the awakening wonder and intrigue swirling in his widened eyes.

"You know what?" Eric said and opened the cafeteria door. "Gym might not be so bad after all."

Chapter Three

Thursday, August 29, 1996

The next morning, Eric was so nervous he wanted to puke. The butterflies in his stomach made focusing on anything but breathing difficult. He wasn't sure if they flapped with supreme dread (gym class) or pure bliss (Andy McCain in gym shorts).

Eric was late getting to school thanks to slowpoke Kate and a minor case of misplaced car keys. She was ten minutes late picking him up, having spent the extra time searching her house for the keys, only to find the EAT ME key chain buried deep in the bottom of her bulky, unorganized bag, where she always kept the keys. Eric gave her grief for it, yelling most of the way to school, but he wasn't really angry with Kate. He was scared, *terrified*, of walking into gym late. The second Kate parked in the senior lot, Eric jumped out and ran to the locker room. Dick would surely be out for blood no matter the reason, but still Eric ran.

And bloodthirsty Dick was. "Where the hell have you been, Anderson?!" he barked the instant Eric rushed past his office door. The other boys were changing into their swim trunks. Eric caught a brief glimpse of Andy McCain's naked behind slipping into a pair of striking blue shorts. It was too brief to enjoy while the fiery Dick dragon breathed down his neck.

"I'm two minutes late," Eric said with too much attitude.

"Do you have a pass?"

Eric just stared at the instructor. Of course he didn't have a pass.

"You know what that means!" Dick shouted. His face lit up and he threw his arms out, motioning to the others. "Gather 'round, men!"

Eric's shirtless enemies flocked around their leader in a threatening circle, covering every surrounding inch. The air reeked of sweat and hungry breath.

"What's up, sir?" Justin Drake asked, eager to a point of obsession.

"Anderson's two minutes late and doesn't have a pass," Dick said triumphantly. "What is his punishment going to be?"

Without skipping a single beat, the boys cheered in unison, "PUSH-UPS!"

Dick smiled. "You heard them, Anderson," he instructed. "Fifty push-ups. Now."

Eric shook his head. "I can't do fifty push-ups," he replied flatly.

"Well, we've got fifty minutes to see you try."

As Dick and the others took ringside seats on the locker room benches circling him, Eric scanned the small crowd for Andy McCain's face. He quickly found it and was surprised but not satisfied to see Andy was near the back of the group, alone. Andy was not enjoying the sideshow circus like everyone else. His hands were tucked under his arms as he leaned against the edge of Dick's office doorway, his face blank.

"Let's go, boy!" Dick ordered, his voice firm and gruff.

"Better get a stretcher in here because this shit's going to kill me," Eric muttered.

Humiliated and enraged, Eric dropped to his knees, assumed the push-up position, and exercised. His weak reps were called out to the soundtrack of fifteen ecstatic boys and one vicious ringleader teacher.

After only ten grueling, bone-breaking maneuvers, Eric was exhausted and unable to move. He propped himself on extended arms and stared at the dirty tiled floor. Sweat dripped from his greasy hair and the longer his elbows remained locked, the more his body shook from the paralyzing pain. Dick and the boys continued to cheer but quickly lost interest once Eric stopped struggling and just stayed in one stagnant position.

"Come on, fag!" Matt Murphy urged.

Dick did not reprimand Matt. He just laughed and watched Eric sweat.

Once his thin arms finally gave out, Eric collapsed to the floor, aching and moaning. The boys applauded and Wes Palmer and David Johnson kicked Eric's legs for an extra laugh.

"All right, men," Dick said, standing up to tower over his students. He adjusted the elastic waistband of his track pants and exhaled slow. "Hit the gym for a game of shirts-n-skins. We'll start swimming tomorrow. Anderson wrecked my mood."

Without pausing, the boys took their instruction, grabbed their T-shirts from their lockers, and left the room with their dry swimsuits still on. Ryan Roberts and Matt Murphy spat on Eric's back as they walked past him. Eric did not react. It wasn't the first time he'd been spat on. He was mildly pleased it didn't splash into his eyes, like it usually did. Matt Murphy had quite a way of shooting right where he aimed.

When the room was empty, Eric forced himself to sit up. He focused his eyes and saw Dick ahead of him, standing tall and looking down. There was a smugness and proud smile to Dick's leathery face. Eric never saw it any other way.

"Next time, get to my class on time," Dick said.

"My bus was late," Eric lied. "There's nothing I could do about it." He tried to catch his breath and stop his hands from shaking at the wrist.

"I don't care if you have to walk your ass to school two hours early, get here on time," Dick said chillingly firm.

Eric wasn't afraid. Maybe a little annoyed, but mostly too tired to care. "What if I don't? Are you going to make me do push-ups 'til I die?"

Dick knelt beside Eric and looked him in the eye. "You don't want to know what I'll do," he warned. "Now get to the gym!"

"This isn't a concentration camp! You can't treat me like this!" Eric protested.

"GO!" Dick's voice ratted the loose tiles on the floor, the wooden panels of the benches, and the doors to the metal lockers. He stood and left the room. Eric watched him walk away. As he did, Dick passed Andy McCain, who was still shirtless in the doorway. He had not moved, from Eric's first aching push-up to the humiliating collapse. Andy stood against the frame of the door, his thumbs now tucked into the waistband of his swim trunks. His face was hard, his jaw clenched tight and his eyes narrow and determined, but he said nothing. He and Eric exchanged a long look, but Eric wasn't sure whose side Andy was on, his or Dick's. But it didn't matter. Eric's arms hurt too much to give it too much thought.

Just as it seemed Andy was about to speak, Dick said, "McCain! Move your ass!"

Andy did as he was told and went into the gym.

Eric moaned and crawled to his locker to change into his gym gear.

***

On Eric's way to second period, a strong hand grabbed him from behind, gripping into the flesh of his forearm. Reflexively, Eric tore free and whirled around to see beautiful Andy McCain standing in front of him. Staring into Andy's fluorescent blue eyes, Eric's heart pulsated in his temples so hard that it blurred his vision. Andy looked back at him with interest although Eric's wanting imagination may have projected the illusion of interest.

"Dick's just trying to get a rise out of you," Andy said, stepping back to show he meant no harm. "Don't talk back and just do what he says. He'll like you a lot more that way."

Eric cocked his head, offended by the suggestion, and said, "I don't want him to like me."

Shiny white teeth gleamed from within Andy's smile "But it'll be easier for you if—"

"Don't say that to me," Eric said. "You don't know what would be easier for me."

"I just meant—"

"You meant to offer up some sympathy from an Innard to an Outtie," Eric snapped, unsure where the confidence came from. "But let me offer you a little insight, Mr. In-Crowd. You want to know what would be *easier* for me? I'll tell you. Not having Dick crawl up my ass and force-feed me push-ups would make it easier. Getting your crew to lay off me for just one second might make it a little easier too. But as far as Dick *liking* me," Eric laughed. "I don't care about that. All I want is to get out of that class and away from people like you."

"That's not fair," Andy politely protested. "We're not all like Dick."

Eric stared at the jock, eyeballing the way Andy folded his strong arms across his chest. Looking at the body ripping out of the tight green T-shirt almost beat Eric's heart right out of his chest. But Andy's apparent lack of understanding kept Eric agitated. Maybe Eric expected Andy to understand him or that they would be more alike. Or maybe Eric was shallower than he thought and just liked the beefy body in the green tee and found that hard to swallow.

"Are you kidding me?" Eric asked, running a hand through his sweaty hair.

Andy flashed the pearly whites again, this time with a hint of frustration. "I'm just saying that you shouldn't let Dick smell your fear. He feeds off it." Andy absentmindedly put his hand under his shirt and played with his navel. "I should know. He's been my coach for years."

"You really don't get it, do you?" Eric chuckled loudly. "I appreciate you talking to me like a human being, but you don't know what it's like for me in that class." He took a deep breath to calm himself. The hand under Andy's shirt was too distracting. "I'm not like you or your asshole friends. I can't take this crap."

For a brief moment, Andy noticed Eric's wandering eyes on his stomach. Andy stopped the belly button play and let his hand drop. The bell rang, signaling the two-minute warning before the start of second period. "I have to go," Andy said, his whites still twinkling. He glanced around the stuffy hall of noisy students and stepped closer to Eric. "You know what?"

With his personal space excitedly invaded, Eric stood his ground and folded his arms.

Leaning in surprisingly closer, Andy whispered, "We're not that different."

With nothing further, Andy jogged off to his next class. Although confused, Eric sneaked a quick glanced at Andy's butt as he left. Its defined rock-hard roundness brought a smile to his face. When Andy disappeared down a separate hall, Eric stood alone among the hustling students, baffled.

Quietly, Eric said to himself, "What the hell does *that* mean?"

Chapter Four

The cafeteria was intense with hundreds of students packed into a large room that was too small to accommodate them. The long metal tables with multicolored plastic chairs covered the floor from wall to wall. At one end of the noisy mess hall, near the kitchen and buffet line, sat Eric, Kate and Nick, in their usual three seats. The choice location was easy: their table was at the extreme opposite end of the cafeteria from Justin Drake's table, which he shared with Wes Palmer, Matt Murphy and the other Innards, including their female counterparts, led by Tara Sanderson, Ashley Fitzgerald, and Danielle Hemingway.

From his chair, although many yards away from the room's popular section, Eric could still clearly see everyone at the Innards' table and vice versa. It facilitated bickering and Justin Drake's tormenting. Eric and his friends were a good distance away, but still close enough for the harassing to continue. And it always did.

The upside to Eric's seat was that while in it he could look right across the room to the spot directly next to Justin. Andy McCain filled that chair daily. So Eric was frequently lost, mesmerized by the way Andy ate a hamburger or sipped soda through a straw.

"Maybe he was just looking out for you," Nick suggested unpersuasively. "Not all straight guys are assholes." He, Kate and Eric had been talking about Eric's interaction with Andy after gym class all

42

morning and into the lunchtime period.

Eric popped out of his spellbound trace and took a drink of his orange soda. He raised an eyebrow at Nick and said, "I guess that's possible. Andy's never been a dick to me, but—"

"So maybe he was just helping out with the Dick Handbook 101 stuff, you know, being nice. That does happen—" Nick paused. "Well, okay, maybe not to you, but I'm sure it happens to other people." He shrugged and turned to Kate for help.

Kate was poised in her seat, her posture perfectly straight with her smooth legs crossed. She sipped on a bottle of club soda and took her time in responding. "Are you goons blind?" she asked calmly and looked at Eric's face. "Andy's putting the moves on you."

Her friends burst into laughter. Blue Gatorade sprayed from the corners of Nick's mouth and onto his shirt and nearly shot through his nose as he laughed, gasping for air.

"You're right, Kate! That's *exactly* what he's trying to do!" Eric teased. "But you foiled his plan!"

"I'm serious. Andy's after you." She sipped her soda through a straw with a natural, know-it-all attitude that effortlessly oozed from her pores.

"I'm not listening to this." Eric awkwardly glanced around the room, looking for any focal point other than Kate's righteous face or Andy's distracting beauty. He settled on the cream corn. But it was too difficult. The corn churned his stomach and Andy made it flutter. Eric gave in and glanced across the room once more. Comfortably packed in with nearly a dozen sporty guys and just as many pretty girls, Andy happily chomped on his lunch and laughed loudly with the crowd. In between bites of his burger, Andy leaned back in his seat and interlocked his hands, resting them atop his head. Eric's interested eyes studied the fleshy lines and muscular curves of Andy's arms, following them from the strong start at the wrist to the shirtsleeve finish. The wavy, well-defined lines disappeared into his fitting T-shirt, toward his shoulders and chest.

"Knock it off, Kate," Nick said firmly. "Eric gets enough shit from everyone else. He doesn't need it from you too."

Again, Eric awoke from his daze and turned to his friends. He tried to nonchalantly reenter the conversation like he had not been gawking at the beautiful boy across the room, but had to take a moment to catch up.

"I'm telling you, I have a feeling about this," Kate insisted. "Let's examine the facts. Andy's never had a steady girlfriend—"

"Holy shit! No girlfriend? He *is* gay!" Nick chuckled. He even smelled sarcastic.

"Let me finish, *ass*, and don't interrupt." She counted her points on extended, manicured fingers as she spoke. "No girlfriend…good dresser…hot body—"

"You've *got* to be kidding," Eric said and looked around the large cafeteria, wondering how he ever got involved with such a crazy young woman in the first place.

"We don't know if he has a girlfriend," Nick offered.

"Oh, please! This is high school. We know everybody's business!" Kate balked.

"I know this is the nineties and it's taken some time, but straight guys do know how to dress themselves now. You don't have to be gay to do that," Eric added. His voice grew faster and his patience grew shorter. "And maybe, just *maybe*, he got that body from playing sports."

Kate folded her arms across her busty chest and sat back in her seat. There was enough force in the reclining that signaled her irritation. She tapped her fingers on her arm for a moment, breathing deeply. Seeing Nick smile only raised her already arched eyebrow even higher and she said, "Don't make me prove my point, bitches."

"How are you going to do *that*?" Nick asked.

She pondered for a moment, spot-checking her fingernails for flaws as she did. "I'll ask him out. If he turns me down—" She flipped a chunk of her shiny blonde hair over her shoulder. "—we'll have our answer."

Eric and Nick were hysterical. The volcanic eruption of laughter filled the crowded room, bouncing off every student's eardrums and back again. They were barked at and booed by their peers, but it didn't silence them. Kate was just too absurd to be stopped.

"I'm pissin' myself!" Nick teetered in his seat. Beaming rays of sarcasm and laughter shined from the depths of his bones.

"So, wait a minute—" Eric wiped the tears from his face and continued, "You're *so* hot that any straight guy can't resist a date with you?"

"You know the rules, honey. I'm blonde and have a great rack. No man can resist me," Kate said. She softened slightly and cracked a tiny smile at her own expense, but she did not back down. Instead, she slid out her chair, stood to her feet and smoothed herself over.

Eric's mouth dropped and his face turned ghostly white. "Sit down!" he pleaded.

"Begging is so unbecoming, Eric."

"*Please!*"

"Yeah, Kate, come on. Don't do this," Nick said, annoyed by her persistence, but he didn't force the issue, knowing there was no changing her mind.

Panic stricken, Eric frantically looked between Kate and Andy, pleading with his eyes to stop what she had planned. "Come one!" he cried. "We were just kidding!"

"Really? I wasn't." She smiled sweetly and pushed in her chair. "Be right back."

As he watched Kate walk to the other side of the room, Eric's heart pounded like a war drum against his chest. The battle cry beat harder and louder as his eyes stayed glued to Kate's slender figure as it approached Andy. She confidently slid in between Andy and Chase Frank, despite angry scowls and mumbles from certain female Innards at the table. They were sure to keep their pretty eyes locked on their male territory as Kate trespassed on the already claimed land.

"She's *your* friend," Nick told Eric. He drank his drink, but never took his eyes off Kate.

"I've never met her before in my life," Eric added. He too was fixated on his pretty best friend, now giggling girlishly and slowly hooking a chunk of her hair behind her ear as she talked to hunky Andy. Eric couldn't hear what they were saying and Kate nodded and laughed so dramatically that he couldn't read her lips.

Eric paid less attention to Kate on her info-seeking excursion and more on Andy's lips, desperately searching for any signal that would confirm the loud voice in the back of his head. It chanted to him with trumpets and harps that he and Super Andy played for the same sexual team. To his disappointment, though, Eric couldn't read Andy any better than the over-the-top Kate. Andy nodded, fidgeted with his ball cap, and spooned his mac-n-cheese as Kate rambled.

Although it seemed to run in slow motion, the actual conversation only lasted a few moments. Eric was surprised to see Kate stand from the In-Table so soon and head back toward him and Nick. Naturally, she exchanged heated words with Justin before her return and scowled back at the female Innards as she passed them.

"Unless you're catching flies, close your mouth," Kate told Eric as she retook her seat beside her friends. She didn't gush. In fact, she didn't say anything as Eric and Nick stared, wide-eyed and waiting. Instead, Kate grabbed her fork and returned to her tossed salad.

"Well...what did he say?" Nick said, seeing Eric was unable to remember English.

Kate smiled and glanced across the room again. Most of the In-Table had returned to snobby business as usual. A few were tormenting overly-tall Phil Parker one table over while a few others went back to the food line to round up ice cream desserts. One face, although trying not to be noticed, stared back at her from underneath the bill of his hat. Kate pretended not to see Andy peering from under the visor and she turned to Eric.

"I told you so," Kate said, smiling proudly. "He turned me down."

Nick burst into laughter again. Eric laughed only briefly because he wasn't sure if she was joking. Kate's eyes were serious but shimmering with a hint of victory. She always got the look when she knew she was right. Eric had no trouble recognizing it.

"So tell me, Kate," Nick said through his laughs. "Did he just come right out and say, 'Sorry, *breeder*, I'm gay so you and your twat can just keep on truckin'' or did you have to pry it out of him?"

"You make my twat sound like a Mack 10 truck," Kate snapped.

"And no, that's not what he said, prick."

Eric finally spoke. "What did he say?" His voice cracked a hundred different ways with only those few words. Nick's laughter dropped upon hearing the urgency in Eric's voice and seeing the holier-than-thou look in Kate's eyes. Eric was intensely attached and taking it more seriously than any of them had intended.

"Well, his exact words were, 'I have to focus on getting my baseball career started so I don't have time to be distracted by a girl.'" Kate didn't look at her friends. She just stuffed another bite of salad into her widely grinning, proud, know-it-all mouth.

"Damn!" Nick's own mouth fell open again. "I've never heard any guy say that before, especially to a hot chick like you."

"At least not any *straight* guy," Kate added.

Eric didn't speak. He just turned his attention back to Andy's table. When he did, he was surprised to see Andy staring back. Knowing he should turn away but being too curious to know the truth, Eric stayed focused.

Andy had purchased an individually wrapped, heftily priced $4 ice cream cone from the rolling ice cream cart at the side of the cafeteria. He sat in his usual seat, the one Eric had burned into his eyeballs, and slowly opened the wrapper to the cone. Every few seconds or so, Andy glanced up from the treat and zeroed in on Eric. Without reaction, though, Andy only stared for a few moments, returned to the ice cream, and repeated.

Eric didn't blink or breathe. Without moving his head or any inch of his body, he glanced around the room, terrified someone might see him staring. From the snotty, brand-named Innards applying make-up or tossing the football amongst themselves to the Freaky-Deak table full of purple Mohawks and studded dog collars to the Pencil Necks with their calculators smoking from the lightning fast keystrokes. Amidst all the cafeteria chaos, no one paid attention to Eric or his obsessive, intensely concentrated gaze across the room to the ice cream eating idol.

Again, Andy glanced up from his dessert and briefly met Eric's gaze, as if to double-check he still had the young man's attention. In seeing he did, undividedly, Andy returned to the cone and freed it from its wrapper. The hot, stuffy temperature of the lunchroom already started melting it and tiny rivers of ice cream raced down from the top of the cone, bursting through the hard chocolaty shell and circling past the sprinkled nuts decorating it. The streams of cream dribbled down the cone and onto Andy's gripping fingers.

As soon as the cold cream touched his hand, Andy once more met Eric's transfixed eyes across the noisy, crowded room. With a flickering, arched eyebrow, Andy brought the dessert to his mouth and bit into it. Ice cream rushed from the cone, down its sides, and onto the hungry corners of Andy's mouth. He stared at his messy hand, inched closer, and with his eager tongue he licked a large glob of chocolate from his knuckles.

The way Andy devoured the chocolaty treat from his hand raced blood to every inch of Eric's body, tightening his pants especially. Andy's thick, juicy lips circled his fingers with an unintended sexiness that made Eric's mouth water and his mind stray to even dirtier thoughts.

Without moving his head, only his eyes, Andy glanced up from the dessert and across the cafeteria. As if guided by radar, his eyes once again magnetized with Eric's uncertain gaze. Andy proceeded with the sultry ice cream show as if knowing Eric was watching, enjoying, and possibly even *loving* it. As if oblivious to any nearby Innards, Andy kept his eyes locked on Eric. Then, without any extreme or rushed movement, Andy's tongue slowly slid out of his hungry mouth and licked another drizzle of chocolate from his hand.

Eric gasped and it took Kate and Nick by surprise. They jumped in their seats and turned their attention to their hypnotized friend. Eric didn't flinch or blink or *breathe*.

"What the hell?" Kate asked. She followed Eric's stare across the room and saw Andy carefully holding the remnants of a half-eaten ice cream dessert. She only witnessed one quick seductive flip of Andy's tongue. Before she could say anything, she noticed Justin, who was sitting closely beside Andy, had spotted it himself and had a typical reaction.

"What the hell're you doing, man?" Justin snapped. His voice startled Andy.

Andy was so shaken, he lost control of the ice cream and it fell onto the tabletop and rolled into his lap. Andy jumped up from his seat, dramatically pushing his chair away from the table. His buddies and several of the popular girls stared at him, laughing.

"Looks like you're giving that ice cream head!" Justin burst into laughter.

Andy dumped the remaining chunk of the dessert onto the table.

"What're you doing?" Justin asked again.

Andy, madly wiping the treat from his T-shirt, said nothing. He just looked up and nodded toward Eric's direction. Every head at the table turned to the other end of the cafeteria. There was Eric, slowly coming out of his hypnosis. Beside him was Kate, waving her nicely polished middle finger.

"Oh, I get it. You're messin' with the fag." Justin's signature grin slithered onto his face. "Watch this," he said and grabbed the wad of ice cream from the table. Justin stood to his feet and with his not-half-bad right-handed curve ball, chucked the chocolate treat across the room. It catapulted through the air to the sound of the Innards' laughter and slammed onto Eric, Kate and Nick's table, splattering only inches from Eric's plate. The melting mess splashed milky droplets onto Eric and Kate's faces and clothes. Nick had seen it barreling toward them and moved before it crash-landed. The second the dessert smacked onto the tabletop, Justin and his friends cackled wildly and Kate breathed fire.

"YOU SON OF A BITCH!" she screamed, jumping to her feet and wiping the sticky ice cream drops from her cheeks.

Eric wiped his face, scooted his chair back and stood up. Instead of creating an even bigger scene with his fuming best friend, he gathered the remainder of his lunch onto his tray, preparing to leave.

"That's right, fag! Run away!" Justin shouted, placing his hands on the sides of his mouth to shoot his voice farther when he spoke.

Every student in the cafeteria and even the cranky lunch ladies fell silent and stared in awe at the ice cream bomb, the laughing Innards, and a hysterically angry Kate.

Nick joined Eric in gathering their lunch trash. "Kate, get a grip and let's get out of here," Nick said firmly.

"ASSHOLES!" she shouted to the Innards, even louder than before.

With Kate in his scope, Justin grabbed the top bun of his half-eaten hamburger and chucked it across the room. It fell short, landing at the Pencil Necks' table instead, near Tammy Lindell's plate. Tammy didn't move. She just wiped the splattered ketchup-mustard mixture from her glasses and kept her head down.

The chucked bread bun infuriated Kate. Her fists clenched. Her jaw tightened. She took a step in the Innards' direction, B-lining for Justin, when Nick grabbed her arm and held her back.

"Let me go!" she screamed.

"You know Spear will kick your ass if he walks in on this!" Nick reminded. "Now get your shit and let's go!"

Kate jerked away from his grasp and took another step toward Justin. She stopped herself though and turned around, leaving her back to Justin. She stared at Nick and then at Eric, who was miserable. He stared at her, his eyes watery but not crying. She knew the look well. He needed to get out, away, anywhere free of the harassment. She nodded and took a deep breath. The muted cafeteria stopped breathing, waiting to see what Kate would do next, as she grabbed her large purse and book bag. When she gathered her lunch items onto the tray, her hand squeezed the closed, half-full club soda bottle and she briefly studied it.

"Come on, Kate!" Nick said again, his patience expired.

"Okay," Kate said with a smile. Her voice was back to its sweet, confident and controlled tone. "Just a second." She opened the club soda bottle and tossed the cap to the floor.

"What're you doing?" Eric said, breaking his silence with a panicked tone.

"Hold on!" Kate corked the bottle with her thumb, violently shook it, and before too much fizz could shoot out, she catapulted the bottle across the room. "Heads up, assholes!" she squealed with devilish delight.

The club soda rocketed across the room. Every student's head followed its path from Kate's hand, over the many tables, until it barreled down, bombing smack dab into Justin Drake's chest. The fizzy liquid erupted onto his face and T-shirt.

"SHIT!" Justin screamed, jumping back from the blow. "YOU BITCH!"

The cafeteria exploded with gasps first, followed by wild, uncontrolled laughter from every student. Kate giggled loudly, basking in the attention and smiling wider with every antagonistic insult the female Innards snapped at her in Justin's defense.

"Are you out of your mind?" Nick said. He grabbed her arm again and kept a strong hold on it. "Let's go before they take you away in a straight jacket!" He left the table, pulling her behind him.

Eric followed. He wanted to run screaming from the room because every set of eyes in the place burned holes in his back. But he didn't. He had made a pact with himself long ago never to show too much weakness and never run away. So he slung his bag over his shoulder and forced himself to casually follow Nick and Kate to the main cafeteria doors.

They had to pass by the Innards' table on the way to their point of exit. Nick's pace was fast, dragging Kate behind him without mercy, preventing her from picking any more fights on their way. Trailing only a few feet behind, Eric tried hard not to look at Andy, but with a crippling weakness for the McCain boy, Eric just *had* to steal one last glance.

As the Innards tended to the wet and war-torn Justin, Andy stood to the side of the large group, his arms folded across his chest, a trademark pose. He wasn't laughing or helping Justin dry off. Andy seemed unaware of anything but eyeballing Eric's walk to the main doors. Before Eric opened them, he took a longer look at Andy. It happened so fast but Eric knew what he saw: Andy nodded ever so slightly and one side of his mouth flickered into a smile for only a moment.

***

For Eric, the school restrooms were only safe for use at certain times of the day. The mornings before classes began and immediately after the last bell of the day were out of the question. It was a jock free-for-all during those peak hours and he steered clear of them like a homophobic plague. He only needed subjection to one violent toilet bowl swirly and one nose-bleeding punch in a school bathroom before he devised an asshole-avoidance schedule. During the middle of fourth or fifth periods was the best time. Most students took their bathroom breaks during lunch, and since fourth and fifth periods followed lunch, the rooms were virtually empty.

Eric usually avoided food and drink throughout the day to ward off even a minor need to relieve himself. He often succeeded but because he was never one to resist the cafeteria's fruit pie dessert, he occasionally needed a toilet badly. "Mother Nature's a mean bitch. When she calls, she hollers," he would tell his teachers, although his sarcasm was rarely appreciated.

Later that afternoon, after the bizarre lunchroom mishaps, Eric excused himself from fifth period Art. The apple crumb pie wasn't sitting well and he needed to answer the bitch's call. On his way to his preferred restroom, the secluded one buried back by the library, Eric turned the corner only to bump into the chest of someone a bit taller. He followed the beefy chest and neckline north to discover Andy McCain's handsome face.

Greeting Eric with a smile, Andy simply said, "Hey."

Eric rolled his eyes, laughed a little with annoyance, and stepped around him. Eric went into the bathroom, closed the door to his preferred stall and wiped off the toilet seat with the cheap school tissues.

Andy followed him and stood outside Eric's stall. "Is something wrong?" Andy asked, his voice echoing in the cold, white-and-green tiled room.

Laughing again, Eric locked the stall door and hung his bag on the inside hook. "That was quite a performance at lunch today," Eric said. Normally, he would have shied away from using the restroom while his hunky crush was in earshot. But not only was there slight refuge behind the closed door, he really had to go!

Sitting on the toilet, Eric could see Andy's sneakers and cargo pants through the bottom of the stall. He was standing outside, leaning against the stall door. "Sorry about that," Andy said quietly. He spoke so softly that Eric deemed it a trick to gain his trust again or, if Andy was serious, he didn't want any possible bystanders to hear him.

"Leave me alone, I'm busy," Eric snapped, but never took his eyes off Andy's sneakers.

"I said I'm sorry," Andy repeated. He paced the area in front of the stall. "We were just kidding around—"

Eric balked. His laughter bounced off the bathroom tiles. "Give me a break!" he said. "I know how you guys work. It was a funny prank. Ha ha! Everyone got a good laugh at the silly little gay boy and you even have to throw some food. Fire up!"

"It wasn't like that, well, I mean, it was, but—" The sneakers stomped the floor. "This is all wrong."

Just as Eric had dreadfully anticipated, the presence of Andy and the conversation chased away his need for the restroom. It happened sometimes. Although in dire need of a toilet, Eric's body grew shy and recluse in the company of cuteness. Irritated as ever, Eric stood up, buttoned his pants and said, "Dammit!"

"What?" Andy asked, confused.

"Nothing," Eric groaned and opened the stall door. He stayed strong and forced himself to go to the sink to wash his hands and not look at Andy's face.

"Come on, man. Justin was just messing around," Andy said, trying a nonchalant approach.

"I don't care. I'm used to this shit," Eric said, drying his hands. "What I'm not used to are pricks like you feeding me lines of bullshit about how you're so much better than the others and you don't stoop to their level and blah blah blah. I forget the rest."

Andy raised his arms above his head and grabbed one of the many painted pipes running along the ceiling. He rested his hands there and leaned his head against one of his flexed biceps. His eyes were quickly moving from corner to corner, searching for something to say. In the awkward silence, waiting for Andy's words, Eric stood there, bored, until his eyes traveled down the curvy lines of Andy's arms to the strong, defined V-shape of his stomach peeking out of his shirt, leading into his pants.

"I don't have time for this," Eric said, popping out of the self-indulgent trance.

Sensing the strong reaction from Eric, Andy glanced down at his own stomach with his arms still stretched above his head. He noticed his raised T-shirt revealed his tight, toned abs and hipbones. He looked at Eric, who was only periodically glancing between him and the floor. Instead of turning away or dropping his arms, Andy extended them further toward the ceiling. His shirt raised even higher, revealing a small navel and a trail, lightly dusted with hair, leading from his belly button into the waistband of his cargo pants.

Eric's eyes shot up and fell into a locked, deep stare with Andy. They didn't speak. Eric tried regulating his breathing, but it only increased as Andy slowly rocked back and forth, still gripping the pipe and showing off his hard stomach. Eric saw more of Andy's skin with each rocked step. Falling back into an intense stare, Andy tilted his head from the left bicep to the right to change his view of Eric. The corners of his mouth curled into a small, deliberate smile. Squinting to decipher the smile's intention, Eric realized it wasn't a smile at all. It was a grin charged with a faint level of excitement, but Eric wasn't sure if Andy was ready to kick his ass or if he was fueled by a curious libido.

Andy dropped his arms to his side and took a step toward Eric. Immediately, Eric stepped back and when Andy took another step closer, Eric took a bigger step back. They continued the bizarre dance until Andy had backed Eric into the bathroom sink. It was hard and cold to the touch and Eric braced himself against it, digging his fingers into its porcelain base. When Andy took one last small step, Eric hopped onto the sink and his butt slid right into it. Andy's grin widened and Eric still couldn't decode it.

Panicking, Eric blurted, "I have to go!" into the bathroom's silence.

Andy only replied with a whispered, "Why?"

Unable to cope with the blindsiding confusion, Eric jumped out of the sink and took a giant step away. He turned his back on the sexy boy and faced the mirrored wall ahead of him. In the reflection, Eric could see Andy standing patiently behind him, brightly smiling, with his strong hands now tucked neatly into his pockets. Before Eric would allow his mind to wander to the interior depths of those pants pockets and imagine what Andy's hands were potentially touching, he dramatically swung toward to the door. He nearly lost his balance in the process since the turn was so swift. Without looking back, he readjusted his fallen backpack strap and moved closer to the door.

Eric's voice cracked when he said, "Later!" He tried not to run too fast from the room but the thunder under his feet quickly chased him away.

In the safety of the quiet hallway outside, Eric refused to look back. But he so desperately wanted to return to the restroom and run his fingertips over the light hair surrounding Andy's beautiful belly button. He wanted to be passionately embraced, *crushed*, inside Andy's well-defined pitcher arms and locked there until the Jaws of Life pried his love-struck corpse from them. But he didn't. Instead, he forced himself to stay strong and fight all of the impulsive temptations. He wouldn't look back. Hell no, he wouldn't! He *couldn't*!

But, of course, he did.

When his head slowly glanced over his shoulder, Eric saw Andy only a few feet away, following him and approaching rather quickly with a confident stride that scared but excited him. Andy's sparkling, mysterious smile rushed blood through Eric's body like Niagara Falls.

Before Andy reached him, Eric, with his head straining to gawk behind his shoulders, ran into a stiff object. Swinging around, Eric saw the stiff was Principal Spear. The tall, burly man was stuffed into his poorly made suit as usual and the thin comb-over hairdo was dyed freshly black to disguise the pure-white. His wrinkly face retreated from a fairly kind, inexperienced middle-aged man to an old-timer ready to feast on the next student for breakfast.

Standing with his arms folded against his chest, Spear drummed his angry fingers on his arms as he stared through his tinted eyeglasses with a bent eyebrow and a narrow gaze. "Shouldn't you be in class, Mr. Anderson?" His tone was gruff and uninterested as usual.

Shaken by the run-in, Eric wiped his sweaty brow and ran his fingers through his now-greasy hair. He dizzily glanced between the principal and Andy, who had now reached them and was standing only a few feet behind Eric. Irritated by Eric's anxiousness, Spear put his hands on Eric's shoulders.

"Is everything all right?" Spear asked, faking concern.

"I'm fine!" Eric said too quickly.

Spear took his own turn glancing between Eric and Andy, two boys he had never before seen together. They ran in separate circles and it was odd for him to see them side-by-side.

"What's going on here?" Spear asked, surprisingly perceptive although unable to pinpoint anything exact.

Eric looked to Andy, partly because he was at a loss for words, and partly because he really wanted to hear Andy's response.

Casually and nonhesitant, Andy stepped close to Eric and swung his arm around Eric's neck. With the inside of his elbow comfortably filled with Eric's head, Andy gave Eric's lean frame a playful shake.

"Well, Mr. Spear, since it's senior year and all, we thought we'd get to know each other better," Andy said. He was upbeat, almost giddy and jolting Eric about in jest.

Spear stared at the star player and his face scrunched, unconvinced. He turned to Eric and asked, "Is that true?"

Before Eric could respond, Andy gave his new buddy another masculine bonding jostle and said, "We never knew how much we have in common."

Spear's face soured at Andy's remark. Andy laughed and stepped away from his unofficial embrace with Eric. He went to Spear's side and patted the principal on the back. "I know it sounds crazy," Andy said. He and Spear took a step away from Eric and together they slowly walked away from the back bathroom hall.

"You always tell everyone to get along," Andy continued. "Well, that's what we're doing, getting to know each other and we're really enjoying it."

"Well, that's great, McCain," Spear said. His tone and attitude changed the instant his head athlete assured him all was well. Whether Spear truly believed it made no difference as long as the issue went away.

Eric did not follow them. He stood still and watched them walk away. Just before Andy and the principal turned the hall corner, Andy looked over his shoulder and did something that only confused Eric further:

He winked.

Chapter Five

Friday, August 30, 1996

As if first period gym wasn't miserable enough, Eric was less than thrilled when Dick announced swimming as the class's first sport. For Eric, it was both a fantasy come true and a living hell rolled into fifty-five minutes. Fifteen sporty boys, shirtless, flexing, and dripping wet: the stuff that dreams were made of. But he knew his mornings wouldn't be an awakened porn film, but rather he would spend those agonizing minutes dodging punches, snapping towels, and verbal attacks on his lean, less muscular frame.

And if a ratty old T-shirt and worn gym shorts weren't unflattering enough, a pair of uniform swim trunks only worsened the fifty-five minutes. Eric was only two inches shy of six feet, but barely a hundred and forty pounds. He was a scrawny guy, but had decent muscle tone. He wasn't strong by any means, but not an unproportioned bag of bones either. Still, standing half-naked beside the likes of muscled hunks Andy McCain, Justin Drake, and the others, Eric was a tiny twig competing against ferocious oak trees.

The shower room in the rear of the locker room, with twenty some shower heads pumping scalding hot water, had a back door that led to the enormous pool room. For cleanliness reasons, the boys always showered before entering the pool, making them ready to swim but freeing up just a few minutes longer to make fun of the boys less blessed in the bodily muscle department, mostly Eric. They humiliated him, throwing shampoo bottles, bars of soap, and whipping drenched towels against his bare skin. It happened junior year too, except one snap of the towel went too far and sliced open Eric's flesh just under his right ribcage. He had to have three butterfly bandages to seal it shut. There was a plus side to the incident though: it got Eric out of swimming for two weeks.

But as always, Eric pressed on and took the beatings with a closed mouth and a trembling heart. When the door to the poolroom opened and Dick appeared on the other side, barking orders for them to line up at the edge of the pool, Eric was relieved the shower assault was over, but petrified to make himself vulnerable at the mercy of the others in a large body of water. Still, he had no choice and filed into the pool area with the others.

The room housed a pool bigger than Eric had ever seen. Even on his yearly summer trip to Vegas with Kate to visit her filthy rich Aunt Janine he never saw a pool so big, and Janine's entire back yard housed a pool an Olympic team would envy. Ann Arbor South prided itself on its pool. It had yet to have a championship team to swim in it, but at least the school was ready for when the team decided to step it up.

Upon entering the cold concrete poolroom floor from the showers on the east side, there were benches and towel racks lining the walls for students. Across the heavily chlorinated water, on the west side of the room, were several rows of high-rising bleachers for spectators to watch events. The south end had two separate level diving boards to spring students into the deep, while the north end had a large electronic scoreboard and a judges' booth for swim meets. At the top of the north wall under the paned windows lining it, was the school's name, printed in bright orange and deep black block letters to represent the school colors.

Dick, armed with a shiny metallic whistle strung around his neck and a clipboard stuffed with unnecessary papers, stood at the head of the pool near the first level diving board. He was in his usual attire, short gym shorts, white polo shirt and knee high socks with yellow and blue stripes around the top pulled as close to his knees as they would stretch.

"Line up, men!" he snapped. "And you too, Anderson!" He smiled viciously at Eric and continued, "Our first exercise is…"

Eric tuned Dick out. It was easy to do, especially when there was so much to look at. With his toes dangling on the edge of the cold concrete pool, Eric stood in between Justin Drake and Matt Murphy. Although petrified and barely able to breathe, Eric couldn't keep his wandering eyes restrained. He tried hard to focus on the still water or Dick's red face but he couldn't resist sneaking illegal peeks at the tantalizing naked flesh of his classmates. It was exciting to see so much bare skinned beauty but the terror of the peek's repercussions was overwhelming. If any one of them caught him sneaking a glance, Eric would surely be drowned. Still, he was so weak. With Wes Palmer's wet chest and hard nipples only a few feet away, Eric just *had* to look, but he made sure the glimpses were so brief no one noticed.

Sick to his stomach with fear, Eric watched the clock on the west side of the room, above the bleachers. Class had only been in session for twelve unbearably long minutes and there were several weeks of swimming still on tap, leaving many more excruciating moments of constant terror to endure.

Suddenly and without warning, Justin Drake's ice-cold hand slapped Eric's shoulder while Matt Murphy's big foot swooped in front of Eric's shins, holding a firm stance. With Justin's slap and Matt's block, Eric lost his balance. Although he fought it with flailing arms and wobbly legs, Eric plummeted into the calm, cool water.

The splash ripped into the room's silence and when Eric resurfaced, the silence was replaced with an uproarious wave of laughter. Justin, Matt, Wes Palmer, and even Dick were beside themselves. Justin exaggeratingly grabbed his stomach and kneeled over, laughing the loudest of all the boys.

Humiliated and treading water, Eric tried to catch his breath and stared up at the pool edge. He took his turn staring at each of the giggling guys. When his gaze paused on Andy McCain, Eric was surprised to see the hunky baseball star and Justin's best friend standing still, his beautiful face expressionless. Andy wasn't smiling or laughing or showing much of anything. With his beefy arms folded tightly against his bare chest, Andy watched Eric closely but didn't engage in the degrading laughter with his friends.

Andy's solemn face surprised but didn't comfort Eric. He was too busy drinking chlorine through his nose to give it much thought. Plus, he had to deal with a fire-breathing Dick.

"Anderson! I didn't tell you to get in the pool!" the gym instructor shouted with a wide, ruthless grin. "Can't you get those bird legs of yours to stand up straight?!"

"He can't do anything straight, sir," Justin quickly retorted.

Dick chuckled and happily patted Justin's back as he paced the pool's edge. In seeing Dick's pride toward the jocks, Eric didn't rat them out. It wouldn't have done any good to tattletale on the young men Dick considered his own sons. Instead, Eric swam to the stainless steel ladder and climbed out of the water. He made sure to take a deep breath in preparation of Dick's impending temper.

"Let's hear it!" Dick ordered, getting into Eric's soaking wet face the instant he crawled out of the pool.

"I slipped," Eric lied, his tone hard and uninterested. He glanced to Justin and Matt, who blew him mock kisses off their extended middle fingers.

Annoyed and unsatisfied with Eric's weak explanation, Dick stepped closer to the skinny wet student, his hot breath burning through Eric's hair. They locked eyes, almost on Dick's insistence. He wanted Eric to know who was boss.

"What do you think, men?" Dick said, never moving his feet or blinking a beady eye. "What should we make our girl Anderson do today?"

"Push-ups!" the boys cheered.

Eric rolled his eyes and tried not to shiver. Waiting for the incoming hard labor sentence, Eric took another look over everyone's shoulders and found Andy McCain nestled in the back of the crowd, watching closely. Andy still hadn't cracked a smile or participated in the tormenting fun. He was quiet, alone in the back, his eyes fixed on Eric.

"No, we won't make him do push-ups today," Dick said. The care in his voice was painfully exaggerated. "But since you love the water so much, maybe you need more time than the rest of these men to practice." He swung around to face his class. "Get into your shirts and shorts, men," he instructed. "You're going to play ball in the gym while Anderson here—" He turned back to Eric and grinned, "—does twenty-five laps in the pool."

"Is that all?" Eric asked bravely, his voice piercing with sarcasm.

"That's what I like, a go-getter." Dick leaned in frighteningly closer. "Make it fifty."

"You're sweet to me," Eric said, unsure of where the words came from.

Dick's grin widened and his crow's feet scrunched tighter, nearly hiding his eyes. "Let's go, men!" he ordered and just as quickly, the boys began filtering out of the pool. Dick looked back to Eric and said, "I'll check on you later. Don't even *think* about getting out of that pool."

With his veiny hands, Dick forcefully gripped Eric's small biceps and pushed him into the water. Eric heard Dick's cackling laughter right before he plunged under the surface. When he reemerged, Dick was gone and the rest of the class was leaving the room in single file.

Andy McCain was the last one in line. Instead of following the others toward the lockers, he stayed behind, walking slow to create a large distance between him and the line of boys. Shuffling his feet and staring at the wet multi-colored tiles on the floor, Andy seemed to use every angle to slow his pace. Not that Eric minded. With Andy moving in slow motion, Eric seized the chance to steal long, juicy looks at the rippling body parts decorating Andy's frame. Even amidst chaos and nearly drowning, Eric still managed to focus enough to appreciate the smooth beauty of Andy's flexed moves.

With Andy still inside the poolroom, the rest of the class left with the door slamming shut behind them. Alone in the silent room, Andy turned to face Eric, who was still in the shallow end of the water, shivering and curious.

"I told you not to piss him off," Andy said, returning to the edge of the pool.

"Thanks for the tip," Eric snapped. He stared at Andy, unsure of why he had stayed behind, but couldn't complain since Andy was in shorts, shirtless, and dripping wet.

"Why didn't you rat them out?" Andy asked. "I saw Justin and Matt push you."

"What's the point? Dick would've turned it around on me anyway. He loves those guys and although that really breaks my heart, I'll try to go on with my life." Eric's sarcasm did not go unnoticed.

Andy laughed. "He's a jock. He doesn't know how to act around someone like you."

Eric cocked his head. "What does that mean?"

"No! I mean someone who isn't athletic or a jock or—" Andy struggled to organize his thoughts.

"Or what?" Eric folded his arms across his wet chest.

Andy shrugged, unsure of what to say.

"I guess that's why you guys treat me like shit. You just don't know how to act around me," Eric mocked.

"I've never been shitty to you," Andy corrected. "We're not all assholes."

"Whatever. Look, I'd love to bullshit with you all day, but can you get out of here? I've got laps to do," Eric said, deepening his voice to sound a little tougher. "And I really don't need Dick coming in and busting my ass again. Plus, I'm self-conscious enough when I'm by myself. I don't need the star player critiquing my athletic abilities."

"What's your problem? I'm trying to be nice." Andy seemed genuine, although Eric might have projected the polite tone since he couldn't concentrate on anything but Andy's drenched swim trunks.

"Are you really being nice or do you feel guilty about having shitty friends?"

"No—"

"You should," Eric quickly added.

"I don't agree with everything they do—"

"You don't stop 'em."

"What am I—?"

"How about saying, 'Hey guys, go to hell!'"

Andy took a step back from the pool edge and laughed. His mouth cracked into a smile and his wet face and hair glistened alongside the bright whiteness of his teeth. His laugh was not condescending, but genuinely amused. As his laughter bounced off the tiled poolroom walls, Andy tickled his navel. Eric's attention peeked. He recalled seeing Andy play with his belly button several times in his presence. It appeared to be a nervous reaction.

"What's so funny?" Eric asked.

"I've never met anyone so pissed off!" Andy said, still chuckling.

"Be proud. You and your friends made me this way."

The laughter stopped and again Andy knelt beside the water's edge. "*They* did," he said calmly. "I've never given you shit."

Again, Eric lost himself for a moment as his eyes surveyed the muscular terrain of Andy's body. By kneeling along the edge, areas of the baseball player's body flexed and bulged in dreamy ways even Eric's imagination couldn't have conjured. Small rivers of water trickled down Andy's shoulders, over the bicep mountains, down the strong forearms to his hands and dripped back into the pool. The droplets moved so slowly, as if knowing their journey was being watched, studied, *envied*, by Eric's eager, wide eyes.

Eric refocused, embarrassed by the unsubtle staring, but noticed, only briefly, that Andy was staring back at him. When their eyes met, Andy's had just left the waistband of Eric's swimsuit. Andy's eyebrow pleasingly twitched so very slightly that Eric wasn't sure if it really happened or if he imagined it entirely.

"You know, there's a lot more people like me out there than there are people like you," Eric said strangely into the silence, his voice cracking.

"People like me?" Andy said, confused. He remained close to the side of the pool.

"Joe Schmoes are more common. Perfect people like you don't even exist." Eric closed his eyes with utter regret the second the words left his lips.

Andy blushed and bowed his head to smile. The embarrassment took Eric by surprise, but he didn't watch Andy long enough to enjoy it. He had his own head bowed, mortified by what he had just said.

"Perfect people like me?" Andy said.

Eric figured he might as well go for broke. "You're pretty much what every guy wants to be," he said, not sure whether to burst into humiliated laughter or scared tears.

"Thanks." Andy's smile grew even bigger.

Finally, Eric bravely raised his head and saw Andy's flattered face. Eric rolled his eyes. "Easy, cowboy. Don't let it go to your head. The last thing you need is a bigger ego," he said with a nervous laugh. "Besides, like you give a shit what I have to say anyway."

Standing from the pool's edge, Andy towered above Eric for a few moments, staring and smiling awkwardly. He had determination in his stance just waiting to spring forth. He went back to the locker room door and, after swinging it open, disappeared inside. Eric frowned at the ball player's exit, but he also heaved a relieved sigh. His system was in overdrive in the presence of the half-naked Andy and he couldn't take anymore of the wet, muscled, flexing body parts, sweet toothy grin, or tickled navel. Most of all, though, Eric couldn't take the polite, energetically charged conversation. There was a strong positive vibe between them that made Eric think or at least imagine there was more at work than two different worlds coming together in friendship.

But, with Andy's departure, Eric was left only with his projected thoughts.

Almost.

The locker room door reopened and Andy returned. Without a second of hesitation, he rushed to the side of the swimming pool and dove in. Waves rushed through every inch of the water, beating against the edges of the pool and soaking every inch of Eric's shaky, surprised skin. He stood, shivering and scared, as Andy disturbed the calm water and stepped back to watch Andy's strong figure swim gracefully under the cool blue liquid. Andy resurfaced only a few feet from Eric's face.

"What're you doing?" Eric asked and took another confused step away.

Andy wiped the water from his eyes. Eric stared at Andy's soaked body as Andy ran his hands through his hair. Waterfalls rushed over Andy's biceps, through his armpits, and down his chest and stomach until returning to the pool. Andy opened his eyes and smiled when he saw Eric's dropped jaw and wide eyes.

"Everyone's playing ball in the gym," Andy said, wiping the water from his nose. "I wanted to make sure we'd be alone."

No words left Eric's awestruck mouth. There were no words. Did he even speak English? For those moments he forgot how to *move*. All he could do—and hardly do at that—was stand in the waist-high water, staring at the beautiful, drenched boy in front of him. He followed the drops of water like road maps over the terrain of Andy's body. The journey started in the north at Andy's broad shoulders and led south to the smooth defined chest and perky, hard nipples surrounded by goose bumps from the chill in the air. From there, the drops led to the hard, toned stomach and then onto the circular navel. It was small, round, and dusted with blonde hair. Eric's eyes followed the hairy trail from the belly button until it disappeared into the waistband of Andy's shorts.

Although aware of his staring didn't stop him from doing it. Instead, Eric slowly followed the defined lines of Andy's arms from the start of his rough hands, gliding over the fleshy forearms all the way up the hilly curves of his biceps until returning to the wide shoulders. He didn't stop there. Following the neckline, Eric's eyes journeyed past Andy's strong, chiseled jaw, his full wet lips and distinct nose, stopping at Andy's wide, awakened eyes.

This time, Eric saw without imagination, that Andy was staring back at him. Andy's eyes wandered over Eric's skin and studied every inch just as closely as Eric had studied him. The tiny beauty mark on Eric's left shoulder, the sharp Adam's apple, and his less defined but equally beautiful muscle tone, it all reflected in Andy's absorbent eyes. The small nipples that had once outraged Eric in a world of Calvin Klein beefcakes, were now under the close inspection of Andy's rough fingertips. But through the roughness came a delicate, caring stroke as Andy's fingers explored the territory of Eric's skin.

Eric knew it with a firm certainty that he wasn't hallucinating. Andy was surveying his body, touching it, committing parts to memory as his coy smile suggested, and it never once made Eric uncomfortable. It raced Eric's blood and excited him in other areas he hoped his swimsuit would conceal, but he never felt the urge to swim away.

A slow breeze swept over the water from the opened windows near the ceiling of the enormous room. It chilled Eric and he held his arms close to his chest to ward off the cold. Andy glided closer to him, rippling small waves as he moved, and gently placed his hands on Eric's goose-bumped arms.

"You're shaking," Andy whispered and rubbed Eric's wanting skin. Their locked gaze never broke or shifted.

With ease and a cool confidence, Andy slid his hands under the water and lightly grabbed Eric's hips. He pulled him closer until their pelvises touched. Eric was initially surprised but eased into relief when he realized Andy's swim trunks were just as tight as his own. Their naked chests grazed together and Eric felt Andy's beating heart pound against his flesh. Andy's sweet, hot breath warmed his face as they stood there, embraced, waiting, and gasping for air. Moving the last few inches closer to Eric's face, Andy's full lips lightly grazed against the wanting skin of Eric's mouth. Eric didn't fight it. His knees wobbled and his heart pounded too fast for him to move or think.

He didn't want to do anything but kiss Andy McCain.

All the years Eric had spent dreaming of kissing him was actually happening and to Eric's overwhelming delight, the hot skin of Andy's lips tasted even better than he expected.

But it was short lived.

Suddenly and seemingly without a sound, the locker room door swung open and Dick stormed into the poolroom. Just as quickly, Andy grabbed Eric's shoulders and dunked him under the water. He repeatedly dipped Eric in and out, laughing and yelling nothing in particular as he did it. Each time Eric resurfaced and gasped for air, he managed to swear and scream at Andy, claw at his arms and chest, and with his sudden strong fury, he even managed to pull Andy under the surface twice.

"What the hell's going on here?!" Dick's voice erupted like a volcano, nearly shattering the windowpanes and the tiles off the walls. He frantically blew his whistle to gain the boys' attention.

Andy ceased the attack on Eric and wiped the water from his eyes. "Anderson was messing with me, sir," he said, standing upright to talk to Dick. "I was teaching him a lesson."

Dick looked at Eric, who was trying to catch his breath. Dick grinned at the drowned rat and let out a hearty laugh. "Good job, McCain," Dick cheered. "Now change your shorts and get to the gym!"

Obeying his orders, Andy swam to the edge of the pool and jumped out. He covered the front of his swimsuit with both hands to hide his lingering excitement. Dick proudly patted Andy's back and ushered him to the locker room door. On their way, Dick turned back to the pool. "Get on with your laps, Anderson!" he ordered. "And stop messin' with these men!"

Exhausted and speechless, Eric stood in the water, watching Dick congratulate Andy once more with another strong slap to the back. Dick led the way back to the locker room. This time, Andy did not trail behind or miss a single step. Smiling and laughing happily, they disappeared behind the main door.

Andy did not look back.

Chapter Six

At the end of first period, Eric was the last to leave the locker room. As always, he took his time changing out of his grubby gym garb and back into his street clothes. He liked to wait for the other boys to change and exit the room before switching outfits. There was only so much fag bashing and towel snapping he could take. There was always the rest of the day for further humiliation, no need to overdose on the misery first thing in the morning.

Also, as usual, Eric was late for second period. He risked detention so early in the school year for tardiness, but he didn't mind. An hour or so in a quiet detention room was better than a rowdy, abusive bunch of boys attacking him as he changed.

As Eric headed for the locker room door, rushing to get to English class, Dick stopped him. "Hey! Anderson!" he barked.

"What?" Eric groaned, annoyed and not in the mood.

"You better stop fooling around with these men!" Dick ordered, swinging his chubby, gray-haired index finger in Eric's face. Dick's forehead turned a frightening shade of red as his voice and blood pressure raised. Winding purple veins pulsated in perfect beat with each swing of his finger. "I don't care what you do outside of my gym," he continued at full force. "But when you're here, on *my* turf, you won't put the moves on my men."

69

"What're you talking about?!" Eric was infuriated. His head quickly matched a similar shade of Dick's red. "That's insane!"

"I know what you were doing to McCain in that pool today and I won't stand for it!" Little drops of spittle flicked from his lips and sizzled on Eric's heated face. "Keep your hands off these men. They ain't like you!"

"Oh, hell no!" Eric shouted. "What does *that* mean?!"

"You know damn well what it means!" Dick took a step toward Eric. Their chests collided and the force bumped Eric right out of the office doorway. He stumbled but refused to lose his balance and grabbed the nearest bench to brace himself.

"You can't treat me like this!" Eric protested with every ounce of courage his body could conjure. But it was no use. Dick heard the cracking in his voice and saw his trembling knees.

"Get the hell out of my gym," Dick ordered.

This time, the firmness of Dick's voice and his clenched fists, wised up Eric. There was no fighting the ex-Army drill sergeant. Unless he wanted a broken nose, Eric needed to get out of there, fast. Trying to hide any fear not yet painfully exposed, Eric grabbed his backpack and left the locker room. In the background, as he exited the gym, he heard Dick's deep, hearty laughter echoing from the office.

Annoyed but relieved to be on his way, Eric headed for English class. On the way, in the crowded hallway stuffed with hustling students, Andy McCain approached him. Without saying a word or slowing his speed, Andy placed a piece of paper, folded nearly a dozen times, into Eric's hand. The exchange was lightning fast. Once their hands touched and the note was passed, Andy kept on his way. He did not stop, speak, or look back.

Eric stepped to the side of the hall, to the most secluded area he could find considering the busyness, and unfolded the note. There were only a few words printed in block letters, strongly pressed into the scrap paper with black ink:

LIBRARY. AFTER SCHOOL. 2:15.

A-

"Huh?" Eric asked, exhausted and confused. He refolded the paper and looked in both directions to make sure no one had seen him or the note. Glancing over his shoulder, he unintentionally locked eyes with beautiful and prissy Tara Sanderson. Surprisingly, Eric couldn't recall ever having a run-in with her, but he disliked her just the same, probably in part of Kate's intense hatred for the female Innards. The snotty, self-righteous bitchiness oozing from Tara's pores made her an enemy like the others, with or without direct contact.

Standing only a few feet away, it appeared Tara had witnessed the exchange between Eric and Andy. Her eyes were narrowed and she watched Eric closely, finally taking a small step toward him. Staring closer with an inspecting eye, Eric couldn't tell if the inquisitive look on her face was confusion or confirmation, like she had uncovered a long-guarded secret and, although surprised by the revelation, was very proud of her discovery. Eric didn't want to find out.

"Freeze, bitch!" he said firmly, pointing his index finger at Tara, instructing the wench to keep her distance.

Tara stopped and swung her hands on her hips. "Excuse me?" she snapped, her mouth open from shock. No one so low on the food chain ever spoke to her in such a way.

"Anything you have to say to me, I sure as hell don't have time for right now," Eric said. He stuffed Andy's note into his pants pocket and hurried off to class before she could respond.

Once he was gone, Tara was left in the hall, her mouth still gapping only slightly. She quickly closed it. "We'll see," she said to herself and went on her way.

***

Eric's feet couldn't get him to second period fast enough. He made it before the final bell rang and rushed to the rear of the classroom. Kate and Nick were already there, sitting at their desks, talking. Eric weeded through the small crowd of students and grabbed Kate's hand.

"I have to talk to you!" he said, yanking Kate to her feet. "Sorry Nick!"

"What the hell?!" Kate said as Eric dragged her to the hallway.

Just as the final bell rang, they pushed their way past the last few students filtering inside and stepped into the hall. Kate and Eric knew Mark Morgan would mark them tardy for the day, but it didn't matter. Eric's news superseded any tardiness.

"Where's the fire?" Kate asked, flipping her hair over her shoulder and staring intently at her best friend. She saw an uncertain determination in his eyes.

As soon as they were alone in the emptied hall, Eric gushed about the thrilling poolroom antics. Every word escaped his mouth in a fast, jumbled rush. The story sped out like lightning, each word faster than the one before. He left nothing out: the empty pool, Andy jumping in, the talking, the touching, the *kissing*! He couldn't contain his excitement while Kate froze. Only her eyes showed movement, growing wider with each juicy word added to the fiery tale. When Eric fished Andy's handwritten note from his pocket, Kate's mouth dropped when she read it.

"Can you believe this?" Eric said, panting.

Kate held the note in her hands, staring at every block-lettered word. Never one to shake under pressure, Kate's hands teetered only slightly while gripping the paper.

"Unless I smoked too much crack this morning, this is for real," Eric said. He was antsy, repeatedly shifting his weight from one foot to the other, waiting for Kate to speak.

Slowly, she folded the note back into its intricately creased pattern and looked at him. "Now, I'm not one to say this," she said, smiling. "But I told you so!"

"Not so loud, *crotch*!" Eric snatched the note from her hand and returned it to his pocket.

"So, wait a minute," Kate said, hooking her hair behind her ears. "He really jumped into the pool with you? Like, splish-splashed, cannonballed, belly-flopped into the pool?"

"It was a little more graceful than that," Eric said and added in a whisper, "But yeah, he did." He rubbed his forehead and, regardless of the isolated location, spoke very quietly so only Kate could hear. "He

72

looked at me, Kate. He really *looked* at me like he could see *into* me instead of right *through* me like everyone else." The excitement exercised his hands, emphasizing the passion in every word through exaggerated movements. "And he *kissed* me!"

Kate's eyes grew wide watching the feverish enthusiasm of Eric's story come to life. "I can't believe you and Mr. Baseball got all porno in the pool! You are such a slut! I'm so proud!" she cheered but quickly added, "I mean, it's so totally clichéd that the school jock's turning out to play for your team, but who cares? This is amazing!"

But, as always, the exhilaration of their mini-hallway party was short-lived. To their familiar disappointment, Justin turned the corner, jogging from the opposite end of the hall, late for class again. Upon seeing them, a wicked proud grin came to his unfairly attractive face.

"Hey, fag!" Justin shouted. "Why're you two out here? Queers and bitches no longer allowed in class?" He laughed at the lame joke but wasn't exactly greeted with smiles as he approached. He painfully slapped Eric on the back and blew Kate a spit-soaked kiss.

"This is your only warning," Kate said, calmly pointing her manicured index finger at him. "Don't call me a bitch again."

Justin rolled his eyes and turned to Eric. "Did you have a nice fall into the pool?" he asked, repeatedly poking Eric in the arm with his hard fingers. "Your ass probably couldn't even do one lap!"

Eric jerked away from the jabbing. "Go infect somebody else!" he snapped.

"Oh! You've got balls today!" Justin poked harder, this time into Eric's chest.

"What the hell is this?" Kate snapped. She smacked Justin upside the head. The loud WHACK! playfully bounced off the hall lockers.

"SHIIIIT!" Justin belted, turning to Kate with his hands clenched into fists. His mouth dropped the smile and slammed shut, tightly clenching his jaw. His flared nostrils exhaled hot, angry puffs of sour air.

"Get your dumb ass inside!" she snapped and firmly stood her ground. Kate had to stare almost to the ceiling to look into Justin's eyes since he was over a foot taller than her. "Why do we have to have the same fight every day?"

Finally, Justin's mouth creaked open to speak.

Kate quickly interrupted. "Nope! I don't want to hear your bullshit!" she snapped, holding her hand up in face. "So get the hell out of here."

To Eric and Kate's aid, old Jonathan Browning, the bald, stocky and usually out of breath Biology teacher, turned the hall corner. When he saw Justin towering over Kate with angry fists and an obviously upset Eric watching close by, Browning B-lined straight for them.

"What's going on here?" he asked, his voice gruff and scratchy from the many cigarette breaks he tried hiding from the students. (Although on a bad day he'd bum a smoke from the first underage student he could find).

"Nothing, Mr. B!" Justin said too fast and too sweetly.

"Get to class, Mr. Drake," Browning ordered, his voice firmer than before.

Justin opened the classroom door and winked at Kate before disappearing inside. Just as she and Eric were about to follow, Browning stopped them. "Is everything all right, you two?" he asked. His interest seemed almost genuine, but when Kate saw him glance at his watch, she abandoned all hope.

"Does it really matter?" she asked with a fake toothy grin.

"Good, good," Browning said, adjusting the wad of papers under his arm instead of listening to her plea. "Try to stay out of trouble. Now get to class." Without another glance, he was gone.

"What the hell's with this place?" Eric asked, frustrated by Browning's dismissal.

"Relax, Norma Rae. No use in trying to change the system now," Kate said with a laugh. She settled back into the supportive best friend role before adding, "So, call me tonight and tell me what Andy says."

"You think I should go to the library?" Eric tried not to sound desperate.

Kate softened and wrapped her arm around his waist. "I think you should proceed with caution," she said sweetly. "You know you want to go, so you should. Just be careful."

"What if it's a trick?" Eric's agitation increased. His eyes swelled with tears and he tried hard to hold them back. "What if Andy's there with Justin and the other guys just waiting to kick my ass?"

"Then call me and I'll come beat the shit out of them!"

Eric laughed a little. "I'm serious, Kate." His voice shook on every syllable. "What if it's a set-up?"

"What if it's not?" she said softly.

Eric's face lit up but uncertainty still glistened in his watery eyes.

Kate took a deep breath. "Look, I don't trust it anymore than you do," she said. "But what if this is what you've been waiting for?"

"I don't want to walk into a trap." He turned away to wipe a tear from his cheek in hopes Kate wouldn't see it but she did. Kate gently grabbed Eric's shoulder and turned him back to face her.

"Do you want me to go with you?" she offered but already knew the answer.

Eric shook his head. "No."

"Then trust your instincts. Think with your head but follow your heart too. If it doesn't feel right when you get there, get the hell out," she said. Her smiling face comforted him, as it usually did. "And call my ass for back-up if you need it."

A smile finally came to Eric's face and he let out a tiny laugh. Kate embraced him inside her loving arms and kissed his cheek.

Four hours, fifty-two minutes, and sixteen seconds until his library date.

***

Andy was at his locker the instant classes ended for the day to dump his Math book. Scrambling through the storage space, Andy couldn't concentrate. His hands trembled and made organizing his History notes difficult. He grabbed his jacket, the notes, and his History book to take home and slammed the locker shut.

When he swung around, Andy almost bumped noses with Justin Drake. "Shit!" Andy said loudly, startled.

"Sorry, man," Justin said and playfully punched Andy's right arm. "You ready?"

"No, man, I have to hit the library like we talked about," Andy said. "Remember?"

"Oh yeah. You need any help with that?"

"No, I got it."

"All right. I'll catch ya later then."

"See ya, J," Andy said and watched Justin run off. Andy clutched his book and turned toward the library hall. When he did, he nearly collided again with another student, the overly pretty Tara Sanderson. "God dammit!" Andy was annoyed.

"Hello to you too," Tara said, smiling sweetly.

"What's up?" Andy asked quickly, trying not to sound impatient.

Tara stared at him her eyes narrow with thought. "Are you okay?" she asked. Her face was calm and non-threatening.

"I'm fine," he said firmly. It was odd for Andy to hear concern in Tara's voice since it so rarely happened and he was uneasy in the presence of her politeness. Once upon a time it meant she was plotting something or pumping him for information, even when they had dated. Standing there in the hallway, though, he noticed a kindness to her face he recognized only in full-blooded humans, not cold-hearted prom queens.

"Are you sure?" Tara's sweetness turned serious. "Why're you in such a hurry?"

"I have to go." Andy turned and walked away.

She paced him and gently grabbed his shoulder. "Wait a minute."

He stopped but didn't turn back. "What?" His impatience was obvious.

"I know you better than you think," she said calmly. "We did date, you know—"

"That was a long time ago." He still wouldn't face her.

"But we're still friends. You can talk to me if you need to."

"I said I'm fine."

She took her hand off his shoulder and said, "You never ran this fast to see me."

Slowly, Andy looked over his shoulder. "What?" His voice was low and focused.

Tara's eyes widened, nervous by the hardened look in Andy's face. "Whoever you're going to see," she said carefully. "You were never this excited to see me."

Chapter Seven

By the time Eric was standing in the quiet hallway in front of the library doors, his head was pounding from a wicked headache. It had been a harsh Friday afternoon, frantically watching every clock in every room in every hallway and on every wrist for hours.

2:19.

Shit! He was four minutes late. Why wouldn't his feet move? He glanced over his shoulder at each end of the hallway, as if searching for a reason not to open the door. But the hall was empty, not a single student in sight.

"Screw it!" he said barley above a whisper.

Eric grabbed the handle and swung the door open. There was a soft echo through the library when it shut behind him. He stood, partially frozen and wobbly-kneed in the doorway and surveyed the monstrous bookshelves and tables for Andy's face. Twirling his eyes so quickly through every inch of the room made him dizzy. Still, through his blurred vision, he kept looking but didn't see the baseball player.

He took a deep breath. And another. And another. And one more. His dizziness intensified with the increased oxygen level. Leslie Rose, the overweight and quiet, but still take-no-loud-prisoners librarian sat at the head of the room, stuffed into a straining chair behind a computer and a mound of returned books. She looked at him only briefly as she stamped dates into the hardcovers. The books and her half-eaten Snickers bar required more attention, whether Eric was nearly hyperventilating or not.

Eric strengthened his shaky gaze and reexamined every nook and cranny of the room. There were no students at the computers or magazine racks, no teachers at the reference desk and no one at the copy machines or even the drinking fountain and no sign of Andy McCain. Eric saw only lonely, burly Rose with her books and candy bar.

"What am I doing here?" Eric asked, unsure of whether he spoke out loud or in his mind. Rose didn't flinch. He turned back to the door.

Just as Eric was about to leave, a flash of red caught his attention. Glancing over Rose's broad shoulders, Eric saw Andy appear from the back library hallway. The hall led to the newspaper archive room and the restrooms. Andy wore a tight red BASEBALL PLAYERS DO IT BETTER T-shirt that, although lame, made Eric's face match the shade of the shirt.

Half relieved and half terrified that the invitation wasn't a joke, Eric stayed in the doorway, fidgeting with his backpack strap. He felt more than a little awkward now that the athlete in the tight tee, with an unintentionally adorable arch to his eyebrow and strong clench to his jaw, headed right for him. As Andy approached, Eric watched every muscle flex through the fabric of the red shirt. The word PLAYERS stretched across the center of Andy's chest and his nipples pitched tiny tents through the letters.

It was *way* too much. Eric turned and made a quick break for the door.

Andy caught Eric and lightly grabbed his arm. "I wasn't sure you'd come," Andy said, speaking softly to avoid setting off the very sound-sensitive Rose.

"I don't know why I did," Eric said, jittery from the strong hand on his elbow. He shook so badly from the gentle touch that his bag fell off his unstable shoulder to the floor. Before he could pick it up, Andy swooped down and grabbed the strap.

"Can you stay?" Andy asked, holding onto Eric's bag. "Can we talk?"

Looking in every direction for who knows what, Eric stuffed his hands in his pockets. Then he folded his arms across his chest. Then back into his jeans as his left foot rocked on its ankle.

"Are you okay?" Andy asked, smiling so subtly that it might have only been a flinch.

"I'm fine," Eric said and heaved a long sigh. He glanced over Andy's shoulder and took another look around the library for any possible Innards waiting to jump out and feed on his unsuspecting soon-to-be corpse. He saw no one, only Rose busting into a Butterfinger.

Eric calmed himself. He took his hands out of his pants pockets and wiped the sweat off. Looking at Andy's face again, Eric saw excitement in the athlete's eyes. Upon closer inspection, Eric saw Andy's hands, still clutching his backpack, slightly shaking. Eric's interest peeked.

"I can stay for a minute," Eric said.

Andy smiled, flashing his heart-stopping dimples, and headed for a secluded table in the furthest corner of the room. Without thinking, Andy pulled a chair out from the table and went to the other side and pulled out a second chair and sat down. No one had ever pulled a chair out for Eric before, except once during freshman year when Jay Edmond and Matt Murphy tied him to a chair, drew cat whiskers on his face, stapled a handwritten sign to his shirt that read PUSSY, and wheeled him through the halls.

Eric glanced around the room again, waiting for the insulting punch line or the other shoe to drop like an anvil. It was too good to be true. A pulled out chair?! Something was up. It was all too familiar, like an orchestrated signed calling card from Justin Drake and the Ann Arbor South Jock Squad. Where were they?

Hiding under the table? Eric checked. No one was there.

Behind the tall true-crime bookshelf? He checked there too. Empty.

On the other side of the huge spinning globe? No. Still, no one.

Andy and Eric were alone.

"What're you looking for?" Andy asked, carefully setting Eric's bag onto the tabletop along with his own handful of books.

"Oh, I don't know, guys with baseball bats and some time to kill?" Eric said, nervously returning to the table and sliding into the selected chair. "Or maybe a bucket of blood's going to fall from the sky?"

Andy laughed but they both looked up to the fluorescent lights. No bucket. No blood.

"Why?" Andy asked.

Eric simply replied, "Habit."

"That's a weird habit." Andy smiled again and it started to irritate Eric. The thick hot air choked him and wore his patience thin. The endless smiles, although titillating, seemed only to buy Andy time, a clever form of avoidance.

"Why am I here, Andy?" Eric asked.

Andy's face brightened at the sound of his name coming from Eric's lips, but a sweaty brow replaced the excitement. "I thought we should talk about what happened this morning." His hands shook harder and he hid them under the table. Steering clear of Eric's face, he kept his head bowed or turned away.

"What about it?" Eric asked nonchalantly, trying to lighten the suddenly intense mood. Seeing Andy's quick descent into nervousness and fear was unsettling.

"I can't stop—" Andy cut himself off. He wasn't ready. His thoughts needed more prep time. He popped off his ball cap and ran his fingers through his short brown hair, harshly rubbing his forehead with the palms of his hands.

Eric awkwardly looked around the room again, not sure what to do. Rose was certainly no help and Kate was nowhere to be found. "You can't stop what?" he asked, turning back to Andy's bowed head.

Andy whispered something but he spoke so soft Eric didn't hear. Eric slid his chair in close, leaned over the table, and said, "What?"

"Nothing," Andy lied, speaking louder and leaning back in his chair. Almost immediately he was back to his old confident self, rocking on the chair's hind legs and smiling brightly.

It was frightening how fast it happened, how fast Andy changed from one temper to the next, from an insecure, possibly hurt young man to a cocky athletic bastard. So fast and almost calculated, Eric realized

SKOT HARRIS

it was the foreseen prank coming to life. Andy was screwing around and the impending punch line finally reared its ugly face.

"You're an asshole," Eric snapped, standing from his seat. "Why did I ever fall for this?" He grabbed his bag and slid it over his shoulder.

The chair legs slammed back to the floor and Andy jumped to his feet. "Where're you going?" he asked with panic in his voice.

"Carrying my bag and pulling out my chair was a nice touch. You get extra points for making me believe you weren't a total prick." Eric left the table and headed for the door.

"Don't go!" Andy chased after him. "Please. I'm not ready. I can't get my words right!"

"Drop dead!" Eric belted, pushing the library door open and stepping into the hall.

"Come on, Eric! Please! I'm serious!" Andy pleaded. His voice bounced off the empty walls. The hall was just as eerily empty as the library. No visible signs of life.

Ignoring every word, Eric walked faster toward the parking lot. He grabbed the new bulky, oversized cellular phone his father had bought him for emergencies. Its dependability and reception was questionable at best, but at the moment, needing a ride from Kate was certainly an emergency and Eric prayed for a decent signal. Before Eric could dial Kate's number, Andy had reached him and grabbed the phone from his hand.

"Do you mind? I need to call in a ride since your ass made me miss the bus," Eric said and snatched it back from Andy's hand. As Eric dialed, Andy spoke.

"Why would I kiss you if this was a joke?" Andy said quietly.

Eric stopped pressing buttons but kept staring at the phone. It took a minute for Andy's words to register and repeat in his head. The only word he could seem to find was, "Huh?"

"I really want to talk to you."

The seriousness in Andy's whispering voice raised Eric's head. Andy's face was tired, anxious, but beautiful as ever and like a sucker, Eric fell for it.

"You're good," Eric said, shaking his head and tossing his phone

82

back into his bag. "But if you're screwing with me, I'm going to turn Kate loose on you and she'll eat your balls for breakfast, *fried.*"

Andy cracked a smile and held out his hand toward the library. "Please."

Annoyed by his own foolishness, Eric sighed and went back inside to their table as Andy followed closely behind. They sat down, facing each other again, but Andy's gaze was less direct and even more distracted.

"Don't jerk me around," Eric said and folded his arms across his chest. "Get on with it."

Andy nodded, thought for a moment, and began, "There was this guy I knew when I was younger." His fingers fanned the edges of his American History book so roughly that every so often a small tear ripped through the pages and echoed through the silent library. But with each tear, Andy only flipped the pages faster.

"His name was Mitch," Andy said quietly. Another rip.

Eric leaned close to hear and he was a little annoyed by the minor book shredding.

"We spent summers together up north in Bayport near the lake. His family had a cottage next to mine." With every word, Andy was tense. His voice cracked and he made no eye contact. "He started visiting when we were 13 and for three summers we were, like, blood brothers. We used to fish and kill shit with BB guns and get into all kinds of trouble and when we were 15, we started chasing girls." His demeanor plummeted even further into avoidance. Eric knew by Andy's tight jaw and clenched fists that he was forcing himself to speak. Eric realized Andy wasn't lying, but dead serious and meant every word. It was no punch-lined prank.

"Are you okay?" Eric asked, grasping for something to say.

"I'm fine!" Andy snapped. He caught the anger in his voice and looked at Eric's face as an apology. "Something wasn't right for me when girls started coming around," he said quietly. "I always liked them. They were cute and all, but something didn't click."

Eric sighed. Although thrilled to be sitting near the sports star, Eric was less than thrilled to hear of Andy's womanizing past. He listened to every word from Andy's mouth and while functioning properly in his presence remained a struggle, Eric had a hard time understanding why he was there. But still, he listened.

Andy continued, "There was always something wrong, something making it hard for me to get with girls. Every time they were around, I was more interested in hanging with Mitch than making out with them." He took his hat off again and scratched his head. "Then, toward the end of the summer, we went to Adventure Land in Caseville, the next town over. We were in the guys' locker room, changing into our suits for the water slide—" He stuffed his head back into the hat and leaned back in his chair, crossing his arms across his chest and staring at the ground.

During Andy's quiet spell, Eric impatiently waited for the conclusion to the story, which he hoped was juicy, although he deduced what was coming due to a quick common sense. But as the story's conclusion drew closer, he wasn't sure what he would do with the information anyway. So again, he just kept his ears open.

Speaking barely above a whisper, Andy said, "The room was empty, at least I think it was, and we were in our shorts. Mitch came running from the bathroom and slipped on the floor. He fell flat on his ass and I ran over to help him up. When I bent down to give him my hand, we were really close to each other and when he looked at me, I guess I saw something there, something that made me just want to…kiss him. So I did."

Eric's eyeballs almost popped out of their sockets. He wasn't sure he heard correctly, but Andy's words replayed at lightning speed in his mind until he comprehended the thrown curve ball. Determined to stay composed, Eric stared at Andy, mechanically nodding every few moments to signal he was listening closely, and tried not to scream.

"I don't remember how long it lasted, but I do remember his beard grew faster than mine and it scratched my face," Andy said with a long pause before going on. "Most of all, I remember the look on his face when he punched me square in the jaw and kicked me away, like I was a monster. He screamed some shit about not being a fag and that he'd beat my ass if I ever told anyone about it. I wanted to say something but

I didn't know what to say. But before I even could, he ran out of the locker room."

Andy's head never rose from the floor. It stared coldly, hard at the torn carpet. "That was the last time I ever saw him," he added. "He left Bayport early that summer hating my guts. But that's cool because I hated myself just as much. After he was gone, I told myself I'd never let anyone hurt me like that and that I'd never be so stupid again. So I pushed it out of my head and refused to think about it. " Andy spoke softly, but matter-of-factly and finally raised his head, his juicy tale concluded.

Although reeling from the revelation that his dream man was now swimming in the same sexual pool, Eric had a few things of his own to say. His first instinct actually wasn't to hurl himself across the tabletop and kiss the beefy ballplayer. Instead, there was a truckload of vicious truths he wanted to bring to Andy's attention. It surprised Eric he didn't have any sympathy or compassion for Andy's story.

"Are you finished?" Eric asked.

Andy nodded with relief.

"Let me tell you a story now," Eric said, taking a deep breath and bravely moving forward. "Those summers, while you were off discovering yourself with Mitch, I was here, where I always am, running away from assholes like Justin Drake and Wes Palmer. No matter where I went in town, they'd find me and harass the hell out of me in some way or another. Let's see, they found me at the movies and made me eat popcorn off the floor. They followed me to Kate's house and let the air out of my Dad's tires. They bombed my mailbox. They egged my house. Do I have to go on?" He paused to breathe. "So while you were off having your self-discovery sessions with Mitchypoo, I was getting my ass kicked. You're making out with some guy wondering what it all means while I'm getting crank phone calls and flaming piles of dog shit thrown through my bedroom window. Call me crazy, but I think that's a little different than your little *90210*-moment by the bay. Do you have any idea what I'd do for my own Mitch?"

"But he broke my heart. I put myself out there for him and it bombed!"

Eric rolled his eyes. "Trust me, you'll find yourself another Mitch. Just look in the mirror. You're not exactly the hunchback escaped from the bell tower or Sloth from *Goonies*, okay? Boys'll be beating down your door when they know you're on the market." Eric's hands moved wildly as he spoke, emphasizing his anger and frustration. "Your little after-school pity party is a bunch of bullshit. We should all have such serious problems. I mean, it sucks your heart was broken years ago, but my heart's broken everyday. Dealing with Justin and Wes and Dick and all these other assholes is my *life*! Do you get that?"

Unexpectedly, Andy listened closely to every word out of Eric's heated, rambling mouth. He reacted only to the horrible things that happened to Eric, not the venomous personal attack fired against him. When Eric mentioned the abuse, Andy's eyebrows lowered or his lips flickered into frowns. And during the verbal battle, the drumming and tearing of the History book stopped and Andy barely breathed as the words rolled off Eric's tongue. Andy couldn't believe what he was hearing, but the real amazement came in seeing Eric remain composed, aside from the strong hand gestures, and so concise as he spoke. It left Andy speechless.

Once Eric's last word was spoken, they stared at each other in silence. The library remained empty, aside from Rose and her crinkling candy wrappers. In the stillness, as if alone entirely with only Andy, Eric calmed himself with a few deep breaths. His nervousness continued to show through his shaking legs, but he paid no attention since he knew Andy couldn't see them under the table. He was screaming inside his skin and his wobbly legs remained a good outlet to release the constricted energy.

"That's amazing," Andy said, flashing his wholehearted smile again. "How do you do that?" Eric made a confused face, making Andy laugh at the expression. "I mean, how do you rip me a new asshole and not even break a sweat?"

Eric fought off smiling as long as he could. He wasn't going to smile; he refused to. But within seconds, his lips gave way to a grin. With a hint of playfulness in his quieted voice, Eric said, "Screw you."

Andy laughed louder and it bounced off every inch of the ceiling and walls. Rose awakened from her book-stamping trance and exaggeratingly SHH-ed the boys at their table, soaking the index finger held to her lips with spit. Andy waved to her with his perfected, charming, guiltless and gleaming smile and she returned to her desk.

"I better watch my ass or Rose's going to rip me another new one," he said, lowering his voice and turning back to Eric.

Sitting with his arms folded across his chest, Eric was ready for some answers. The pretty person sitting across the table was delicious eye candy, but his still-racing heart couldn't take much more. "What about Tara?" he asked, trying to force depth into his quivering voice.

"What about her?" Andy asked, uninterested.

"Didn't you used to date?"

"We were only together for, like, two months. I had to keep suspicion down."

"So you used her?" Eric was appalled.

"No, well, yes, NO!" He paused to think. "She's great. We're still friends."

"What's going on?" Eric asked, finally brave enough to ask his most important question. "I'm not Mitch so I don't know what was going on in the pool today. Why am I here?"

Andy's nervousness returned and he reached for the History book. Eric quickly snatched it away from his fingers and slid it off the glossy tabletop. The BOOM! it made upon impact with the floor was even louder than their SHH-ed laughter. They didn't look at Rose, though. Eric stared only at Andy's face, waiting for a response, demanding one with his eyes, and it was clear he didn't want Andy distracted from the answer.

In a soft, frightened voice Eric had never heard before, Andy spoke. "I wanted to talk to you about what happened." He broke the locked gaze with Eric and stared at the table. He scratched his bitten fingernails into the creases of the soft wood. It made tiny indents and occupied him for only a moment. He cleared his throat and said, "At the end of junior year, something happened to me that I've been thinking about a lot, especially every time I see you." Andy didn't look up from the impressed tabletop fingernail designs. He stayed turned away, unsure of what he would find in Eric's eyes.

"What are you talking about?" Eric asked, lost by Andy's rambling. He moved his head in several directions, trying to relock with Andy's wandering gaze.

"At the end of last year, I was leaving school and I passed by you and Kate heading for the parking lot. Your friend Nick might have been there too," Andy said, trying to buy himself some time by recalling every little detail. "It was the end of the day—"

Eric impatiently interrupted, "Get to the point, please."

Andy licked his dry lips, took one last deep, brave breath and continued, "When I passed you, I heard you laugh. I don't know at what, but you were laughing, like, *really* laughing and I had never heard you do that before."

"Probably because you've never been around me," Eric said, chuckling. "I don't get it."

"Your laugh sounds just like Mitch's."

Eric's jaw nearly hit the table. He closed it quickly to avoid showing too much emotion. But under his skin, his veins were adrenaline racetracks. "What?" was all he could say.

Once again, Andy's eyes wandered. "You sound like Mitch," he repeated softly, bowing his head. Eric could only see the top of Andy's ball cap and he suspected Andy was crying. He had wondered, imagined, *dreamed* of what Andy's beautiful face looked like crying, with tears on his cheeks and dripping off his chiseled chin. Deep down Eric hoped, if for only a second, to catch All-Star Andy cry and reveal he was actually human. But he didn't. When Andy raised his head, there were no tears.

Andy cleared his throat and adjusted his hat. "When I heard you laugh," he said. "It did something to me."

Eric's attention was completely undivided. He even stopped paying attention to his knocking knees under the table and every so often they tapped the tabletop or leg. Andy didn't react either. He was too focused to notice.

"It's like I wasn't alive until I heard that loud-ass laugh!" Andy smiled at the memory. Eric blushed and nibbled on his fingernails. "It's really hard to explain. Just hearing it reminded me of the feelings I had for Mitch."

Eric was instantly sobered from his buzz. "So you see Mitch when you look at me?"

"No, no! Don't get me wrong," Andy quickly said. "You reminded me of my *feelings* for him. Forget the way shit went down between us. He sparked something in me that I didn't even know was there. He made me realize I'm gay." He was uncomfortable with the words once they were spoken out loud. "I don't care about Mitch. That's not what this is about."

"What is it about?" Eric asked, desperately wanting to know the answer but painfully trying to appear strong and uninterested, like his life's happiness didn't actually depend on it.

"It's about me and what I've locked away and ignored for so long, *too* long." Andy was on a roll. His face lit up and he spoke with an unexpected confidence for the first time that afternoon. "After Mitch left, I shut myself off from any feelings I had about guys. I hated that part of myself because I didn't understand it and I didn't want to. That's why I'm so hardcore into sports. I play ball to get this anger out. If I can beat the shit out of something on the field, I don't have to beat the shit out of myself at home." He ran out of breath and had to rest.

In the awkward moments as Andy regained his senses, Eric said nothing. He couldn't even think. He could only check his gapping, awestruck mouth every few seconds for drool.

Andy sat up straight in his chair and refocused. "I don't see Mitch when I look at you," he said. The sweet, charming Andy-McCain-trademarked voice had returned. It brought soothing warmth to the conversation and made Eric's mushy insides run even gooier. "I see what I'm missing and what I shouldn't be avoiding."

Under the table, Eric's legs almost shook him out of his seat. Adrenaline-charged jolts of energy shot through his excited body, almost bursting through his toes and fingertips.

"Every time I see you—" Andy stopped, refusing to rush the story, and searched for the right words. He began again, "When I was nine, way before puberty or Mitch came along, I picked up my first baseball bat. It was a gift from my dad. He taught me about the game and I really took to it. Pretty soon, it was my life. You know how it is when you're nine—"

"Not really," Eric corrected with an embarrassed smile. "When I was nine, TV was my life. Well, that and playing with my Superman action figures. Funny how Superman was always getting it on with Batman more than Wonder Woman."

They laughed and Andy's smile had a different gleam to it. It shined brighter, as did his eyes, in the presence of Eric's laughter.

"Playing ball was the first thing I ever really focused on and fell in love with. There's something about the way the ball cracks against the bat that thrills me to this day," Andy said, a little embarrassed by the admission. "But I never really understood my love for the game until I was ten and hit my first homerun. We were playing the Hogan Hawks and I cracked one so far into left field and won the game. I can't really explain how I felt when I saw it fly over the other team's hands and heard all my buddies cheering for me. It was so amazing!" The more Andy remembered, the faster the words came and the wider his smile grew. "I knew at that moment that *this* is what I'm going to do for the rest of my life. *This* is going to define me and make me who I am and I never want it to end."

"That's great, Andy. We all need those moments to make us feel alive," Eric said. He was almost as excited hearing the story as Andy was telling it. "And you're lucky because you get to relive it every time you're on the field."

"I'm even luckier now," Andy added.

"What do you mean?"

"What I've been trying to tell you, the reason you're here is that—" The corner of Andy's mouth rose just enough to show a hint of a dimple. He breathed deeply and let the rest flow. "Every time I hear you laugh or see you smile, it's like I'm ten years old again and just hit my first homerun."

For three years, since he was an Ann Arbor South freshman, since he first laid eyes on the unattainable and beautiful Andy McCain on the football field that first sports season, Eric had dreamed in countless different ways of hearing those words from the star player. Well, maybe not those *exact* words because even Eric's imagination couldn't have come up with the beauty and passion in Andy's voice.

"What did you say?" Eric asked, certain he was hallucinating.

Andy fully flashed his dimples, blushed, and sweetly said, "I love to hear you laugh."

"You don't even know me—"

"I want to."

"Is this really happening?" Eric glanced in every direction, searching for answers or hidden cameras or something to help him grasp the reality of the situation.

"You said I'd find another Mitch," Andy said. "I think I have in you."

Eric instantly snapped back to reality. "Do lame-ass lines like that really work?" he asked with a laugh. "No wonder you never had any luck with the chicks."

Andy's face reddened. "Knock it off," he said quietly. "This is hard enough."

Ignoring the sexuality angle for a moment, Eric realized the danger Andy faced by expressing his true self and deep feelings to him. If any of the Innards caught him in the library at that moment, it would kill his popularity rating. But looking closer at Andy's dimpled face, Eric saw no fear and fading uncertainty. There was an awakening light in Andy's eyes, a brightness beginning to glow with the honest confessions.

Andy was coming to life.

"Well, don't grow too attached to my laughter," Eric said with a childish grin. "I only do it when I'm nervous."

"I make you nervous?" Andy asked, excited by the possibility.

Eric's eyes narrowed. "Don't flatter yourself," he teased and was surprised just how quickly flirting worked its cunning way into the conversation. It wasn't forced or awkward but had an unrehearsed and almost perfected flow that they willingly danced to.

"Why're you telling me this here, at school?" Eric asked. "What if they catch you?"

"Who?" Andy asked innocently, but knew damn well *who*. "The guys? Don't worry about them."

Eric persisted, "But—"

"I knew you've never meet me outside of school. You'd think it was a trap and you'd never go for it," Andy explained. "I had to tell you how I felt before I blew up and this is the best way I could come up with."

"But it's social suicide for someone in your circle to even *talk* to someone in mine."

"So what?"

Eric cocked his head. "Okay, Mr. Badass," he joked. "They'll be—"

"I don't want to think about it. I'll just hide it like I always have."

Eric wasn't surprised by Andy's response. He expected it. "Well, don't worry, they won't find out. I'm not going to tell them. I wouldn't want you to go through the hell I go through," he said. "But I don't recommend hiding yourself for too long. It's really stressful and causes ulcers and premature wrinkles."

"Why haven't you tried to hide it?"

"Well, I didn't think I was parading around like Super Queer in a mini-skirt and tube top, but thank you." Eric laughed at his own wit.

"That's not exactly what I meant." Andy shook his head at Eric's unstoppable sarcasm. "You could've gotten into sports." Andy's response was so natural and honest, as if sports were the answer to everyone's problems, as they had been for him for so many years.

Eric smiled. "Coach Porter tried to get me to join the track team sophomore year because I ran so damn fast. I guess he heard about it through Dick for some reason," Eric said. "But the only reason I can run is because I've had a lot of practice running away from Justin Drake and his goons my whole life."

Eric never regretted his decision to turn down Coach Allan Porter's offer to join the track team. Every now and then, though, Eric wondered if he had joined and somehow proven himself an athlete, gay or not, if the Innards tormenting would have been less severe. Eric never lost sleep over what could have been.

"Point is," Eric continued. "I don't think sports would've solved my problems."

"So hiding it was never an option?" Andy asked.

"I tried hiding it," Eric said. "But figuring out who the hell you are is hard enough, let alone trying to cover that person up to be someone else. It's too much work. Plus, these guys pull the anti-gay shit on me whether I deny it or not. Whenever it happens, it feels like every single one of my bones are breaking at the same time. So if I'm going to suffer through it anyway and get my ass kicked no matter what, I might as well be true to myself. Otherwise, what's the point?" A small smile reflected his tiny sense of pride. "Besides, I don't want to go all Terminator on their asses. Prison suits are *so* unflattering."

"How can you joke about it?" Andy asked.

"Beats the hell out of crying."

Andy frowned. "That's depressing."

"Wasn't meant to be," Eric said. "I'm okay with it. Well...I've learned to deal with it. The point is your secret's safe with me. I'm not going to tell your business."

Relieved, Andy slid his hand across the tabletop and very softly grazed the skin of Eric's knuckles. Eric's hand opened and his index finger met Andy's and they hooked together. Eric's body boiled with exhilaration and when his skin touched Andy's and he felt the scorching heat from the athlete's touch jolt through his flesh. The touch lasted only a mere second before Eric withdrew his hand. It was too soon.

Andy released a satisfied, assured sigh, not at the removal of the embraced hands, but at Eric's secrecy promise. "Thanks, Eric," he said and stood up. "Come on, I'll drive you home."

Eric laughed at the obvious joke. "What if someone sees us?"

"They won't," Andy assured with an unknown confidence.

When Eric stood from the table, he reached for his book bag. Andy beat him to it and snatched the bag from the tabletop. "I got it," Andy said, slinging it over his shoulder.

Eric formed his signature deadpan stare and shook his head. "It's okay, Romeo, I can carry it," he said, reclaiming the bag. "Thanks for the strange chivalry, though."

"Just trying to be a gentleman," Andy teased and left the table.

It took Eric a moment to convince himself he wasn't dreaming and motivate his feet to follow Andy. The overwhelming day was still sinking in and he wasn't sure if any of it was real. If it was, could he trust Andy? Could he trust any of it? There was only one way to find out: move forward. If he didn't take the chance, he'd wake up supremely pissed off from the dream.

Until then, to hell with it.

He was going to enjoy the ride.

Chapter Eight

With cheap but good food as their forte, Kate and Nick regularly visited the Jupiter Coney Island Restaurant. Located downtown, the old store was still Dicked out in a groovy 70s vibe, with brown brick walls and deep orange vinyl booths to coordinate, as well as dark brown hard tabletops and an array of oddly displayed pheasant artwork. The wait staff was mostly punk high school kids trying to scrounge an extra buck, leaving the service less than stellar. Still, it was quiet and a great place to eat, hang, bitch, and enjoy good company, as Kate and Nick did probably more often than necessary.

"Andy better not be screwin' around," Kate said, flipping her menu open. She sat across from Nick in their usual corner booth. She always took the seat facing the interior of the restaurant so she could see everything and everyone in the eatery to feed her feverish hunger of people watching. "Eric doesn't need anymore shit."

"You're right," Nick agreed, sulking for only a moment in his default seat with his back facing the restaurant.

"But what if he's not?" Kate added. "Let's pretend for just a second that Andy's, like, wholeheartedly, over-the-top bonkers for Eric and it's genuine and it's real—"

Nick gave her his attention. "Okay—"

"That would be really great for him, for both of them. I think it

95

would—"

"Sounds like there's a big *but* coming on."

"I don't think it's going to work."

"What do you mean?"

She paused for a moment, nibbling on her bottom lip as she gathered her thoughts. "We've all read Romeo and Juliet and we've all seen West Side Story," she said. "The Sharks and the Jets sure as hell never got along. And look at Tony. He died in the end!"

Nick made a face. "What are you talking about?"

"Two people from two different worlds coming together? That's never a good idea."

He rolled his eyes and laughed. "Overly optimistic today, huh, Kate?"

"There's just going to be a lot of bullshit to deal with if they start seeing each other," she said. "It'll make West Side Story look like Sesame Street."

"That's a little dramatic."

"Not that I won't enjoy the scandal of seeing Justin *Thinks-He's-Hot-Shit* Drake finding out his boy's all about ditching chicks for dicks—"

Nick sighed. "Try a *little* class at the dinner table, please?" he begged. "Besides, we don't even know if Andy's gay or not."

"Oh, please, I already—"

"Yes, I know you already had your Homo Reader Meter go haywire," Nick interrupted. "But until Eric confirms that for us, maybe we should mind our own business."

Kate rolled her eyes and studied the menu again. She snapped her gum and was quiet, which worried Nick. When she glanced back to him, Kate's face was serious and he was ready to listen. "What if Andy *is* just messing with him?" she asked calmly and concerned. "Like it's some cruel joke they all came up with to hurt him?"

Nick shrugged without worry, trying to ease her stress. "Eric'll know what to do," he said confidently. "And if he doesn't, he'll figure it out. That's how it works. If it is a joke, he should know how to throw a punch by now. He's learned from the best." Nick smiled at her.

"Bite me," she snapped jokingly. She grabbed her bulky bottomless-pit of a purse and pulled out her own clunky cellular telephone. The second she started dialing, Nick exploded.

"Put that away!" he ordered with a frustrated laugh. "You're not calling him!"

"Why not? I sorta feel like I pressured him into going. If something happens, I—"

"I love you, Kate, and not to burst that self-centered bubble you're living in, but the harsh reality is that Eric's not thinking about you right now," Nick explained. "If all went according to plan, which we hope it did because we're his friends, then he's only thinking about Andy. So chill out and put your phone away. It's a piece of shit anyway."

"You're mean to me," Kate snapped but did as she was told and dropped the cell into her purse. She sipped her iced tea, thinking. "Won't it be weird, though? If they do get together, I mean," she said. "It'll be so totally sickening because Eric's dreams'll be coming true with Andy and I'll be left with your sorry ass."

"Sweet-talking me isn't going to get me to pay for dinner," Nick teased. "Now shut up and order your food."

Chapter Nine

By the time Andy and Eric reached the parking lot, the energy between them was so electric that their generated sparks almost set their T-shirts on fire. As they approached Andy's 1991 dark blue Ford Escort, it was clear neither of them were ready to part ways.

"What time do you have to be home?" Andy asked as he unlocked the passenger side door for Eric.

Eric shrugged, confused by the question. "Well, my curfew's eleven," he said, glancing at his wristwatch. It wasn't even four o'clock. "But I doubt it'll take you that long to get me there."

"Let's go somewhere," Andy said anxiously. Eric made a funny face, making Andy laugh. "Just to talk! I swear!"

"Where'd you have in mind?"

"My apartment's just a few blocks away," Andy suggested with no hidden agenda.

"Your apartment? What kind of a girl do you think I am?" Eric joked.

Andy blushed and shook his head in jest. "I can take you home if you don't want to go."

"No, it's okay," Eric said with a little too much enthusiasm. To recover, he added, "As long as you're not going to stuff my bloody body parts into an acid barrel, then I'm game."

"You're a smartass," Andy said playfully.

Once they sat into his car, Andy started the engine, pulled out of the parking spot and drove the Escort down Owen Road and then onto Caroline Street toward his apartment. Eric was surprised it really was only a few blocks from the school. As they pulled into the parking lot, Eric's heart raced with excitement as he stared out the windshield at a large complex full of many buildings. Made of brown brick and beige siding, the apartments were accented with sporadic trees and shrubs that were losing color and leaves with the approaching autumn. Watching the many numbered buildings pass by, Eric anxiously awaited for Andy to stop the car. His dream of seeing the inside of Andy's home, where he lived and breathed and ate and *showered*, was only a few moments away!

Andy parked and shut the engine off. He reached across Eric's lap, pulled the handle to Eric's door, and swung it open. Unsure of how to react, Eric sat there. Andy winked at him, stepped out of the car and said, "Come on!"

"Won't it be weird introducing me to your parents as what, a new friend?" Eric said, shutting the door behind him and joining Andy in the parking lot. "Are they home?"

"I live alone," Andy said, fumbling through his key chain for the house key.

They walked across the lot to the main entrance of apartment building 3108. He typed in a short code into the number pad beside the double entrance glass doors. A second passed, a green light popped on and the door buzzed open. Andy stepped aside, allowing his guest to enter before him. Eric smiled and went inside. The door shut loudly as Andy led the way up two flights of stairs to the third floor.

"Why do you live alone?" Eric asked, following Andy down the hall to apartment 33. "Are your parents dead? Oh, was that an insensitive question?" Eric bowed his head.

"Yes, it was an insensitive question," Andy said, laughing loudly. "But no, they're not dead." He slid the house key into the deadbolt and turned it counterclockwise. The bolt jerked open and Andy opened the door. Again, he stepped aside and Eric went in ahead of him.

Once inside, Eric's eyes swirled in every direction. He wanted to see everything, every inch, all at the same time. The apartment was small, *tiny,* with only two rooms. The main room was sectioned into a few tinier areas. The couch and simple entertainment center separated the living room from the kitchen; the countertop, sink, and refrigerator separated the kitchen from the bedroom; and the mattress and a straining overhung clothesline packed with T-shirts separated the bedroom from the living room. Tucked secretly in the corner between the floor mattress and the living room television was the bathroom. It was a separate room with a door, but peeking inside, Eric realized the door had to open slowly to avoid hitting the toilet, which was nearly connected to the freestanding shower.

The walls were a cream color and simply decorated. An old baseball game schedule was taped to the fridge and *Interview With The Vampire* and *Seven* movie posters hung on the wall behind the television. Eric thought about the random, seemingly unrelated butch movies for a moment. When he made the hunky Brad Pitt connection, they both made complete sense.

The only item in the cramped space that really caught Eric's attention rested on top of the television: an old grass-stained baseball neatly displayed in a square glass case.

"What's that?" Eric asked, very interested in the obviously treasured item.

Andy's face reddened and he said, "The homerun ball from when I was ten."

Eric smiled, touched by the sincerity of the souvenir and continued on his mini tour.

Overhead lights lit the kitchen and living room areas and turned on with a flick of the same switch. A large picture window covered the wall above the bed. Andy went to it and closed the pre-installed white blinds.

Regardless of the claustrophobic vibe of the closet-sized apartment, Eric loved it. It smelled of sweet cologne, hair gel, chlorinated tap water, and dirty cleats. It was lived in and had a subtle and small charm.

"Well, this place is depressing as hell," Eric joked and turned to Andy.

"I know," Andy said, shrugging. "But I'm hardly here to take care of it."

"You never answered my question," Eric reminded. "Why do you live alone?"

"My parents are dicks. I came out to them and—"

"You *what*?!" Eric almost crapped his pants.

Andy smiled and shrugged. "I wanted them to know who I was. I didn't want to go through this alone and my parents were always there for me—" He stopped himself and pushed a counter-full of dirty dishes into the sink. He flipped the faucet on and hot water splashed in every direction. Andy paid no attention. He just scrubbed the dishes clean.

Staring at the mad dishwasher, Eric quickly understood the reaction. "So they freaked?"

"That's the happier version," Andy said with an uneasy smile. "My Dad swung a few punches, my mom yelled a few 'You're-going-to-Hells' and we haven't really spoken since. I moved out a while after that. I had too much going on and didn't want to deal with that too."

Eric stepped around the counter and stood beside Andy, their shoulders touching. "That sucks," Eric said, grabbing a glass with a protein shake stain on the bottom.

Andy laughed and nudged Eric's shoulder. "Do your parents know you're gay?" Andy asked, more than ready to shift the conversation's attention away from himself.

"My dad's a workaholic. I only see him at work but we don't talk enough for me to know him and he sure as hell doesn't know me," Eric said with no real reaction. "My mom's great. They're divorced and she's stronger than steel because of it. She knows I'm gay in the way mothers just know these things about their kids, but she doesn't know how rough it is for me at school. I don't have the heart to tell her. Maybe she knows but we've never actually talked about it. She's just quietly waiting for me to bring it up."

"Any plans to do that?"

"Not so much!"

Andy laughed. He slid his wet hands through the dishwater and lightly grabbed Eric's fingers. The touch took Eric by surprise and he flinched, splashing water on Andy's T-shirt. Embarrassed, Eric laughed nervously. Andy never noticed his wet shirt. His eyes were on Eric and he grabbed his hand again. Eric stopped laughing and tried to calm himself. It was hard just remembering to breathe. He had to turn away from Andy's gaze every few seconds or cardiac arrest would surely attack. In turning away, Eric glanced over the countertop to Andy's mattress. He noticed strong movement from a pile of crumpled blue jeans near the bed. When the pants started to grunt, he had to speak up.

"I think something's growing in there," Eric said.

Andy laughed and replied, "Sort of." He dried his hands and went into the living room. He clapped twice and cheered, "Buddha!"

As soon as Andy spoke, a tiny, sandy-blonde Chihuahua wearing a white leather collar sprang out from a pant leg and leaped toward Andy. The eight-inch tall attack dog barked and grunted its way to Andy's hands. Once there, he was content and calm to be scratched and kissed by his owner. Eric went to the couch and sat down. Andy joined him with the small dog in hand.

"This is Buddha," Andy said, raising the dog's leg to wave.

"Can I rub his belly for luck?" Eric said with a laugh. Seeing Andy so smitten with the tiny creature confused Eric. "*Buddha?* That's a joke, right?"

"No," Andy said, shaking his head in a way that suggested Eric had just insulted him.

Eric smiled as an apology. "Is there a story behind it?" he asked with genuine interest.

Setting Buddha beside Eric, Andy grabbed a beefy treat from the kitchen, tossed it to the dog, and rejoined them on the couch. He seemed suddenly nervous and on edge, avoiding eye contact with Eric and fidgeting with the sleeves of his T-shirt.

Eric said, "It's okay if you don't want to tell me."

Andy softened and smiled. "I'm not avoiding. It's just hard to talk about," Andy said. "It has a lot to do with my parents. Things are more serious than what I told you a second ago."

Eric nodded and waited for the juicy tidbits of the story.

Andy continued, "My parents don't accept me. I came out to them after all that shit went down with Mitch because I didn't understand what was happening to me and I wanted their help." He took a deep breath and paused, pretending to search for the right words, but Eric knew he was only stalling.

"What happened?" Eric urged with care.

"My mother told me there's better things I can be doing with my life than screwing guys up the ass," he said firmly, choking back tears.

"What?!" Eric exclaimed, immediately outraged and ready to attack.

"And my father doesn't get involved in anything that's not related to his work, so he wasn't any help. He just smacked me around for my mom's sake and left it at that." Andy's voice shook more as he continued, "So I moved out when I turned eighteen. I had some money saved and a good job and I just had to get out of there."

Unsure of what to say, Eric thought for a moment. "Not to change the subject," he said off topic. "But what does this have to do with Buddha?"

Andy scratched the wispy blonde hairs between the dog's ears. "I got him right after my parents and I stopped talking," he said, snuggling with Buddha and kissing him. The affection Andy showed the animal made Eric wish he were a sandy-blonde Chihuahua. "I went through a rough period after Mitch and my parents. I was so desperate to figure out what my problem was that I tried a lot of things, like different religions. I even called one of those teen grief hotlines. The counselor I talked to said I should get a dog because it would help with the loneliness during my...what did she call it? My personal inner growth transition or something like that."

Eric laughed a little and asked, "Did it help?"

"The hotline or the dog?" Andy teased. Eric cocked his head. "Buddha's been my rock, if you can believe it," Andy added and scratched a grunt out of the beast. "I love this little guy. I'm not supposed to have animals in the apartment, but I figured an ankle-biter wouldn't be too much trouble."

As Andy talked, Eric watched his mouth move and heard the words, but it was different. The young man, the sports star, the funny, beautiful student was taking shape. Andy was morphing, growing, and becoming even more than the dreamy mythical megastar Eric had conceived him to be.

"You really called a hotline?" Eric asked.

Andy nodded. "I was messed up. I didn't know who I was or what was happening to me," he said, losing volume to his voice. "I didn't understand why I was falling for the quarterback and not the head cheerleader." When his face turned red, Andy turned away to hide the embarrassment. When his eyes swelled with tears, he made sure to hide those from Eric too.

But Eric saw them and he heard the surprise cracking of the tough-guy's voice. Eric wanted to embrace him and lean Andy's sobbing head against his caring shoulder like all the sappy movie-of-the-week specials he had seen on television. Part of him wanted to take a picture of that moment to lock away for years to come, the moment when he saw Andy McCain, Ann Arbor South's strong-as-steel superstar, show that underneath the popularity and muscular frame, he was actually human. After all the semesters and seasons Eric mentally built Andy's pedestal of perfection higher, it turned out they were the same. On the inside, they were both hurt, confused young men desperately searching for understanding, but praying just as hard to simply blend into the crowd.

"Wait a minute, you fell for the quarterback?" Eric said, thinking. "You don't mean Chase, do you?" He softly pressed his hand against Andy's arm. The gesture let Andy know he understood Andy's feelings, but they didn't have to talk about them any further. So much seemed to be understood through silence. "Please tell me you're joking! *Chase Frank*? Eww!"

When Andy finally composed himself enough to turn back to Eric, he was greeted by a warm, accepting smile on Eric's face. "You're an asshole!" Andy said, flashing his pearly white grin and deep dimples. His eyes glistened from a few stray tears, but the light was back in them, shining brightly. "And screw you! Chase is a good-looking guy!"

"Yeah, I guess, in a train-wreck sort of way," Eric added with a laugh.

The laughter was infectious and both boys couldn't contain it. As it filled the apartment, Andy reached over and tickled Eric's stomach, chest, and arms. Eric playfully fought the baseball boy's advances as much as he could, but Andy was too strong and determined. Eric wiggled and squirmed his way off the couch and his butt smacked against the hard wooden floor. He was laughing so hard it didn't hurt. Andy continued, climbed on top of Eric and showed no mercy.

The roughhousing was nonstop until Eric finally found Andy's unexpected weak spot: under his arms. Twisting his fingers into Andy's clamped armpit, Eric tickled inside it and the reaction was instant. Andy bolted off Eric's body and quickly backed away.

"That's a dirty card to play," Andy said, protectively tucking his hands into his pits.

Eric sat up and lowered his eyelids, staring intensely at Andy. He rose to his knees, crawled over to him, and made another move for the underarms, but Andy's steel wall of hands was impenetrable. "All right," Eric said, backing down. "I'll leave you alone. Although you deserve an ass-kicking badly!"

Gleaming dimples accented Andy's smile. With the smile and a deep giggle, Andy, for the first time that afternoon, sat back onto the couch, leaned his head onto its back and relaxed. He nestled into the cushions as his arms and legs slid into cozy positions to which they seemed comfortably accustomed. Andy took his ball cap off to reveal serious hat-hair and snuggled deeper into the couch.

Witnessing it excited Eric. The tiny gesture of Andy relaxing thrilled him to the core. Watching him made Eric realize and truly believe that Andy was now, surprisingly, comfortable in his presence. Andy had finally relaxed to the point of easing his muscles and releasing the hard tension and rugged facade he carried around at school.

But there was something else.

Andy put his hand inside his shirt to tickle his navel. Knowing it was a nervous reaction and seeing a flash of Andy's smooth skin widened Eric's smile. It pleased him that although Andy was now comfortable around him, there was still an element of surprise and uncertainty in the air. Even inside the walls of his own apartment, Andy was still pleasantly on edge.

"You say you work with your dad?" Andy asked, keeping his eyes closed.

Eric made himself comfortable on the couch beside Andy. "Yeah. He owns an engineering company," Eric said and watched Buddha wrestle with an old, chewed up baseball glove. "I do some computer work, answer phones, run errands. It's good money and he's flexible with my hours."

"It must be cool working with your old man," Andy said with a childish innocence and longing. Eric knew Andy missed his own father.

"I guess. That's why I took the job in the first place, to be closer to him and learn whatever I could." Eric thought for a moment and his face saddened. "But that never happened. He's worked right down the hall for three years and I still don't know who he is."

"What a waste."

"Tell me about it." Eric felt a possible tear welling in his eye and, refusing to show weakness, he quickly asked, "What about you? What do you do?"

"Landscaping in the summer and fall, like mowing lawns and shit," Andy said with genuine enthusiasm, but added with less excitement, "And while I'm waiting for summer to roll back around, I wait tables at The Crow's Nest."

"That dump? Not that I've ever been. It's just a little too redneck-on-the-loose for me."

Andy laughed. "It's a little rugged," he agreed. "But it's good money."

"And you've got bills coming out of your ass, I'm sure."

"You got that right." Andy frowned. The reference was hitting too close to home.

Eric saw he was uncomfortable and lightened the mood by saying, "It better be good money. Isn't that a karaoke bar? Anyone who has to work while listening to dying cats serenade each other with drunken renditions of *Endless Love* better be breaking the bank!"

Andy softened and smiled again. "Do you always talk this much when you're nervous?"

Eric's mouth dropped open and his face turned bright red. "Excuse me?" His voice cracked and he couldn't lose the embarrassed grin now plastered to his face. "Do you always touch your stomach when you're nervous?"

Laughing, Andy sat up straight. His eyes had a determined stare. "What are you thinking about right now?" he asked randomly.

"I'm thinking about pissing my pants and running, screaming, from the building," Eric said, still giggling.

"No, really, what are you thinking about?" Andy insisted. "Whatever it is, tell me and be honest. I want to know."

Eric made a funny, confused face, unsure what Andy meant. But the closer he stared at Andy's face and the more Eric calmed himself and eased out the embarrassment, he saw Andy was serious and truly interested in his response.

"Okay," Eric said, taking the bait. "I'm wondering what I'm doing here."

"I know," Andy quickly agreed. "I can tell. You seem guarded, like you're holding back."

"You have to give me time," Eric said, taking a deep breath. "Everything's happening so fast. I mean, I never thought I'd be sitting on Andy McCain's floor looking at Brad Pitt posters and talking about religious dogs. That was never on my dream-come-true list, well, maybe a little, but still! It's a lot to take in."

"What else?" Andy asked, anxious and energetic.

"I don't know—"

"Yes, you do." Andy read Eric well. "What else are you thinking?"

There was an honest, excited tone to Andy's voice that comforted Eric. "I'm thinking..." Eric trailed off, buying himself time. "It figures you work landscaping."

Andy smiled, surprised by the admission, and said, "Is that bad?"

"No, it's just that I get winded walking to the mailbox and here you are mowing lawns and planting bushes and whatever—"

"I have to be outdoors doing something with my hands. I can't sit at a desk all day," Andy said honestly. "I'd go crazy if that was my life."

"And I'd rather work with computers than bust my ass planting shit with my hands," Eric said, sighing. "So much for having anything in common. That's what I'm thinking. Why am I here? We don't have anything to talk about."

"I think we've been doing just fine."

"Yeah, I know, but—" Eric lost his focus.

Andy inched closer to him until their hips and upper thighs slid together on the couch cushions. He looked hard at Eric's face and said, "It wouldn't be very interesting if we had everything in common." He put his hand on Eric's leg. "You're here because I want you to be."

Eric bowed his head, trying to hide his excited ear-to-ear smile.

"Do you want to be here?" Andy asked.

"Of course I do," Eric said too fast and raised his head.

Andy shared his smile. "Then the rest will work itself out." He leaned even closer and pressed his full lips against Eric's. From there, everything seemed to fall into place.

The boys lost track of time.

Eric barely made it home by curfew.

Chapter Ten

Six Weeks Later - Sunday, October 6, 1996

Kate stared at the Jupiter Coney Island menu, holding it with her right hand and twirling a chunk of her blonde hair in her left. She always spent too much time staring at each of the menu's four pages. It was a pointless ritual since she always ordered the same deluxe hamburger platter with fries and a side salad. Maybe she just liked testing Eric's patience.

"Come on, *Rain Man*, make a decision. I'm hungry," Eric said firmly. His menu was already face down, ready for the server to collect. He never looked at it. The grilled ham and cheese sandwich with lettuce and mayo on the side was his entrée of choice each and every time.

"Give me minute. Maybe they added something new," Kate said, just to be difficult.

"Since yesterday?" Eric fed the playful banter.

Kate closed the plastic menu and slapped it on top of Eric's. The greasy waiter with the bad acne pounced on their table, took their usual orders, and returned to the kitchen. Once he was gone, Kate smiled at Eric with her typical, devilish grin.

"What are you and Andy doing for Sweetest Day?" she asked.

Eric rolled his eyes and sarcastically replied, "We're heading over to your mom's house to tag team her."

"Great! She could use the workout with you two strapping young lads," Kate teased. "But really, are you guys doing anything?"

"Get serious!" Eric balked, scrunching his nose at her ridiculous question.

"Well, you don't have to look at me like I've got a third boob!" Kate snapped and folded her arms against her two-breasted chest. "I was just asking."

"What are we supposed to do? Go on a date?" Eric said harshly. "Oh! Better yet, we should double with Justin Drake and his skank-of-the-week!"

Kate didn't appreciate Eric's defensiveness but she knew it wasn't personal since he had been overly emotional for weeks. Eric was ecstatic by the flourishing relationship with Andy, but irritable because of its top-secret classification. No one knew about their involvement together except Kate and Nick and Andy refused to tell anyone else.

"I'm sorry I mentioned it," Kate said calmly. "Let's not talk about it."

"What do you want to talk about?" Eric asked as he cooled down.

"I don't know. You pick."

"All right…" Eric said and thought for a minute before adding, "Can you tell me why the hell swimming has to last six weeks in gym? I mean, we're not exactly training for the Olympics here. Why does Dick have us in the water for almost the whole quarter?"

"Maybe he likes boys and he's too shy to admit it." Kate smiled at her own ludicrous comment. "Or he knows you hate it with a passion and he does it just to torture you."

"I wouldn't put it past him," Eric said. His face quickly turned serious and he added, "I'm just scared, though, because every day the guys get more restless and more pushy with me. I can only be dunked so many times before they want to do more, you know?"

"When's it over?"

"Next week, thank god!" He took a drink of his ice water with no ice, just the way he liked it. "But it's not like things are looking up for me after that. I still have seven months in that damn class. Tell me *that* doesn't haunt my dreams."

"At least Andy's in there with you...well...that's sort of a good thing."

"If we could talk to each other, yeah, it'd be a good thing."

"I thought we weren't going to talk about this," Kate reminded.

"It's okay," Eric said. "Sorry I was a dick."

"I'm use to it, sweetie," Kate said lightheartedly but regained control when she said, "It sucks that you guys have to act like you don't even know each other at school." When Kate saw her defensive attitude put Eric on edge, she eased up. "I understand you have to because Andy's friends will kick his ass and it'll be a wild uproar between The Sharks and The Jets—"

"The *whats*?" Eric made a funny face.

"Nothing," Kate said, rolling her eyes. "My point is that I know it'll be a bloody, messy nuclear meltdown if anyone finds out you're dating each other and that sucks."

"Tell me about it!" Eric laughed, trying to make it sound casual.

There was something in Eric's laugh, though, a tiny crack that raised Kate's eyebrow and lowered her painted eyelids. She heard something he was trying to hide. It only took a quick survey of Eric's nervous actions—taking too many fast sips of his iceless water and staring at the blank paper placemat more than her face.

"You want Andy to tell everyone he's dating you," Kate realized.

Eric's eyes widened with surprise. The positive, somewhat fearful reaction to her on-target inquiry confirmed her curiosity. Eric fiddled with the white paper wrapper to his straw, tying it in several knots before it ripped to pieces. He kept his eyes away from Kate's face, unable to admit what she already knew was true.

"You are so transparent," Kate said. Her voice was upbeat to lighten the awkwardness. "You want him to take on the world and move mountains just so you can be Homecoming Queen. My god, could you possibly be any more obvious?"

Eric hid a smile with his hand but Kate saw it.

She took a breath, nibbled on a soup cracker, and said, "What's going on?"

Eric looked at Kate's face and relaxed in seeing her caring eyes. He paused to gather his thoughts, took another drink of water, and said, "I don't want him to spill his guts, but...well..."

"Come on, Eric, this is me you're talking to," Kate said.

He smiled and continued, "It would be nice to be acknowledged. It would be nice to go somewhere in public where we actually know people. We've been seeing each other for almost six weeks and we only go to that old movie theater in Fenton, which is an hour away, or those shithole restaurants in Flint, which is even farther."

Kate nodded. "I've been to those hole-in-the-wall dives with you and you're right, they're shitty," she said. "But don't forget you spend most of your time buried in Andy's apartment with the blinds closed, which is a little too gay serial killer for me. I mean, when I was there with you last weekend, it was so boring! There are only so many movies you can watch before you need to get the hell out of the house. Of course, with you and Andy cuddling and talking to each other more than me, well, that's just a drag anyway."

"Don't get me wrong, I really like him," Eric was quick to point out. "It might even be more than that. This is a dream come true for me."

"I know," Kate said. "He more than likes you too. You're just saying there're a few flaws in the dream."

"Yeah, well, sort of." Eric confused himself and had to pause. He tore tiny pieces off the paper placemat. "When we're alone together, he's really nice to me. The way he looks at me and touches me—"

"I don't need all the slutty details!" Kate's inappropriate defense weapon—sarcasm—always managed to sneak its way in.

Eric continued without even responding to it. "When he's around his friends at school or when they call his apartment when I'm there, he becomes a different person," Eric explained. "He's never mean to me or anywhere near as bad as the guys at school, but it's still—"

"Shitty."

"No," Eric said, thinking for a moment. "More like disappointing."

"It's not the knight in shining armor fairy tale you thought it would be?"

"No, it's not that. He plays the role of the knight pretty well," Eric said, blushing a little. "We're just not allowed to be together in this kingdom and that kills the fairy tale."

"Enough of the medieval metaphors," Kate said. "You're hurt because he won't take a stand against the others and you have a right to feel that way. He should stand up for himself."

"But it's not just the guys he's scared of," Eric added. "He's going to stay quiet forever."

"What do you mean?"

"He's got this great dream of being a Detroit Tiger, which will happen because he's an amazing baseball player—"

"You might be a little biased," Kate interjected. "But yeah, he's good."

"He's going to stay closeted," Eric said, cringing at the words. "He doesn't want his team to know he's gay when he goes pro. He wants to make millions by playing ball and signing Nike endorsements. He wants to retire at an early age but still work as a sports commentator on some TV news channel, but he doesn't want anyone to know he's gay."

"So is he just going to have random man-whores until he settles down and gets out of the spotlight?" Kate asked, confused and annoyed.

"He says there'll be enough time for love later in life, after his career."

"What kind of bullshit is that?"

"I don't know. I mean, I love the thought of Andy in a Tigers uniform and I want that dream to come true for him, but it's sickening to think he'll live his life to please other people."

"You know I love you and I'll beat anyone's ass for you until the day I die so don't take this the wrong way," Kate said. "But you don't really have any room to be saying this shit to Andy when you're a victim of it too. You're telling him to stand up for himself and fight holy wars if he has to, but you're not doing that."

"What're you talking about?"

"Your relationship with Andy's a perfect example. You're playing by his rules and keeping it top secret even though you don't want to.

You want to confess your love by dancing across the mountaintop like a damn singing nun, but the truth is, you're keeping your mouth shut and letting Andy call all the shots. That's not like you. It never has been. You've put up with so much bullshit in your life that you vowed never to let some guy silence your voice."

"That's before I was in a relationship," Eric said quickly. "It's easy to rattle off all kinds of insightful crap when you're single and alone."

"Calm down, queen. I'm not trying to step on your evening gown or piss on your Mariah Carey posters," Kate said carefully and continued, "You mentioned Andy's dream of being a Tiger and how he has all these plans sketched out and ready to roll, but what about your dreams?"

Eric's face went blank and he looked away.

"You've been talking about taking pictures for the New York Times since we were kids. You've had a camera glued to your palm for years—"

"What's your point?" Eric snapped.

"I haven't seen you take a single picture this year—"

"I have too!"

"Andy McCain memorabilia doesn't count. It's nice, but I can only look at so many pictures of his dirty cleats before I want to puke."

"What the hell's your problem?" Agitated, Eric's expression was hard, almost angry.

Kate shook her head, signaling she meant no harm. "I'm not picking a fight, Eric," she said softly. "I just hate to see you lose yourself and give up what you love for some guy."

"So what, Kate? We gave up a lot to be together. I let my photography slip and he gave up football this year—"

"Did he give it up for you or is he just too scared that his friends will find out he's gay?"

Eric wasn't mad at Kate but was pissed at her words, fearing they were right. With watery eyes, Eric said just above a whisper, "He's not just some guy."

"I'm sorry I said that," Kate was genuinely regretful. She slid her arm across the tabletop and lightly squeezed Eric's hand. "I'm not hating up on you guys. You know I love you and I like Andy too. I'm just looking out for you."

Eric nodded and took a deep breath to ward off the tears. "I hate it when you make me think," he said and laughed nervously.

"I really am a bitch, huh?"

Her smile dried Eric's eyes and loosened him up. "Then what's your advice, Miss Crawford?" he asked, preparing himself with a deep breath.

She wasted no time answering his question. "Sooner or later, no matter how hard you try to hide it or make your own rules around it, someone will sniff it out," she said.

"But I don't want to live my life in fear, well, not any more than I already do."

"You didn't let me finish," Kate said, smiling brightly. "If you're in the eye of the storm and it's inevitable that the shit's going to hit the fan no matter what, until that moment comes—"

"Yeah?"

"Enjoy every fucking second of it."

Chapter Eleven

Monday, October 7, 1996

At the end of the day, the thunder under Andy's feet couldn't propel him fast enough. Racing toward the senior parking lot, he had only one thing in mind: Eric. On his way, dodging through the thick maze of students and ignoring any friends trying to talk to him, Andy passed Tara Sanderson. She gently grabbed his arm.

"Where's the fire?" she asked, seeing the hard determination in his face.

Her clutch startled him and awakened his daze. "Oh! Tara! Hi!" Andy said, impatiently pacing the floor in front of her. His gaze never left the end of the hall, where a huge wall of windows looked out to the parking lot.

"You're in a hurry a lot these days, huh?" Her voice was sweet but not overly concerned.

"I really have to go," he said, inching toward the hallway's end.

"You might want to be careful," Tara said firmly. "People aren't as blind as you think."

Andy's head spun around, his wide eyes zeroing in on her bright face. "What?"

Her pretty smile grew as she readjusted her backpack. "Have a good day," she said and patted his arm. She flipped her bleached hair and turned on her heel.

Tara's sexy hips swayed as she strolled away. Andy watched her but couldn't force himself to speak. He was too scared to hear the explanation of her puzzling comment.

Instead, he ignored it and returned on his important journey to the parking lot. Maneuvering through the crowd of students, he turned the English hall corner only to abruptly slam into a fellow classmate: the ever-delicate Kate Crawford. Andy almost pissed himself. Avoiding Tara Sanderson was one thing, interacting with Kate was something else entirely, like trading one of Hell's angels for the devil herself.

Immediately the tension between Andy and Kate was so thick it nearly fogged her contact lenses. She brushed herself off from the minor collision and smiled as sweetly as she could, but it didn't fool Andy. He stepped back for breathing room and broke the awkward silence with a simple, "Hi."

Kate smiled again but with an agenda. "Let's cut the crap, okay?" she said, moving close to the border of his personal space. "I know whenever we're around Eric together, we get along. Maybe that's for his sake or because me and Nick are the only ones who share your secret with him. Whatever the reason, I think we both know it's uncomfortable between us."

Andy shrugged, neither admitting or denying her claim.

"Maybe you don't like me. I'm a hard person to get along with. That's not exactly late-breaking news," she continued. "But I want you to know that I like you and I like the way Eric's been since you two got together."

"What's your point?" Andy said, surprising even himself by the snappy tone to his voice.

Kate was surprised too. "Okay," she said. "I'll give it to you straight...no pun intended."

Andy laughed nervously and glanced at his shoes, his sleeves, and his backpack strap, anywhere to avoid her judgmental eyes. The defined dimples on his scared face softened her demeanor and she took a small step back. "It's like this, Andy," she began. "Whatever your plans are with Eric aren't really any of my business—" She hooked a lock of hair behind her ear. "But if you knew me any better, you'd know I never mind my own business."

Andy laughed again, albeit forced and frightened.

"He's my best friend and I adore him, so your plans *are* my business," she added. "I've seen what's been going on between you two and it's really exciting. But you have to understand something. I trust Eric and I respect his decisions but I also know he doesn't always make the best ones."

"Oh, now I get it," Andy said with a sigh. He took his baseball cap off and ran his fingers through his short hair. "You think I'm a bad decision."

"I didn't say that," Kate quickly corrected. "It's just that the Innards don't exactly have the greatest track record with him. They've done some pretty shitty things. I just want to know if you're going to be true to him or if you're just screwing around."

Disappointment and panic swept across Andy's face. He repeatedly shook his head and gushed, "No, Kate! Of course not! I promise you!"

"I know you've got this whole God's-gift-to-the-teenage-eye thing working pretty well for you and Eric's always been a sucker for the muscley-chiseled-jaw-dimpled-cuteness thing you've also got going on—"

Her flattery made him uncomfortable. Andy squirmed in his shoes and reached under his shirt to scratch his stomach. "Yeah, so?"

"Don't play into it," she replied without thought. "He's star struck like you're Madonna or Jesus or something and I don't want you to take advantage of that. He's never had a friend like you before, let alone a boy—" Kate stopped herself. She couldn't say *boyfriend*. Unlike most of the English language, Kate wasn't shy of randomly tossing any word into a conversation. But *boyfriend* in a sentence about her best friend just didn't fit yet. It was too tricky for her to utter. She recovered by saying, "He's just not ready for any of this."

"Neither am I," Andy replied, firmly standing his ground against the lioness. "This is new to me too, Kate. Eric's not the only one taking a chance. I'm just as scared."

"I know," she agreed, like she had thought about it much more than she'd ever admit. "And because you're so much higher on the food chain, you've got a lot more to lose and that scares me because I don't know how it'll affect him."

"I'm not going to hurt him," Andy said. Any doubt in his voice was overshadowed by his increased agitation. He paced the hallway floor, searching for a place to keep his hands—stuffed inside his pockets, tucked tightly under his arms or inside the bottom of his shirt. "Why do you care so much? I know you're his best friend and I dig that, but aren't you taking it a little too seriously?"

"No," Kate replied without a single second of hesitation. She smiled a little, but not in the defensive, proud way she did before punching someone in the snout. Seeing Andy pace and fidget made her realize he wasn't angry or a threat at all. Maybe annoyed, but he was mostly scared, not only of her but of his own feelings too. Talking about them brought them to life and made them real in a way he had not fully considered and that terrified him to the core. Her smile comforted him, but he made sure to remain guarded.

"I know I'm a flaming crotch," Kate said casually and without regret. "But Eric's like family to me and I have to look out for him. He'd do the same for me. I'm good at taking someone's word, Andy. Give me your word and I'll believe you. But if you break it, I'll break your legs off and beat you with them."

Not knowing whether to laugh or cry or run screaming, Andy bravely stood tall and put his ball cap back on his sweaty brow. He confidently looked into Kate's impatient eyes and said, "I give you my word."

A wide, white smile accented Kate's pretty face. The way Andy looked back at her with honesty in his now watery, fragile eyes filled Kate with assurance. "Wow!" she said, shaking her head with a giggle. "You've got it bad."

Finally, Andy softened and cracked his signature grin.

"I just want you to be good to him," Kate continued. "He really likes you and I've logged enough hours on the phone talking about your ass to last ten lifetimes so treat him right. Too much has happened to him and the last thing he needs is to deal with getting over you."

She grabbed a mirrored compact from her purse, checked her look, and readjusted the bulky bag on her shoulder. Glancing back to a stunned Andy, she smiled. "Tell Eric to call me later. See ya!" she said and took a few steps in the opposite direction.

"Wait a minute!" Andy said. He matched her steps and gently touched her shoulder.

Kate turned back and Andy searched for the words. "I know he's been through a lot," he said softly. "And I really want to start something with him, something serious—"

"Yeah," Kate said, unsure of the conversation's direction.

"And I know I've just started getting to know him, but…why doesn't he open up?" Under his shirt, Andy twirled his fingers through the small hair patch below his navel. His soft tone was casual but desperately trying to sound nonchalant, like the answer to the life-and-death question didn't matter.

But Kate knew it did.

"Why doesn't he tell his inner most thoughts or spill his guts to you?" she asked, growing more comfortable with Andy as they talked.

He looked back into her eyes and she saw genuine interest and urgency in them.

Kate shrugged a little and said, "Think about it. Why should he? He's been chased and shit-kicked by you guys for years. A little attention from you isn't going to make all of that go away. If anything, he's more confused than ever."

"But he doesn't have to be." As soon as the words left his mouth, Andy realized how silly they were. "I know that's easier said than done, but—"

"That's just it. You can't turn trust on and off," she interrupted but saw it didn't satisfy him. She flipped her hair over her shoulders and thought for a moment. "Eric seems very perceptive. When we're at the mall or a restaurant, he always notices the people around us, the waiters, the customers, the smelly homeless guy on the street everyone else ignores. He sees it all. And he's got a great sense of direction. He always remembers where we parked, what isle we're in, street names—"

"Yeah?" Andy said, anxious to hear her point.

"It turns out he isn't observant at all. He's scared," she said. "He's scared of straight guys who're going to talk shit or kick his ass. That's why he always knows where the door is or where the car's parked, so he can make a quick getaway to save himself. He doesn't trust anybody, hence the loud-mouthed exterior he puts on—"

"Kind of like you?" Andy quipped.

"We're not talking about me."

"But why's he like that? Why's he so scared?"

"Is there no brain behind your pretty face?" Kate snapped. "*You,* dumbass! You, Justin, Wes, Matt, the baseball team, you guys are the reason he's like this. You're the reason he can't trust anyone."

"But he can trust me."

Kate gently put her hand on his arm and said, "You're going to have to earn it."

Chapter Twelve

During the initial weeks of his growing romance with Andy, Eric trudged on through the wretched gym class while the tormenting never ceased. The boys only worsened the torture as Dick watched with a proud eye. The only moments that motivated Eric to make it through were brief glimpses of Andy in his gym shorts, tight T-shirts or wet swim trunks. He had, of course, perfected the art of sneaking peeks at the athlete without anyone spotting him. And every once in a while, but very rarely, he caught Andy sneaking a quick look at him as well. Luckily, the required jock straps contained their excitement.

"All right men, line up!" Dick's thunderous voice echoed through the poolroom as the boys took their usual stances near the edge of the water. Eric had learned to stay at least two steps behind them to prevent another *slip* into the pool. Each time he neared the edge, he reminded himself that the six-week session of swimming was nearly complete.

Dick blew his whistle. "Get in the pool!" he ordered, and tossed his clipboard to the tiled floor.

At Dick's instruction, the boys splashed into the water, most of them tried to out-cannonball the other. The air was thick with unrest and Eric felt it. He slipped into the water as quietly as he could and paddled to a lonely section away from the overbearing beasts. But the tension mounted as the vicious boys spotted his secluded spot and exchanged devious glances.

"Why're you over there by yourself, fag?" Chris Golden asked. His early-grown hairy chest pumped hard with laughter.

The room fell silent, with only the rippling sound of waves bouncing softly off the walls as all the boys turned in the water to stare at Eric. Dick, standing by the edge of the pool with the whistle around his neck and his arms folded across his chest, just grinned.

Like lightning, Chris, Justin Drake, and the others pounced on Eric's defenseless frame. Digging their hungry claws into his thin flesh, the boys took turns dunking Eric beneath the surface of the water. Each plunge followed one more brutal than the first. Eric frantically grabbed at whatever he could, Chris Golden's swim trunks, Chase Frank's long arms, Wes Palmer's ankles, Justin's left wrist. But the fight was unfair with the athletes harshly overpowering him.

After several torturous moments, Eric stopped fighting. All he wanted was a fresh, uninterrupted breath of air but the boys kept him from it. The abuse lasted for several agonizing, laughter-filled minutes before Eric finally broke free from their clutches and swam to the pool's edge. He didn't really break free, though. The boys just gave him a little room to squirm before continuing the chase. Eric made sure to hoist himself out of the water as they headed toward him, thirsty for more.

The instant Eric's bare feet landed on the cold, slimy tile, Dick's voice was shouting as usual. "What're you doing, Anderson?!" Dick barked, although everyone knew by the grin glued to his face that he had witnessed and enjoyed the attack.

"Are you going to let them do this?!" Eric yelled. "They're going to kill me!"

Dick smiled and calmly said, "Don't egg them on."

Eric's mouth dropped. "Are you kidding me?!"

"Get back in the pool, Anderson," Dick demanded. "I'll deal with you later."

"No fucking way!"

The boys half-laughed, half-gasped at Eric's remark. Dick stepped closer and leaned into Eric's face. "You better watch your mouth, boy," he whispered with a fiery kick.

Dumbfounded and furious, Eric stared back to the laughing boys. When his eyes landed on Andy, Eric couldn't see at his face. Andy had his head firmly bowed to the water.

"Get your ass back in that pool!" Dick's thunderous voice now cracked with lightning.

"I'm sick of this shit!" Eric shouted and marched to the towel bench to dry off.

Dick blew on his whistle and pointed to the water. "Get in that pool!" he shouted. "I haven't dismissed you!"

"I don't care!" Eric yelled. "And stop blowing that whistle! I'm not a dog!" Clutching the towel, Eric went to the locker room door. Dick followed him and grabbed Eric's right arm, digging his fingers in tight.

"Who do you think you are, you little shit?!" Dick demanded to know, tightly pressing his sharp fingernails into Eric's bicep.

Eric jerked his arm twice but Dick's hold was too strong. "Let me go!" he shouted.

Dick yanked Eric's arm, pulling him back toward the pool. "We're not done!"

"What're you going to do, drown me?!" Eric screamed and violently tugged his arm loose from Dick's cold grip. Without skipping a beat, Eric turned back to the locker room door. On his way, his wet feet slipped and he fell on his ass. As his bony tailbone bounced against the slick tile, the room erupted with laughter.

"Not so light on your feet after all, huh, Anderson?" Dick mocked.

Without an ounce of pride left, Eric stood up and once again faced the boys in the water. He found Andy's eyes without a need to search through the judgmental faces. His wanting heart had learned to navigate through the painful attacks and find silent solace in Andy like an angelic needle in a continuously cruel haystack. In the water with the others, Andy stood aside from them, his arms folded hard across his chilly chest, his eyes filled with a watery hurt. But Andy didn't move. He stood there, silent, breathing heavily and allowed the abuse to continue. Not even a single, small ripple disturbed the water around him. He stood so very still.

Eric paid little attention to him. Andy's folded arms infuriated him, not only because he needed help but because Eric was mad at himself for foolishly expecting more than he should have. Andy never promised him help or safety from any future attacks. Andy never promised him anything.

The steely truth to their arrangement suffocated Eric's lungs worse than the pool water.

Humiliated, angry, and physically aching from head to toe, Eric held his breath. Maybe if he slowed his system down, he'd be able to stop the tears welling in his eyes. He turned away from Andy's quiet neglect and kept turning until his back was to the rest of the class, as well as Dick and his nonstop screeching whistle.

With insults thickening the humid air and his lungs, arm, and ass pounding with pain, Eric disappeared into the safety of the empty locker room.

***

There was no time to waste. Once the poolroom door slammed shut, Eric heard the bulky chain of keys Dick kept strapped around his neck jingling toward him. Eric raced to his gym locker, grabbed the first few pieces of clothing his hands touched and ran out of the room. Just as he turned the corner from the exit, Eric heard the poolroom door swing open and the boys loudly encouraging Dick's rampage with cheers and splashes.

As if his sneakers were on fire, Eric ran as fast as his legs could carry him toward Principal Spear's office. On the way, he multi-tasked running for his life and changing his clothes. He slipped into the blue T-shirt and gray cotton gym shorts he had snatched from his locker. Stopping only for a moment to pull the shorts on over his wet trunks, he continued on his quest for the office. The halls were empty and quiet, but Eric's head pounded with replays of his attackers' screams and joyous tormenting shouts.

When Eric marched his soggy body into the reception area to Principal Spear's office, Rebecca Bates, the hoity-toity secretary whom everyone suspected did much more than answer phones for Spear, was behind a desk overly decorated with photos of her odd-looking young children. She didn't look up when the heavy glass office door opened. Her mid-morning bagel and cream cheese had her undivided attention.

Eric stood at the counter at the front of the room, his wet hair falling in his face, dripping off his chin and onto the wooden countertop. "Excuse me," he said, tapping his pruned fingertips as he waited.

Bates chomped another bite of food. She was oblivious to anything other than the cream cheese she intricately spread over the lightly toasted bagel. But the very instant Eric walked passed the counter and entered the "Staff Only" area of the office, she was on her feet and in his face.

"What are you doing, young man?" she demanded to know, her voice muffled by a messy mouthful of food.

"I need to see Mr. Spear," Eric said, shivering from a chill.

"Do you have an appointment?"

"Do you have any scheduled?" Eric asked, glancing around the silent, empty office.

She wasn't amused by his sarcasm and asked, "Why do you need to see him?"

Holding his wet arms out, Eric stared at her, his eyes wide and his eyebrows cocked. "I want him to check out my swan dive," he snapped. "Is he here or not?"

"Watch your mouth, young man, and have a seat," she ordered as harshly as she could. She walked away, disappearing behind a wall leading toward Spear's office.

Eric remained standing, tapping his toe impatiently.

Bates returned and said, "He'll see you—"

Before she could finish, Eric brushed passed her and B-lined for the principal's door. It was open and Spear was inside, sitting at his desk, focused on a stack of ruffled papers. Eric tapped on the door to get his attention.

"May I help—" Spear stopped himself when he recognized Eric's well-known face. "Well, Eric, what a surprise."

"It shouldn't be. I'm here almost as much as you," Eric said coldly and out of breath. His wet hair and body soaked his T-shirt and his slippery shoes made for quite a dramatic entry.

"What happened to you?" Spear's laughter was annoying, bouncing off every inch of the golf-shrine office, off the framed high scorecards and the mounted putter below the bronzed 5-iron. His red, puffy, chuckling face only worsened Eric's anger.

"Those assholes almost drown me in the pool!" Eric spoke so loud he was sure he heard Rebecca Bates choke on a chunk of cream cheese down the hall.

The foul attitude of the imposing student silenced the principal's laughter. He sat up in his chair. "I beg your pardon?" Spear said, clasping his hands together and resting them on the desktop.

Taking a step closer into the room, Eric spoke even louder than before. "Dick and the other guys in that class are going to kill me! They almost drowned me!"

"Now, now, Eric, calm down." Spear's voice was condescending at best. "Are you sure it wasn't just a little fun gone wrong?"

Eric's head cocked and lowered like a bull ready to attack the matador with its horns. "No!" he screamed. "These guys've been giving me shit since the sixth grade, so NO! It's not a little fun gone wrong!"

Spear was chillingly calm, unshaken. "Sixth grade?" His smirk dripped with doubt.

"Is there an echo in here?" Eric stood his ground.

"You must be mistaken," Spear assumed. He glanced up only a few times from his desk, paying no attention that Eric was wet, shivering and scared.

"The pool water didn't flood my brain. I know what I'm talking about."

"They are very good guys, strong athletes, well-mannered—"

"WHAT?!"

"Maybe if you tried to be more like them, you know, fit in with their crowd, you wouldn't project so much of this supposed hatred."

"Spare me the psycho-babble-bullshit! I don't want to fit into their crowd!" Eric charged further into the room and pounded his fists on Spear's desk to emphasize his frustration. "I just want them to stop!"

Rolling his eyes and sighing, Spear tossed his hands up, surrendering. "What do you want from me?" he asked, "How can I make this go away?"

"I want you to nail their balls to the wall and get rid of Dick!"

"Leon Dickson has been with this school for more than twenty-five years. He's obviously doing something right."

Eric's eyes nearly popped out of their sockets. "Is this the fucking Twilight's Zone?"

"You're skating on very thin ice, Eric. Do not use that kind of language in my school."

"Thin ice? There is no thin ice, unless I was just trapped underneath it when those bastards were drowning me!" Eric's voice gained such a thunderous momentum that Bates came to check on them. Spear waved her away.

"Eric, I'm very busy," Spear said, groaning with disinterest. "So—"

Shocked and now shaking with scorching adrenaline, Eric stood still, unable to catch his breath. "The least you can do is get me out of that goddamned class!" he demanded.

"I already warned you about your language, young man!" Spear snapped, his voice increasing in volume. "As for transferring you, I can't do that. It's too late into the semester and, frankly, I think gym class is good for you, so you'll just have to stick it out. And if you use language like that with me again, I'll serve you with detention for two weeks."

Eric was hysterical. "I almost drowned and you're telling me to suck it up?"

Spear was beyond annoyed and frustrated. He heaved a long sigh. "Eric—"

"Do you know you're breaking the law by not protecting me?" Eric said. He had done his research. "I've come to you a hundred times with the same old shit and you never do anything about it. You always tell me to 'Stick it out' or watch my language—"

"Eric—" Spear's forehead glistened with early signs of sweat.

"The truth is you *have* to do something, by law. It's your job to keep me safe in this school." Eric breathed a proud, fiery flame. "So maybe you should figure something out fast before I get my parents involved or a lawyer or the press or anyone who'll listen to me."

Spear stood to his feet and towered over the shorter, out-of-breath boy ahead of him. "You've got some nerve coming in here and demanding such things," he said. His steely tone stayed strong. "And yes, I know you've come to me with concerns before—"

"And you don't do anything about them!"

"Did you ever stop to consider that maybe I have a hard time believing your stories because you and that noisy girlfriend of yours are always involved in some kind of trouble?" He stepped around his desk and stood close to his pupil. "You're always rambling on and on about one thing or another. It's hard for me to keep them straight." He spoke casually and even chuckled a little, waiting for Eric to join the lighthearted approach.

Instead of busting a gut, Eric stretched his legs and straightened his spine to stand as tall as he could. "I think skipping detention *once* with my noisy girlfriend is a little different than getting the shit beat out of me by my classmates and my gym teacher," he said, lifting his right T-shirt sleeve. Underneath the cloth, where Eric's flesh burned from Dick's grip, were the early signs of rough, blackening bruises in the shape of a grown man's fingers. "Don't you, Mr. Spear?"

The principal's generic smile faded at the sight of the brutal marks. He stepped back and returned to his seat behind the desk. He wasn't accepting defeat, just buying himself time to think. Without looking at Eric, he fiddled with a few pencils and papers on the desktop for several moments before pulling a yellow form from the filing cabinet behind his chair.

"I'll give you study hall first period," Spear said, keeping his head on the long form and away from Eric's face. "Your gym requirement will be waived."

Standing at the head of the desk, Eric finally caught his breath.

***

There was a deep, obvious satisfaction in Eric's proud grin as he strolled into the counseling office. His hair hadn't dried yet and his damp T-shirt still clung to his thin physique, but no one would've noticed anything aside from the ear-to-ear smirk.

"You're back again?" Elizabeth Tilly said, glancing up from her desk only briefly.

"I need to see Mrs. Hatcher," Eric said, overly sweet.

"Didn't you clear everything up at the beginning of the year?"

"Is she here?" Eric was impatient.

Tilly motioned toward Hatcher's office and said, "Make it quick."

Somehow, Eric managed to stretch the smile even further and coat it with a gleaming glaze of arrogance before walking toward the counselor's office. When he reached Hatcher's doorway, she was immediately annoyed.

She said, "Eric, it's been several weeks. I already told you I can't—"

Eric pulled a slip of yellow paper from his pocket and handed it to her. "I've got my Get-Out-of-Gym-Free card," he said, oozing with pride.

Hatcher snatched the note from his hand and read it. She sighed and rolled her eyes. "It doesn't say what other gym period you are to be placed in," she noted.

"He waived the requirement for graduation."

"You little shit. How did you do this?" She was firm, but a tiny laugh expressed a hint of amazement.

The five-minute warning bell rang before second period. "Oh, I have to go," Eric said, intentionally ignoring her question. "I'll pick up my new schedule after school."

He smiled once more and his left eyebrow curled upward in a victorious arch. He turned on his heel and left the office.

On his way out, Hatcher shouted once more, "How did you do this?!"

Chapter Thirteen

Eric spent too much time after school in the darkroom of Pamela Murray's photography classroom developing one last picture of the marching band for the school newspaper. He was so late and made Kate so impatient that she left, stranding him without a ride home. He hurried anyway and hauled his ass to the bus lot, hoping his bus would miraculously still be there, waiting for him. Of course, the only thing actually waiting for him was the stinging bite of the cheese-wagon's exhaust choking the air.

"Dammit!" Eric snapped and glanced around the empty lot. He wasn't sure what he was looking for since the area was for school busses and faculty vehicles only. Still, he looked in every direction for help or guidance or Kate's eyes to scratch out for leaving him there.

Then something caught his eye.

Parked at the end of the drive was Andy's old beat-up Ford Escort. Leaning against the outside front passenger door, with his arms folded in the muscle-flexing way Eric enjoyed, was Andy McCain, smiling and waiting patiently like the hero of an 80s romance flick.

Somehow finding motivation to move his feet, Eric walked the few yards to the Escort. His cheeks blushed and his heart raced as he drew closer. "Can I have a ride, sir? I'm broke as a joke, but I'd be more than willing to work it off somehow," Eric teased.

A boyish grin came to Andy's face that Eric had never seen before. It was the first glimpse Eric had of a truly horny baseball player thinking dirty thoughts.

"I'm sure we can work something out," Andy said and opened the passenger side door for Eric. "But I hear you drive a hard bargain."

"I'm worth every penny." Eric laughed at his own lameness and sat in the car.

Andy circled the car, hopped into the driver's seat and started the engine.

"How'd you know I'd be here?" Eric asked.

With his hand on the gearshift, Andy paused to think. "I just knew."

***

Eric wasn't surprised that Andy drove them to his apartment instead of taking him directly home. They spent so much time there that Eric couldn't think of anywhere else they had ever been together. But it didn't matter. Eric loved the subtle charm of the little home but even that didn't matter, as long as they had somewhere to spend together.

Except on that afternoon, after Eric's near-drowning incident in gym class that morning, there was an unsettling tension between the two boys. Andy avoided it and drove quietly to his apartment. Eric tried to do the same, but by the time they reached Andy's front door, he couldn't keep his mouth shut any longer.

"You were pretty quiet in gym today," Eric said, blatantly enough so Andy would recognize the guilty insinuation.

Andy heard it like a hundred ringing church bells. "What did you want me to do?" he asked calmly. They walked inside and Andy tightly locked the door behind them.

Quietly and without force, Eric said, "You could've stopped them."

"How could I have helped without crucifying myself?"

The disappointment and hurt on Eric's face made Andy realize the severity of the insensitive remark and regret it.

"Eric, you know what I mean," he said to recover.

"Not really," Eric said and sat on Andy's sofa. Buddha scurried to his feet and barked for attention and Eric scratched the dog's head.

Before Andy could climb out of the hole he dug, the telephone rang. He quickly answered it.

"Hey Justin!" Andy cheered. Eric cringed at the sound of the prick's name, but was more surprised by how quickly Andy popped back into chipper jock-mode upon hearing his friend's voice. Andy saw Eric's watchful, disgusted eye fixate on him but Andy had no reaction, nor did he end the conversation early. Justin did most of the talking since Andy only nodded and grunted a few times into the phone. He only really spoke once.

"Yeah! What you guys did to Eric Anderson in the pool was great! That fag had it coming!" Andy said with an all-too-easy chuckle.

Eric's mouth dropped, his eyes bulged, and he released a disbelieved half-laugh-half-scream. It turned into a cough and he bent himself over the couch to catch his breath. The fit lasted the rest of the conversation. Andy nodded twice more and grunted again.

"All right, J. See you later," Andy said and hung up. He looked to Eric and, oblivious to Eric's coughing fit, said, "You have to go. The guys are coming over."

Without warning, Eric leaped off the couch and grabbed the hardcover math book from the kitchen counter. Screaming and crying, Eric spun around and chucked the book in Andy's direction. Pages flapped wildly in the air as it bombed across the room. Andy ducked as the hurling hardcover whizzed past his ear and smashed against the picture window above the bed, cracking the glass.

"What the hell?!" Andy screamed and ran to the broken window. "Are you crazy?!"

Standing in the kitchen, Eric breathed heavily, his face puffy from crying. His heart crumbled as Andy paid more attention to the cracked glass than to him. Eric went back to the couch, slung his backpack over his shoulder and grabbed his jacket. "Go to hell," he said so quietly that Andy didn't even hear him.

Andy did, however, turn to see Eric at the door. "Where're you going?" he asked, rushing to Eric's side. He finally noticed Eric's tears and after a few more seconds, he realized what had happened. "Shit!"

he shouted. "Eric, I'm sorry—"

"How dare you say that about me." Eric's eyes were drying. Anger replaced the tears.

"Eric, I just—"

"First of all," Eric said without acknowledging that Andy had spoken. "I don't have *anything* coming from those assholes—"

"I know! I'm sorry!" Andy gushed. "But I can't let them suspect anything!"

"—and second," Eric continued, ignoring Andy once more. He spoke softly but with an increasing volume that put Andy on edge. Raising a shaking index finger, Eric leaned into Andy to emphasize his next point. "Don't you *ever* call me a fag."

"Eric, come on!" Andy begged. "I'm doing this so I can be with you!"

"Bullshit!" Eric shouted. "You're doing this so you can be *you*, so you can be hot shit with the boys and still get a piece of my ass on the side!"

"Is that what you think I'm here for, your *ass*?" Andy asked, shocked. "We haven't even done that yet. That's not what this is about."

"Maybe not," Eric said. He ran his fingers through his hair and let out a little scream. "I just don't want to be with someone who's going to throw me out of his apartment every time his friends come over." He was already exhausted by the argument. "Being popular is too important to you and you're so concerned with looking straight that you can even *see* straight!"

"That's not true—"

"Oh, please! My born-on date isn't yesterday!" Eric adjusted his backpack on his shoulder and returned to the front door. Buddha scurried up and nibbled on his shoelaces, growling with determination. Eric knelt beside the ankle-biter and scratched the furry puff of hair on his head. From the floor, Eric glanced up to Andy, who was standing with his arms firmly folded across his chest to keep them from shaking.

"I don't want to hide my feelings for you. In a perfect world or even in a perfect school, I wouldn't have to," Eric said, giving Buddha one last scratch before standing up. "But Ann Arbor South sure as hell isn't perfect. You're not going to change and neither are my feelings." His eyes swelled with tears again and he quickly wiped them away with his shirtsleeve. Eric was determined to stay strong and not embarrass himself by crying again. "So I guess the only way to change the situation is to end it."

Andy's lower lip quivered and his eyes moistened with tears. His arms dropped out of the fold and reached for Eric but quickly drew back. Then they reached again and again they stopped. Andy didn't know his boundaries. He wanted to grab Eric, shake him, hold him, but knew it wasn't welcomed. "You can't leave," Andy said quietly. "Not now."

With an extended arm, Eric's fingertips softly touched Andy's shoulder but only for a moment. He jerked his hand back and clutched his backpack. "I learned a lot today, watching you in the pool as they did all that shit to me. You just stood there." Eric tried to stay calm. "I guess I thought or hoped you'd be some shit-kicking knight in shining armor, but I was wrong and I can't do this to myself. I can't follow these rules. It's not enough for me to see you at secluded library tables or in dark movie theaters or in your apartment with the blinds closed. I can't live in fear of your friends or what they'll do to us if they know we're sneaking around behind their backs." Eric turned to the door and forced himself to turn the knob.

"Eric, please!" Andy was frantic. He took a step closer to the door and gently grabbed Eric's shoulder. Eric jerked away and Andy backed off. "Don't go! You can't!"

Without turning around or glancing behind him, Eric added, "Don't worry, I'll make sure they don't see me leaving."

Eric took a step out the door, but Andy grabbed him with stronger force and pulled him back into the apartment. "You can't go! Please!" Andy begged. He held onto Eric's shoulders, making Eric look at him. Andy's face was tear-stained and hurting. "Don't go! You can stay!"

Eric's eyes squinted, his head cocked, and he said, "Do you mean that?" It wasn't a real question and Andy didn't respond. Eric shook his head, annoyed, and wiped his tears. "I didn't think so." He pushed

Andy aside and walked out of the apartment.

"I'm just so fucking scared!" Andy screamed into the hallway.

"Of what?" Eric snapped, turning back. "Of Justin? You're scared of your best friend? No, you're scared of being who you really are."

"I don't know how to be a fag!" Andy shouted, paying no attention to any potential listeners behind the other closed apartment doors.

"Oh, and what, *I* wrote the Flaming Queer Handbook? Go to hell, Andy!"

Eric left before Andy could speak. He ran to the stairs, forcing each step, knowing if he gave Andy even a second longer to respond or shed another tear, he wouldn't leave. He'd probably never leave and fall back under the spell of Andy's hypnotic blue eyes.

Eric was outside the apartment building before stopping for air. He tried to keep his head pointed east, toward home, but it kept wandering north, toward Andy's window. The blinds were open again and Andy was standing on the other side of the broken glass, looking down at Eric on the sidewalk. Eric saw him mumble a few words he couldn't understand. Maybe they weren't even words, just cries. Andy pressed his big hands to the window and kept his teary eyes on Eric.

To his own surprise, Eric followed his head and not his heart. He took a deep breath, turned back to the east, and headed for home.

***

Eric made it two blocks from Andy's apartment before the teary-eyed water works sprang into full force. Sitting at the corner of Adelaide and Caroline streets, on a lonely white bench in front of the town's only homemade candy store, *Sweet Intentions*, Eric cried and waited for Kate. He called her a block earlier and painfully cried for a ride. Although Kate had dried his eyes countless times over the years, Eric never needed his best friend more than he did while sitting on the wooden bench.

Without question or hesitation, Kate arrived within minutes and parked her car a block away from the candy store. The sidewalk was not busy with pedestrians, but the streets were heavy with traffic, which thickened the tension in the air. As she approached Eric, Kate slowed her pace to quiet her loud shoes. Eric's head was bowed in his hands. Kate knew he was crying. She knew it the moment he called her, nearly hysterical and begging for her to pick him up.

Instead of bursting into her signature loudmouth theatrics, Kate softly slid onto the bench beside Eric and kept her mouth shut. Eric did not look at her, but he was aware of her presence.

A few overly curious pedestrians walked by, gawking at the sobbing boy on the bench. Kate glared at them and sent them on their way. Even still, Kate said nothing. She put her hand on Eric's back, gently rubbed it, and waited for him to start.

Finally, in a soft whisper, Eric said, "He chose them."

Kate only listened and rubbed the back of his shirt.

"Justin called and the guys were coming to the apartment, so Andy kicked me out." Eric wiped his face and sat up, facing Kate for the first time. She saw tear-stained cheeks and angry eyes. "He told me I had to get out and we said some pretty nasty things to each other. He was crying. I was crying. It was really ugly and…I left."

Again, Kate held her tongue.

"I know our relationship has to be top secret," Eric continued. "I have no choice in that. Andy made the rules and at first I was all for it because, well, this is *Andy McCain* we're talking about!" He smiled a little. "But I never thought it'd get like this, him choosing them over me. I guess I wasn't thinking at all and maybe I'm just kidding myself. It's not like we belong together anyway."

Kate nodded and wasn't going to speak, but Eric stared at her, waiting, *needing* her words. She cracked a comforting smile. "It's hard being Clark Kent and Superman at the same time. Andy doesn't know how to lead a double life and figuring it out is exhausting. I'm sure he didn't mean the things he said," she told him. "And don't say you don't belong together because I've seen the way he looks at you like a little kid on Christmas morning. He really likes you, Eric. He's just torn between you and the guys and he doesn't know how to choose."

"Well, I don't want it to be like that!" Eric said with a desperate laugh.

"I know, sweetie, and he shouldn't have to choose," she said. "I wish I could pull a solution out of my ass, but I can't. He's going to have to work it out for himself."

"What am I going to do?"

Kate thought for a moment. "Maybe you should just chill out for a while and see what happens," she suggested, her voice confident. "That's shitty advice but I don't really know what you should do. I mean, I could tell you that whatever's meant to be will be and it'll all work out in the end, but you're too emotional to think like that right now."

Eric nodded.

"If you want to kick his ass, you know I'll help," Kate added. "But something tells me you don't want to do that. So take a breather and cool off."

"You think?"

She stood up, held out her hand, and said, "Come on, I'll buy you that fruity shake you like at Jupiter. The one that gives you the shits."

Smiling a little and taking a deep breath, Eric held Kate's hand. She helped him to his feet and they headed for her car.

"And you never know," Kate added. "Andy might surprise you."

Chapter Fourteen

Wednesday, October 9, 1996

At Kate's insistence, Eric ditched school the next day. He didn't want to see Andy and definitely didn't want to see Justin or the other boys. Staying home, though, wasn't the best decision since it only left him with too much time to think about anything and everything.

At the end of the school day, Eric met up with Kate and Nick as classes were letting out. Eric had to pick-up his English books but mostly he needed to be with his friends. When they arrived at Eric's locker, Kate hugged him and Nick squeezed his shoulder.

"Let's grab some food," Nick said.

"Good idea," Eric agreed, comforted by Nick's casual tone. "Let me just grab my stuff."

The second Eric's fingers lifted the locker latch and he looked inside, he saw a small glass box tied with an old pair of dirty shoelaces sitting on the top shelf. Propped against the box and partially concealing it was a piece of white drawing paper, folded twice and marked ERIC in familiar block letters.

"What's that?" Kate asked, peeking over her friend's shoulder.

Eric pulled the folded note off the shelf. In doing so, he exposed the entire glass package and clearly saw the item for the first time.

Beautifully displayed inside the small case was an old dirty baseball. Eric instantly recognized it as the ball from atop Andy's television: the treasured souvenir from Andy's first homerun as a kid. The ratty blue shoelaces circling the baseball's box were from the cleats Andy wore the day he ran that homerun. Eric had never seen them before but knew the story well since he had asked Andy several times to repeat it. The passion and exhilaration in Andy's eyes when he told it was nearly as thrilling as the story itself.

"What is it, Eric?" Kate asked again. She gently shoved him aside and grabbed the displayed ball from the locker shelf. Looking closer, she realized what it was. Naturally, Eric had told her the homerun story a hundred times. "You've got his balls in a case. Well, *one* ball," she said and giggled sweetly.

Eric rolled his eyes and unfolded the accompanying note. He recognized the paper as a piece torn from the art sketch book he had left at Andy's apartment. The large, hard stock paper opened to reveal only a few block-lettered words written in black charcoal pencil:

THOUGHT YOU'D LIKE THIS.
A-

"What's it say?" Kate impatiently asked. "Come on!"

Eric's eyes widened and his gaze slowly rose to meet her face. She stared at him with her eyebrows raised and snatched the note from his hand. Nick read it himself over Kate's shoulder.

"Holy shit!" she said in a whispered excitement. "Not much of a romantic note, though." Glancing back up, she saw Eric's expression had not changed. Shock had frozen itself to his face. But he said nothing. He reclaimed the piece of paper, reading it repeatedly.

"How'd he get in here anyway?" Kate asked. "Does he have the key to your heart *and* your locker?" Her smile was bright. "That's so cutesy it makes me want to puke."

Finally, Eric spoke in a whisper, "What's he doing?" He glanced over his shoulders, keeping the note and gift tightly guarded. "What if someone sees?"

Kate barely heard him but didn't dare ask him to repeat it. She shrugged and said, "Maybe he doesn't care anymore. Maybe you're more important."

"Did you know about this?" Eric's nerves clouded his logic.

"Yes, we conspired through smoke signals and midnight meetings in a back alley downtown," Kate laughed. "Of course not!"

Before Eric, Kate and Nick could examine the note and the million different angles to which it needed examining, the smell of Justin Drake's expensive and overly used cologne filled the air. Kate choked on the tangy scent. She knew the trouble it brought.

"What's going on?" Justin's condescending voice came from over their shoulders. Turning without surprise, Eric, Kate and Nick saw Justin leaning against a nearby locker, smiling widely and ready to pick a fight.

"I'm sure as hell not in the mood for your shit right now," Kate warned. "So just get out of here and save us the grief for once!"

Justin stepped closer. "Naw, I don't think so!" he said and viciously snatched the unique note from Eric's hand. Towering over the others, Justin held the paper above his head as Eric and Kate leaped for it without success. Nick stood back, observing, waiting for the worst before getting involved.

"You son of a bitch!" Kate screamed, clawing at Justin's chest and arm, trying to retrieve the note. "Give me that!"

Unfazed by the tiny young woman, Justin read the note at arm's length. "HA! Who's this from, your *boyfriend*?!" he said, his voice proud, exhilarated and most of all, righteous. "It is! I knew it! Who this *A* guy?"

"Get out of here!" Kate yelled again. Her repetitiveness annoyed even herself.

Justin ignored her and turned to his makeshift audience. "HEY EVERYBODY!" His voice bounced off the hall walls and demanded the attention of every student within earshot. Many gathered around Eric's locker and listened closely as Justin continued, "Anderson got a card from his *boyfriend*!" His voice playfully tickled curious eardrums with a childish ring. With the note in his hand, he waved it in the air for all to see. The ever-increasing crowd of on-looking students jammed the hall, all of them stretching for their chance to see the mysterious love letter.

Kate took a big step toward the annoying instigator and brutally slapped her small hand across his left cheek. It smacked hard against his prickly skin and echoed off the metal lockers and judgmental students' faces. The slap stunned Justin, stumbling him back a few paces. He stared at Kate, partly bewildered but shocked only slightly.

"You're an asshole!" she shouted and swung another slap at him. He ducked and the blow missed. "LEAVE!"

The gathered crowd blocked the hall and stopped student traffic. Snotty, self-righteous Innards and anti-Erics and anti-Kates stood behind Justin, scowling, pointing fingers, and laughing. But surprisingly, a smaller scaled group of peers stood behind Eric and Kate pointing their own angry fingers at Justin and his groupies. Apparently, the Innards weren't as all-around popular as once believed.

Rubbing his stinging cheek, Justin regained his senses and retook his power stance ahead of Kate. "You stupid, *bitch!*" His hot breath scorched its way through her pretty blonde hair.

Immediately, Kate's face burned a fiery red and her fists closed so tightly that her knuckles were pure white. "I'll show you a bitch!" she screamed and pounced toward Justin's smug face. Nick finally involved himself and together with Eric, they moved fast and restrained Kate before she could fill her fingernails with Justin's flesh. She struggled as Nick locked his arms around her waist.

The increased excitement and anger swept through the onlookers. A few even encouraged Justin to "Hit the bitch!" but he didn't take the advice. Instead, he leaned against a nearby locker and tucked his hands into the pockets of his jeans. Watching Nick and Eric try to restrain the crazy girl brought a smile to his face.

"Check this *bitch* out," Justin said to the crowd as if performing for them. "She's just pissed 'cuz I figured out her faggy friend's got a boyfriend!"

The students laughed and gobbled up the drama. "Who's his

boyfriend?!" one of them called out from amidst the chaos.

"Who knows?! But his name starts with 'A'," Justin said.

"You idiot!" Kate shouted. "If you just think about—" Nick quickly covered her mouth to silence her. She wanted to spill her guts, but Nick wouldn't let her temper or meddling mouth ruin Andy's reputation or his future with Eric.

"What's that, *bitch?*" Justin oozed with pleasure in emphasizing the one word that truly got under her skin.

As Kate continued her fight with Nick's arms, Eric stepped away from them and approached Justin. "Give me the note back," Eric said, panting from the struggle.

Justin laughed wildly at the request and didn't oblige. Instead, he waved the paper for all to see and repeatedly read it aloud for all to hear. As the repetitive words bounced off every set of attentive ears in the hall, Andy McCain fought hard to make his way through the crowd. He pushed and shoved and cleared a path to the center, where Justin was tormenting Eric and Nick had a death grip on Kate. Andy exchanged a quick but comforting glance with Eric before turning his attention to Justin.

"What's up?" Andy asked him.

A fast, eerie silence fell over the hall.

Justin's face brightened upon seeing his friend. "Check this out, dude!" he said, happily handing the note to Andy. "He really is a fudge-packer!"

Andy took the creased sheet of paper from Justin. After refolding it into its original pattern, Andy handed it back to Eric and asked him, "Are you all right?"

"I'm fine," Eric said, nodding. "He's just being a dick."

Andy lightly touched Eric's arm and looked back to Justin. "What the hell's your problem, man?" He asked. His voice dropped deeper.

"What're talking about?" Justin's eyebrows bent toward his nose. "What do you care?"

"Come on, J. Are you really that stupid?" Andy said, straightening his back and spreading his shoulders to prepare himself. "Who do you think gave that to Eric?"

"Some guy whose name starts with—" Justin stopped himself. His eyes narrowed as the puzzle finally came together. His eyes darted between Andy's face, the note in Eric's hand, and back to the baseball in the locker. Justin's face flickered with a hint of recognition at the ball. Returning his attention to Andy, it took only a few quick moments for Justin's look to alter upon realizing the truth. He no longer recognized the friend ahead of him. He leaned back to get a full-size view of Andy and to distance himself from what he feared was true. "You—" Justin almost choked on his own breath. "You sent that to him?"

"Yeah, I did," Andy said, filling his chest with a deep breath. "And if you want to fight someone over it, fight me. Leave them out of it."

Taking a big, plague-avoiding step away from Andy, Justin shook his head and ran his fingers through his hair. He grunted and moaned, trying to keep the thoughts from seeping into his mind. But the more he fought them the more they consumed him and with each handful of pulled hair or grinding of a few teeth, the truth of Andy's sexuality came to life.

Justin exploded.

"YOU'RE A FAG?!" he shouted, boldly stepping into Andy's face.

Without even blinking an eye, Andy stood his ground and said, "What if I am?"

"NO! YOU CAN'T BE!" Justin screamed, tearing at his hair. "WHY?!"

Bravely, Andy replied, "Because I love him."

A deafening gasp came from the crowd. The air was hot and sticky with so many sardine-packed students in the hall. No one moved for fear of missing a single second. Eric's heart stopped and Kate's eyes popped from their sockets. Nick held her waist with his right arm and put his left hand on Eric's shoulder.

"If you want to kick my ass, let's do it," Andy added. His nostrils flared and his fists trembled. "But stay away from Eric. He has nothing to do with this."

Justin verged on hyperventilating. His whole body shook with pure anger. His jaw locked and his squinting eyes stared furiously at Andy.

Only seconds passed between their words before Justin was overwrought with hysterical rage.

"YOU SON OF A BITCH!" Justin released his cocked fist and cracked it against Andy's jaw. The blow tumbled Andy into the crowd, scattering students in every direction. Several frightened girls screamed and a few antagonistic boys pushed Andy back to his feet and into Justin's thirsty reach.

Kate's struggling intensified and Nick tightened his grip on her. Eric stood on the sidelines, terrified and helpless. The rest of the crowd cheered and yelled and fed the chaos.

Andy didn't back down. He stepped up to Justin and waited for the next blow. But he never tossed a punch of his own, as if the beating was deserved, justified, and wanted.

But Justin didn't swing another hit. He stared at Andy, unsure if he even knew the ball-playing stranger standing in front of him with a bleeding lip. Although unsure if it was actually there or a bizarre lighting illusion from the overhead fluorescents, Andy thought he saw Justin's eyes watering. He wasn't crying, but was possibly, if it was actually possible, emotional, upset, hurt to the point of tears.

There wasn't enough time to find out. Justin took several steps away from Andy.

"Go to hell," Justin whispered. He turned on his heels and walked away.

The move shocked everyone. The crowd silenced and even Kate stopped fighting Nick's restraints as they watched Justin disappear toward the parking lot. Just as quick, before the inevitable appearance of the clueless faculty, the crowd began to dissipate. The action was over and no one wanted to be responsible for pointing any fingers to an authority figure if questioned. The name-calling continued as the crowd thinned out. Most of Justin's henchmen chased after him, knowing they'd put him in better spirits.

Walking up to a shocked and scared Eric, Andy's bloody lip curled into a smile. "Are you okay?" he said sweetly, like nothing had happened.

Eric didn't say a word. He only stared at Andy's bruised face.

Andy glanced at his watch. "Shit! I have to get to work," he said and took a step closer. Leaning in toward Eric's cheek, he lightly kissed it, paying strong attention to avoid smearing the blood from his beaten lip onto Eric's skin. "I hope you like the baseball," he whispered.

Still, Eric was quiet. He didn't even move. Andy lightly squeezed Eric's arm and walked away, smiling at Nick and the restrained Kate as he passed and left the hallway. After Andy was gone, there was no commotion from the three remaining friends in the emptied hallway. With the hall now eerily vacant, Nick thought it safe to release Kate.

The second Nick removed his hands from her mouth and waist, Kate made a dramatic mad dash in the opposite direction. "Later, bitches!" she yelled without turning back. Her bulky bag and beautiful blonde hair flapped in the air as she ran away. "I've got shit to finish outside!"

"Kate—" Nick lost interest in reasoning with her. It was no use. She was off to viciously hunt Justin down like wild prey and instead of stopping her, Nick turned his attention to Eric.

The hall had emptied so fast that Nick hadn't realize he and Eric were alone. He looked in both directions without a single person in sight. Even creepy Mrs. Frisby, the slow-on-the-go hallway monitor, and her wicked limp were absent. When his eyes refocused on Eric, Nick found his friend still stunned and speechless.

"Nice to know a good ol' hallway fist fight still attracts the teachers," Nick said, trying to break the tension with sarcasm.

There was no reaction from Eric. He just stared at the tiled floor, silent.

"Andy's got balls of steel," Nick added. "That was really brave."

Eric only nodded slowly.

Nervous in the awkward silence, Nick playfully slapped Eric's arm to shake him back to attention. It worked a little and at least brought Eric's eyes to his face.

"What just happened?" Eric's voice was soft and so unsure that it almost sounded scared. "Why did he do that?"

"He thinks you're something special," Nick said.

Again, Eric was at a loss for words.

So Nick added, "You have to talk to him. Catch him before he goes to work."

"What am I going to say?" Eric whispered.

"You'll think of something," Nick said. "When you see him, the words'll come to you."

Eric finally came back to life through the power of Nick's touching words. He cherished the rare moments when Nick expressed his care. "Thanks for standing up for me," Eric said.

"It's what I'm here for." Nick smiled but before it got too emotional he added, "Now go!"

***

From Eric's locker, through the main sport trophy hallway, passed the stank cafeteria and sweat sock smelling gymnasium, and outside to the senior parking lot, Justin and his smug buddies laughed. Spewing insults and swinging powerful pretend punches, the boys enjoyed themselves, proudly slapping each other's backs in a sick sort of congratulatory dance as they exited the school. Justin seemed to adjust quite nicely to the sudden absence of his best friend. His boys knew just the right insults and jokes to reverse his bad mood.

Kate was not joining in the post-abusive celebration. She followed close behind the boys from the very second Nick released her back into the wild. She was unseen. Justin and the others were too caught up in their overloaded arrogance to notice the tiny young lady breathing fire on their tails.

The moment everyone stepped into the parking lot, lit brightly by the fall sunshine, Kate could remain silent no longer. Her stiff fists shook at her side, filling with adrenaline gun powder, ready to explode.

"HEY!" she screamed into the gentle, cool breeze.

Justin and the rest of the boys, including Matt Murphy, Chase Frank, and Jeremy Flint, paused in the lot and turned toward the shout. Upon seeing a supremely pissed off Kate Crawford, Justin broke into laughter. The others joined him and chuckled even louder than during their vain parade away from Eric's locker.

Without hesitating any longer, Kate made a mad dash across the lot with no one but Justin Drake in her scope. To the nasally soundtrack of jock squad laughter, she ran as fast as her legs would carry her. Even in the craziest and uncontrolled of moments, Kate's hair flowed beautifully in slow motion, looking fabulous and somehow presenting her as less threatening than the wicked war-hungry witch she was.

The very instant she reached Justin, Kate released her cocked fist into the tight flesh of his face. The curled fingers forced their way into Justin's right eye socket, squashing it without mercy. The hard hammer to the skin disturbed the stillness of the air. Even the cool breeze held its breath in shock.

The blow knocked Justin into the arms of Matt Murphy. Justin grabbed his face, protectively covering his stinging, beaten eye. Matt quickly boosted Justin to his feet and gave him an extra push toward Kate.

"YOU *BITCH!*" Justin shrieked. Instinctively, his fingers curled into fists. He stepped even closer, towering over his tiny attacker, angrily breathing into her face.

Before he could speak again, Kate brutally slapped his right cheek, intensifying the burn to his eye. "How do you like it?!" she snapped. "You son of a bitch!"

She reached up with both arms to hit him again. Impulsively, Justin reacted fast to protect himself, swinging his own arms and hands at her to block the incoming blows. In doing so, his open palm struck the side of her head, slamming against her ear and upper neck. With an angry force propelling it, the hit sent Kate's shiny blonde hair flying in every direction as she tumbled to the asphalt. Her ass hit first and skidded on the rough pavement a few feet before spinning her onto her stomach and abruptly stopping face first into the ground. Her bulky purse burst its contents onto the parking lot, spewing an endless supply of make-up, nail files, photographs, and unpaid parking tickets.

"DUDE!" Jeremy Flint snapped. He stepped up to his friend and snatched Justin's arm from the air, where it was still hovering. "What're you doing?!"

Although Justin's strike to Kate's ear wasn't entirely intentional, it didn't matter. Justin, Jeremy and the other boys froze, staring at a quiet

Kate, still on the ground, her back facing them. She stirred a little and slowly rolled over. Her hair, a shiny tangled web, covered her face as she carefully sat up straight. She didn't look at her attacker or his cohorts. Instead, she slowly stood to her feet. On the way up, she noticed her smooth legs had several pavement scraps, as did the artificially tanned skin on her arms.

Still, she was quiet as she casually and calmly brushed off the butt of her dark skirt. Taking a deep breath, as if to prepare herself for the worse damage of all, Kate glanced at her manicured fingers. The acrylic nails on her left index finger and right ring finger were broken; the latter dangled by only a tiny piece of skin. Without flinching, Kate chewed it off and spit the fake nail to the ground.

She gave her hair a once over with her hands to smooth the tangles and return some kind of order to the style. When she flipped her blonde locks from her face and finally returned her gaze to Justin, the boys gasped. Her eyes were red with anger. Almost supernaturally, Kate leaped into the air from her stance several feet away and attacked Justin, screaming no particular words as she crashed into him. He fell to the asphalt, his back slamming against the curb. With Justin on his back, Kate straddled him. She was relentless, intensifying the attack with every blow, punching and clawing at his clothes and face. Only devilish shouts erupted from her mouth and the repeated pounding of fists on flesh came from her hands. Kate fought with an animalistic hunger that kept Justin's friends shocked, speechless, and unable to move.

It wasn't until they saw Justin raise his hand to fight back did they finally get involved. Jeremy Flint leaned into the brawl and, with more muscle than he expected to use, pried the ferocious Kate from Justin's body. She scratched at Jeremy's arms and kicked at his legs, trying to break free. But Jeremy's grip on her from behind, through her armpits, was too awkward to overcome.

The temporary defeat was more than worth it when she saw Justin emerge from the fight, his lip bleeding, his eye red and rapidly bruising, and his red Polo shirt shredded from his muscular back. Justin stood to his feet, disoriented and shirtless, the cotton corpse a tattered pile on the dirty parking lot. Kate's claw marks decorated Justin's chest and stomach in a random, reddening pattern. Being short two fingernails didn't slow her down.

Justin tried to hide his humbled, badly bruised ego by spitting a wad of blood at Kate's shoes, but it fell several inches short of her toes. He didn't have the strength to try again but refused to back down. Breathing like rabid attack dogs, a whipped Justin and a constrained Kate didn't speak. They just stared at each other, ready for round two, to the death.

"What the HELL is going on here?!"

Every head in the parking lot, including the thickening crowd of gawkers, turned to see Principal Spear, fuming, his arms folded tight against his chest. It was unclear exactly how much of the attack he had witnessed but it made no difference. He saw enough and was so furious, little droplets of snot flew from his overly flared nostrils. Staring at Kate and Justin, Spear studied them, judging them, trying to make his disappointment known without words.

Kate winked at him.

"My office," he said hoarsely and unamused. "NOW!"

As Justin gathered his torn T-shirt, Spear escorted him, his friends, and a few select witnesses to his office. Three other teachers arrived on the scene to help round up the chosen students. Spear personally took a firm hold on Kate's arm. As she and the others were sternly escorted away from the parking lot, Kate cracked a tiny, itty-bitty smile.

She giggled a little too.

***

The mid-afternoon sunlight burned Eric's eyes when he stepped into the senior parking lot, hoping to catch Andy before he left. Near the tennis courts, Eric saw a thinning crowd of students and Spear escorting a laughing Kate and a swearing and shirtless Justin away from the lot. Kate waved to Eric briefly before reentering the school. Eric rolled his eyes and returned his attention to his search for Andy. Almost instinctively, Eric's eyes zeroed in on the athlete at his car. Eric smiled, surprised but pleased at how quickly his mind could find him without effort.

As Andy dropped his backpack and a few loose books into the trunk of his Escort, Eric jogged over to him, smiling cautiously.

"Got room for one more?" Eric asked, pointing to the car's passenger seat.

Andy's face lit up when he saw Eric. "Sure!" he cheered. "But I should warn you, I'm on my way to work and I'm having coming-out impulses."

"I'll take my chances." Eric walked around the front of the car and leaned against the driver's door, lightly grazing Andy's shoulder. A comfortable silence arose as they enjoyed the sunshine and cool breeze. Andy innocently played with Eric's shirt and slowly slid his fingers up the sleeve to tickle Eric's bicep. Eric laughed and enjoyed the welcomed teasing, but his mind was preoccupied.

"Do you want to tell me why you did that?" Eric asked.

Without hesitating, Andy looked at his face and simply said, "For you."

"You know it'll be all over town by tomorrow."

Andy nodded. He removed his hand from Eric's shirt and nervously kicked a pebble around the parking lot instead. "I know," he whispered.

"Why'd you go through all that just to give me an old baseball?" Eric asked.

"It wasn't about the ball," Andy said. "Well, sort of. I wanted to give you something special. I've never had a real relationship before so I don't know what to give the one you love, so I gave you something that means a lot to me." He breathed deep, kicked the stone, and continued, "And I wanted everyone to know how I feel about you so I took a chance."

Eric lost his focus. His concentration sidetracked halfway through Andy's rant. "You're in love with me?" he asked, holding his breath.

Andy looked closely at Eric's excited, dancing eyes. "Don't flatter yourself too much, cowboy," Andy teased. "But yeah, that's what this is about."

"I'm not worth all this though—"

"You're worth so much more," Andy said softly. "But I don't know what else I can do to make you happy."

"Trashing your popularity, spilling your guts in front of half the school, telling your best friend to fuck off, I think that's enough for one day," Eric said with a laugh. "But it's not about making me happy. You didn't have to do that if you didn't want to."

"I know." Andy looked at Eric's face. "I did what I had to do so we can be together."

"But—"

Andy interrupted Eric by pressing their lips together. The kiss was long and warm and a little salty from the cut on Andy's lip.

"Don't change the subject," Eric said half-joking, breaking from the kiss.

Glancing to the edge of the parking lot, Eric saw that the curious and noisy crowd, which had egged on the violent fight between Kate and Justin, had thickened again and turned its attention to Eric and Andy. With Kate and her beaten prey dragged off to the principal's office, the crowd needed fresh blood for their entertainment. Although Eric was no batch of fresh blood, Andy provided a new canvas for them to paint with their attacks. The air filled with insulting shouts, vicious laughter, and a few tossed soda cans.

"FAGS!"

Uncomfortable and nervous, Eric took a step away from Andy's car for distance and to avoid feeding the hungry mob with more fuel. He went to the passenger side of the car to separate them even further. "Are you ready for this?" he asked Andy.

"QUEERS!"

Giving the pebble one last swift kick across the lot, Andy took only a brief look at the increasingly agitated swarm of students. "It's no big deal," he said. His attempt to hide emotion was pathetic. By his reddening face, sweaty brow, and heavy breathing, Eric knew Andy's blood was boiling.

Eric tried to talk. "Andy—"

"BUTT FUCKERS!"

"Come on, I'll drive you home before I go to work," Andy said without acknowledging Eric's voice. He dropped his keys on the ground and fumbled to pick them up.

"COCKSUCKERS!"

From the passenger side of the car, Eric could hear the keys jingling loudly. Andy couldn't steady his hands to unlock the door. Circling the vehicle again, Eric took Andy's keys and opened the lock. The sweat thickened and dripped from Andy's forehead.

"Want me to drive?" Eric offered.

"What? No. Why? No. Get in," Andy said quickly. He hopped into the front seat, unlocked the passenger door, and started the engine.

Before getting inside, Eric turned to the crowd. It had thinned a little and the shouting was less intense but still there. He was surprised they hadn't approached the car or picked another fight. But with ringleader Justin hauled away, there was no one to guide them.

The closeness of the storm still made Eric nervous. He sat inside the Ford and locked the doors. He looked to the driver's seat. Andy, the strong-as-steel sports star, was sweating heavily and his lower lip quivered.

"It's going to be a lot different tomorrow," Eric said, instantly hating the obvious words.

Andy's fists curled around the leather steering wheel and twisted back and forth. He was quiet, staring out the windshield. His breathing was fast at first but regained control before he said, "It'll be fine." The few words were forced.

"Didn't you think about this part?" Eric asked as carefully as he could.

Andy shrugged and looked out the passenger side window at the still-taunting group. He studied them with a surprised, somewhat betrayed eye, as reality began to set in. When his gaze drifted to Eric's face, he cracked an uneasy smile. "Guess not," he said with a low sigh. "But if I have to go through some bullshit to be with you—" His mouth curled into an unsure smile. "I'll do what I have to do."

Eric shared the smile, pleased by Andy's bravery however forced or fronted. "By the way," Eric said nonchalantly as Andy put the car in gear. "I love the baseball."

Chapter Fifteen

Thursday, October 10, 1996

"Did you talk to him last night?" Kate asked Eric as they walked through the senior lot the following morning.

Before Eric could say anything, Nick caught up with them and smiled.

"Hey," Eric said.

"Hi," Nick replied but kept his attention on Kate. His smile turned to a wide grin.

Instantly, Kate knew the reason. "Okay, okay," she said. "Maybe I got a little carried away in the parking lot yesterday." They kept walking and her voice was never apologetic.

Eric and Nick laughed.

"I was just defending you and maybe it got out of hand," she told Eric. "If it makes you feel any better, dickhead Spear gave us two weeks in detention together. Better yet, Spear is making me buy Shithead Justin a new shirt. Can you believe it? Spear said something about how he can't have his students ripping each other clothes off. I told him he made it sound like underage porno but he didn't dig that so much. So I have to buy some cheap twenty dollar Polo."

The boys' laughter was louder.

"Well, it'll be an early Christmas present for your boyfriend and a way for you two love birds to make amends," Nick joked.

Kate flicked him off.

"At least Spear didn't call your parents or expel you," Eric said. "Your mom would've make lawn mulch out of your ass."

"Yeah, but after two weeks alone with Justin Drake, I'd rather be expelled or dead," Kate said. "But how are you doing? How's Andy?"

"We're nervous about today. That's for sure," Eric said.

"Why're you even here? You should've ditched to let everyone cool off."

"*Ditch*? That's great advice from the girl with two weeks of detention," Nick joked.

"Andy didn't want to ditch. He wants to deal with it now," Eric said. "But he thinks it's not going to be that bad, like nothing's changed."

"Is he delusional?" Kate asked.

"No, but I'm really scared of how everyone's going to react," Eric said as they walked through the main doors of the school. "Because I'm sure everyone knows about it by now."

"Are you kidding? Of course they know. The whole town knows by now," Kate agreed. Nick nudged her to ease her insensitivity. "But so what if they know?" she added, trying to recover. "You guys like each other and that's what it's all about anyway. Screw everyone else."

"But Andy's not used to any of the bullshit I go through. If the guys are this brutal to me, what're they going to do to one their own? He was hot shit yesterday but now he's—"

"Look, Eric, it's none of my business, but Andy doesn't deserve any sympathy," Nick interrupted. He was calm as usual. "If he didn't want to deal with the incoming shitstorm, then he shouldn't have told hundreds of people he's dating a guy."

"Shooting for the Sensitivity Award today, Nick?" Kate snapped.

"I'm not trying to be a dick," he quickly added. "But Andy knew what he was getting himself into. Hell, he brought it on himself. I'm sorry, Eric, you know you're my boy. I'm happy for you, but if Andy thought he could come out and crown you his boyfriend and not have to deal with a hellacious backlash, then he's taken one too many baseballs to the head. This school's just not ready for their Golden Boy to be a faggot."

Immediately, Eric and Kate's jaws dropped.

Nick panicked. "You know what I mean!"

"I can't believe you just said that!" Kate belted, punching his arm.

"No, it's okay," Eric said, sighing. "You're right, Nick. Andy knows it's not going to be the same, but I don't think he's ready for what's about to happen." He paused and tried to think. It was hard for him to concentrate with so many students and faculty members staring, whispering and pointing at him as he walked the halls. Kate did her best to ward them off and Nick ignored most of them as Eric tried to do, but it wasn't easy. "I just don't want him to go through everything that I do."

"I know, man. I'm sorry," Nick said, squeezing Eric's shoulder for support.

"Maybe we're thinking too much," Kate lightheartedly offered. "Andy was Mr. Hottie McPopular yesterday. I'm sure he'll rule the throne again today." She forced an all too toothy grin, painfully showing doubt in her own words.

***

When Andy arrived to gym class the morning after his love confession, he sensed an obvious change in the atmosphere. The air was different, thicker, hotter, like everyone had been blowing off steam, yelling about something or someone and pumped the room full of angry, heavy unrest. As he approached the locker room, Andy heard shouting from inside. The instant he reached the doorway and the guys saw him, the room fell silent.

Standing strong in the sticky metal doorway, Andy watched the boys, his friends, frantically finish changing into their gym clothes. Several of them, panic-stricken, wrapped towels or T-shirts around their half-naked bodies to keep Andy's queer eyes from indulging in any fleshy part of their smooth anatomies.

It took only a few moments before the boys started to filter out of the crowded, sweaty room. On their way out, while passing Andy at the door, the boys took their turns verbally attacking their once worshiped friend. They muttered, spat, and yelled loaded insults. Each shouted word was followed by an even louder laugh. The insults and accompanying laughter ballooned so fast that after a few seconds it all blurred together in an enormous, overwhelming hot ball of hatred that nearly set the room on fire.

Through it all, Justin Drake smiled and stared at Andy with disgust, but Andy wasn't sure if he saw Justin actually participate or toss his own insults. It didn't matter. Justin's ear-to-ear grin was participation enough.

Andy stood there and took the abuse, all of it, every word and every laugh. It happened so fast there was no time to comprehend or lash out as he was verbally attacked for the first time in his life. Andy McCain, Ann Arbor South's star athlete, was now nothing more than the new fag, the new Eric Anderson.

But Andy refused to back down or show mercy. Instead, he went to his locker and changed into his gym shorts and shirt, breathing deep and preparing for war. From a few remaining former friends scattered among the lockers, there were snickers, slurs and snapping towels as his jock-strapped behind slid into his shorts. Still, Andy kept his mouth shut and his fists contained.

And took it.

Several moments later, as the last of the boys filed out of the locker room and into the gym, Andy was last in line, keeping a safe distance from the spewing spitballs and insults. When he passed Dick's office, Andy's name erupted from inside.

"McCain! Get in here!"

Andy backtracked and returned to Dick's doorway. "Sir?" Andy said.

Dick stood from his chair and slowly strutted toward Andy. "I've been hearing things," he said firmly. "Crazy things!"

"What, sir?" Andy asked, taking the biggest preparation breath his lungs would hold.

Dick leaned in close and whispered, "You queer or something, boy?" His scorching hot breath hissed out of his gapped-toothed mouth and burned Andy's skin.

Andy's heart raced and blood steamrolled its way through his veins. "What?" he asked, almost vomiting on the adrenaline choking his throat.

Chuckling, Dick shook his head and adjusted his gym shorts. "You used to be a great athlete, McCain," Dick said with pure disappointment. "You could've gone all the way. I got you in with my recruiting buddies at State for Christ's sake! What the hell was I thinking?"

"I'm still a good athlete, sir," Andy assured through tightly clenched teeth. His fists were clenched even tighter, his white knuckles nearly split out of his skin.

A silence swept over Dick for only a moment as he fiddled with the whistle around his neck. He locked eyes with his once star player and Andy saw Dick's disappointment had turned to disgust.

"Be warned, McCain," Dick finally said, his voice low. "You have no friends here."

"Sir!"

"Get your ass to the gym!" Dick ordered and stormed away.

***

"All right, I have to give a form to Spear," Kate said, dropping the last of her books into her bag and shutting her locker. Glancing up, she saw Eric and Nick staring at her, confused. She rolled her eyes and said, "He wants my mother's signature on a sheet he gave me, telling her about the fight with Dipshit and the tour of detention."

"You forged it, didn't you?" Eric said, shaking his head.

"Of course I forged it. Are you kidding? You said yourself my ass is grass if Mommie Dearest hears about it," Kate said, digging the white crumpled form from her purse. "So I'll catch you studs later."

"See you in Forgery 101 this afternoon," Nick said.

Kate flipped him the finger over her shoulder and walked toward the principal's office.

ANN ARBOR SOUTH '96

Nick turned back to Eric and jokingly said, "What an asshole."

Eric laughed but before he could add anything witty of his own, beefy basketballers Ryan Roberts and David Johnson plowed past him and Nick. Ryan's fender-sized shoulder rammed Eric's arm, knocking Eric back into the row of lockers.

"Hey, fag!" Ryan said, towering over Eric and breathing heavy into his face. "You better pray for your butt-buddy 'cuz he's got it coming to him good this morning!" He chuckled loudly. David Johnson's sinister laughter added harmony to Ryan's delight. The guys were gone just as quickly as they came, leaving Eric no time to speak. After Ryan and David turned the corner, Eric looked at Nick.

"What'd they mean?" Eric asked. Fear shot through his wide white eyes and pale cheeks.

Nick was quiet, unsure of how to answer.

"They're going to kick his ass, aren't they?" Eric was sick to his stomach.

Somehow knowing it was true but unsure how to break such terrifying news, Nick kept quiet.

"I have to help him!" Eric cried, taking a step toward the gymnasium hallway.

"Easy there, Rambo," Nick said, finally finding his voice and grabbing his friend's arm. "If you go running into the gym, they'll beat your ass too."

"I can't just let it happen!" Eric was fighting off tears. "I have to do something!"

"Like get your ass kicked? I don't think so." Nick kept a firm grip on Eric's bicep.

The final bell rang. They were late for class.

"Nick, come on!" Eric begged. "I have to go!"

"No!" Nick snapped and gently shoved Eric in the opposite direction. "Go to study hall. I'll check on Andy."

Eric's face lit up. "Really?"

Nick rolled his eyes regretfully, wondering why he ever opened his big mouth. Such moments reminded him of why he chose not to get involved in other people's business. Then again, Eric wasn't other

159

people. He was his best friend and since Andy's safety was so important to Eric, it was important to Nick too.

"Get to class. I'll check out the gym. I'm not Rambo either, so I don't know what the hell I'm going to do," Nick said with a goofy smile. "But I'll do what I can."

"Thanks, Nick," Eric said gratefully.

Nick ushered his friend off once more and headed for the gym.

***

Andy did as Dick viciously instructed. When Andy joined the others in the gymnasium, Dick was instructing the boys to form two separate teams for a game of shirts and skins basketball. The swimming section of the semester ended early with no distinctive reason. Unofficially, Dick called it quits after Eric took the humiliating fun out of it. Andy knew Eric's threats to Principal Spear played a larger roll in its abrupt end.

It was on to basketball. When Dick declared it shirts and skins, there were too many uncomfortable protesting moans from the class, no doubt due to Andy's sudden sexual transformation. Never mind that just the day before, Patrick Johnson had been playfully stripped of his gym shorts and jockstrap by the losing team when the shirts and skins game got a little too out of control. Still, there was a traitor among them now, parading around as a friend, and no one wanted to make himself vulnerable to Andy's animalistic sexual impulses. Dick squashed the skins idea and all the boys kept their shirts on.

Dick selected Justin, complete with a puffy purple and blueish-black eye about the size of Kate's fierce tiny fist, and fellow meathead Chris Golden as team captains. Andy walked into the group as Justin and Chris took turns picking players from the boys in the class.

Andy stood against the wooden bleachers along the wall leading back to the locker room with the others, still optimistic that things might magically turn around in his favor. Justin chose Wes Palmer as his first choice and Ben Miller was Chris's selection. These careful decisions surprised Andy. Not only was he Justin's best friend and the best Ann Arbor South basketball player next to Chris, but Andy had always been the first pick for any choosing team. Since elementary school, everyone fought to have Andy on his team. It was a matter of winning or losing the game and if you didn't have Andy McCain on your side. Other teams even offered monetary bribes for loyalty to certain teams.

But now, as Justin and Chris made their selections, Andy wasn't second, third, ninth, or twelfth choice. They went through the entire class. Even smelly, abnormally tall Phil Parker and chubby "Helmet Hair" Daniel Hedman were chosen before Andy, making him the last man standing against the rickety old wooden bleachers. The next choice rested with Justin and he fell silent when it was his turn to pick. Fronting one of two angry teams staring at Andy, Justin avoided inviting his former best friend to his team at all costs. He turned to Dick.

"Chris can take McCain," Justin said generously. "We're strong enough without him."

Chris immediately protested. "No!" he shouted. "We're strong too. You take him, J."

"You can use all the, uh, *help* you can get," Justin said with a wicked grin.

"Not that kind of help, you prick!" Chris snapped.

The bickering continued as Andy looked on, breathing deeply, his arms folded tightly against his chest. He glanced at the EXIT sign and considered a quick getaway, but couldn't bring himself to let everyone's uproarious laughter chase him out. He refused to give them the satisfaction. So he stood his ground, keeping his trembling hands hidden in his armpits.

Dick finally stepped into the argument, smiling as if proud of his feuding students. With little deliberation, he looked at Andy without really seeing him and said, "Get on Justin's team."

***

"How did I get myself into this?" Nick asked himself as he hurried down the empty hallway. Not only was he ditching first period Science, he was also risking detention for being in the hall after the final bell without a pass. He prayed Mrs. Frisby, the elderly hall monitor with the pronounced left limp, was not yet at his end of the school. She usually started her rounds in the Art and English wing at the opposite end of the building. If all went accordingly, Nick could get to the gym without detection, stop any attack on Andy, and make it back to Science class without Frisby catching him.

"And while I'm at it, does anyone else need saving?" Nick mumbled to himself.

***

Once the basketball game began, Andy was only allowed on the court once. Andy intended to make the most of it. If he could play his best and shine like he always did on the court, maybe the boys would remember their friend and not think of him as a gay stranger.

The instant Andy's sneakers hit the floor, he dribbled the ball expertly, racing toward the basket. At the same time, Wes Palmer barreled up from the opposite end, his shoulders tight, and headed straight for Andy. Their eyes locked and like a wicked game of chicken, neither backed off. Andy's hand never left the bouncing ball as his feet ran faster and his lungs breathed harder.

Within seconds, Wes Palmer's steely shoulders slammed into Andy's chest. The blow knocked Andy off his feet, crashing his back onto the hard gym floor. The once-hero's fall didn't stop Wes's attack. He towered over him and as Andy refocused from the drop, Wes kicked him, blasting the toe of his tennis shoe into Andy's ribcage.

"Son of a bitch!" Andy screamed and attempted to stand.

There was no time for Andy to rise. By the time of Wes's first kick, the rest of the boys in the class were hovering around Andy, breathing fire and thirsty for blood. Seeing the angry look in the eyes of his friends finally made the attack real. Andy's bones shook but he refused to let it show. He looked to Justin, who stood at the front of the group with his white-knuckled fists at his side, and saw a familiar anger he knew well. It was the same disgusted, annoyed anger Justin had toward anyone below him, on a lesser level, for the nobodies, the Outties, the fags.

But Justin didn't throw the next punch. He stood by as Chris Golden kicked the other side of Andy's stomach. Ben Miller followed it with a punch to Andy's jaw. David Johnson and Matt Murphy took turns kneeling beside him and pummeling their fists into his chest, shoulders, and face. All the hits soon turned into a hurricane of abuse as all the athletes joined in the attack, laughing wildly and releasing the frustration of Andy's betrayal through the beating.

"HEY!" an unfamiliar voice shouted into the gymnasium chaos.

The fighting ceased and everyone in the hot room turned toward the gym's rear entrance. They saw Nick Murphy standing in the doorway, his wrinkled forehead and flared nostrils dripping with fury.

"What're you doing?!" Nick shouted and took a step into the gym. He was cautious, though, and kept the gym door open in case he had an angry mob of jocks swarm after him. The gym door led back into a quiet back school hallway, full of old stacked chairs and soda machines, the perfect place to dump and hide a body. So Nick kept his distance.

Before the boys could react by attacking Nick too, Dick appeared from the locker room. He passed Nick but said nothing. Instead, he went directly to the sweaty mess in the center of the gym. "Move!" Dick ordered to his students, waving his arms in all directions.

The boys fanned out from their huddled crowd to show a beaten and bloody Andy curled on the floor. Andy's shirt was shredded, his shorts were missing, and his face was already swelling and turning an ugly shade of purplish-black.

"Get out of the way!" Dick motioned for the boys to spread out further. They did and Dick knelt beside Andy.

Sitting up very slowly, groaning in pain, Andy spit a wad of blood from his mouth and ripped the remaining shreds of his T-shirt off his bruised chest.

"What the hell're you doing, McCain?!" Dick shouted. His voice cut like glass through Andy's head. "Can't you even play a game of ball without egging these men on?!"

Through badly beaten, swelling eyes, Andy looked at Dick and whispered, "What?"

"I can't leave your faggoty ass for one second, can I, McCain?!" Dick's voice rose with each breath. "Get your ass out of here and cleaned up so these men can finish their game!"

Barely able to stand, it took Andy several tries to make it to his feet. As with his shorts, one of his shoes was missing, leaving him in a single shoe, one sock, and his jock strap. Once standing, Andy moved toward the locker room. Every inch of his body ached and made breathing difficult. Even after the attack, the boys didn't stop their teasing. Wes Palmer violently slapped Andy's bare behind as he walked away. The SMACK! echoed loudly throughout the gym, bouncing off the rafters, and left a welted handprint on Andy's flesh.

As he shuffled toward the temporary safety of the locker room, Andy noticed Nick at the rear doorway through blurry eyes. Nick walked completely into the gym, letting the door shut behind him. He went to Andy to help him to the locker room and begin cleaning him up.

"Can I help you, Mr. Murphy?" Dick snapped so loudly it startled Nick.

"I think you've done enough," Nick said bravely without looking at Dick. His attention was on Andy as he put his hand on Andy's shoulder and led him toward the lockers.

"That'll be quite enough of that!" Dick's voice gained momentum as he rushed toward them. The on-looking jocks stayed behind, smiling and enjoying the show.

Andy walked so slow from the pain that he and Nick didn't even get a few feet before Dick reached them. Dick grabbed Nick's arm and snatched it off Andy's shoulder.

"Get to class!" Dick demanded. "This is none of your business!"

Shocked by the sheer craziness in Dick's demeanor, Nick took a step back. "But—"

"GO!" Dick shouted, firmly shoving Nick's chest. "Or my men will take care of you too!"

Nick exchanged angry, confused glances with crazy Dick and his henchmen athletes. Realizing Dick meant business, Nick took another step toward the door. He saw Andy again, shaking, nearly naked, and beat to hell. Nick unzipped his hooded sweatshirt and bravely stepped passed Dick to put it over Andy's shoulders.

"I'll get Eric," Nick said softly into Andy's ear.

Andy said nothing and clutched the sweatshirt.

Nick went to the gym doors. He glanced back to Dick, who was viciously digging his fingernails into his wooden clipboard. Shocked and scared, Nick opened the door and ran to find his friends.

Chapter Sixteen

Study hall was a supreme drag. It was better than gym class, but Eric couldn't thrive in such a quiet atmosphere and that's what it was: quiet. Packed with only a handful of students, mostly braniacs studying hard for their pre-college classes, it was a calm, work-at-your-own-pace hour of boredom. The students were left alone to fend for themselves and only on rare occasions would an instructor check on them. Eric used the time constructively, writing in his journal or finishing homework. More recently, though, the time was spent daydreaming about Andy's beefy baseball biceps.

The classroom was so calm and rarely disrupted that no one stirred when the door was opened. It was usually a student arriving late. So when the door opened and Nick and Kate rushed in, mad and determined, the peers paid no attention. They kept their noses buried in their books.

Eric recognized the unique combination of Kate's sweet perfume and angry breath. He glanced up from his desk and, upon seeing the deep concern on his friends' faces, became worried. As they grew closer, Eric saw tears in Kate's eyes if only briefly. He almost panicked, since tears only appeared on her face in rare, heartbreaking, once-in-a-lifetime moments.

Slowly, Eric stood to his feet and stared at Nick for answers. "What happened to Andy?" The words barely escaped his mouth without choking him first.

"We have to go," Nick said. His voice was calm, but his eyes gave way to distress.

"What'd they do?" Eric's eyes flooded with tears.

"He—"

"They kicked his ass!" Kate interrupted and slung Eric's bag over her shoulder. She took his hand and pulled him out of the classroom.

Together, they headed for the gym. On the way, Nick updated Eric on Andy's horrific beating and Dick's icy cold disregard for it. Nick was caring enough to leave out most of the violent details and kept it generic but as honest as possible. Although hurt and pissed off, Eric wasn't sidetracked by crying. He was too focused on finding and helping Andy. He refused to lose control.

If only his feet moved faster!

***

The gym was an eerie, sweaty ghost town when Eric, Kate and Nick burst through the doors. There was no Dick, no jocks and not even a stray basketball in sight. With the annoying hum of the overhead industrial lights buzzing in their ears, they split up briefly to check separate parts of the enormous room. Eric checked the back hallway, leading to the storage room but found nothing more than stacked chairs. Kate glanced into the janitor's closet, a silly move since three mops and a bucket barely fit into the small space, leaving no room for a classroom of beefy athletic boys and their insensitive instructor.

Nick ventured toward the locker room. On his way, he passed a dented metal trashcan, tipped on its side and pushed along the wall next to the bleachers. He stood the three-foot tall can back onto its base and peeked inside. In it Nick saw a tattered uniform T-shirt and Nike gym shorts. Both items were speckled with blood. Nick's worrying intensified but he left the clothes in the trashcan. Eric and Kate didn't need to see them. Nick said nothing and rejoined his friends in the center of the gym.

"Where are they?" Eric said, trying hard to stay calm but the adrenaline sizzling through his veins shook his bones.

A faint, repetitive tapping echoed in the distance. They turned their attention toward the noise as it slowly grew louder. From the opposite end of the enormous room, geek-supreme Brandon Warren appeared, rolling a basketball rack and bouncing a ball beside him as he wheeled the cart. Brandon was Dick's quiet, pencil-necked teacher's aid. He took attendance, gathered and maintained equipment, and remained uninvolved while Dick and his "real men" enjoyed a life of sports. Brandon appeared from the rear equipment room with the balls and an air pump to refill any flats.

Without hesitating, Eric, Kate, and Nick ran to Brandon's end of the gym, eager for answers. Hearing the stomping shoes frightened Brandon and he tried to retreat back to the storage room. Nick quickly grabbed his arm.

"Where is everyone?" Nick demanded to know.

"I don't know," Brandon said, squirming out of Nick's clutch. He never made eye contact with any of them.

"Bullshit!" Eric shouted. "Where are they?!"

Surprised by the defensive tone, Brandon stepped back, gripping his ball cart for support. "Haven't seen them," the fair-skinned, blonde assistant said. His scared voice quivered like his shoulders under the pressure.

"You're lying. Tell us where they are. Where's Andy?" Nick said, his voice even firmer.

Brandon was silent and continued to inch toward the back room.

"I can't believe this!" Eric shouted and ran his fingers through his hair.

Nick added more force, "Brandon, god dammit—!"

"Nick," Kate gently interrupted, smiling brightly. "Let me try." She approached Brandon and slowly flipped her hair over her shoulders before looking deep into his pale green eyes. "Now," she said, her voice sweet as honey. "Let's cut the bullshit, okay? Tell us where they are."

Brandon repeatedly shook his head but his gaze never left Kate's cleavage.

"Brandon," she said, still fronting the kindness. "Come on...tell me."

Shrugging, Brandon said, "I don't know."

Like lightning, Kate's manicured hand death-gripped Brandon's throat and squeezed tightly. "Where are they?!" she snapped as her nails bled into his flesh.

Brandon panicked. His left hand clutched the ball cart, jerked violently and tipped it over, sending seven basketballs bouncing in every direction. He tore at Kate's tiny fingers with his hands, trying to free the pain and breathe again. But she matched him move for move, squeezing tighter but never losing the stone-cold smile on her pretty face.

"Where's Andy?!" she shouted. Her friends made no attempts to stop her.

Finally, the pain forced Brandon to surrender. He pointed to the door in which his own attackers had just come through, which led back to the Psychology and American Government hall. Kate loosened her throttle to let him speak. "The nurse's station," he said, barely speaking through the throbbing soreness of his throat.

"And the others?" Kate snapped, shaking his neck once more.

"I don't know—"

"Wrong answer!" Another shake.

"The parking lot, I think," he said. Tears rolled down his pale cheeks.

"And Dick?" Kate wanted it all.

Brandon pointed to the locker room. "The office."

She released her grip and gave him one last shove. He lost his balance and fell onto the fallen basketball cart, crying.

Turning to her friends, Kate was ready for war. Like any good soldier, her breathing was regulated, her vision focused, and her nerves strong as steel. Without words, the three of them simply exchanged glances before Kate hugged Eric, squeezing him tight in her arms.

"Go find him," she said softly. "We'll take care of this."

"What're you going to do?" Eric asked but didn't care to hear the answer. It didn't matter. He backed away from their embrace and looked at Nick.

"We'll find you later," Nick said with a smile.

Eric nodded, turned, and ran for the First Aid Office.

After he left, Kate and Nick glanced at each other. "You take the parking lot," Kate said with a strong certainty. "I'll take Dick—"

"Whoa!" Nick said firmly, grabbing Kate by the arm. "Unless you've got some sort of weird rape fantasy, *I'll* take Dick and you wait for me before manhandling the boys outside."

But the wicked gleam in Kate's eyes said it all and as Nick headed for the locker room, she strutted to the parking lot.

***

The First Aid Office was more of a few combined cubicles than an actual office. It had only three very tiny rooms and an even smaller reception area, where the on-duty nurse doubled as the office secretary. When Eric rushed in through the glass door, the room was empty, no student patients and no secretarial nurse at the reception desk.

"Hello?" he said impatiently and loud enough for anyone in the small four-room vicinity to hear. "Excuse me!"

Still, no appearance of life and no nurse. Eric stepped around the reception desk and went to the first of the three rooms. Nothing, only an empty cot and a rolling stainless steel cart with gauze, ear swabs, and tongue depressors. Eric checked the second room.

Jackpot.

In a matter of speaking.

Lying face-up on an un-cozy cot was a badly bruised Andy McCain. Shirtless with purpling flesh around his ribs and chest, Andy had his arms draped over his eyes, blocking the bright fluorescent lights. Eric's eyes scanned the young man's body, from the bruised biceps into the armpits, over his chest, complete with a few random tapped bandages, and stopped on the white paper privacy gown draped over Andy's crotch from his waist to his knees. A little swatch of cloth from a jockstrap peeked through the paper. Beside the cot was Nick's bloodstained sweatshirt, balled onto a chair.

Eric took another step inside. Andy never flinched at the sound of the door. He only moaned from the pain. "It's not working," Andy said softly.

"What's not working?" Eric asked.

Startled, Andy jerked on the cot and almost lost his balance. He moved his arms, perched himself up a little, and opened his eyes. His blackened and bruised left eye shocked Eric and he cringed at the sight of it but didn't turn away. Andy wasn't pleased to see him and Eric's reaction only worsened the moment.

"The pain killers," Andy said flatly and returned to a less-painful position on his back. "I thought you were the nurse."

"No," Eric said and cracked an uneasy smile. "I didn't look good in the outfit."

Andy didn't laugh. Eric rolled his eyes at himself, annoyed and unsure.

The room was silent and tense. Eric stared at Andy's beautiful body once more, now a canvas of bruises, shoe prints, and dried blood. Softly and with caution, Eric spoke again, "Where're your clothes?"

"They tore them off," Andy said, his voice firm, fighting the urge to cry.

With a deep breath, Eric slowly took a seat on a small stool beside Andy's cot and used Nick's sweatshirt as a cushion. He carefully put his hand on Andy's ankle and squeezed it. Andy didn't jerk away from the touch, which surprised but pleased Eric.

"You were right, you know," Andy said, barely whispering. He gave into the pain and cried, but he covered his beaten face to hide the tears. "About what it would be like for me."

Gently squeezing the ankle again, Eric replied, "I didn't want to be right."

Very slowly, Andy rose from his back and swung his legs around, dropping his feet to the floor. The paper gown fell to the floor too, leaving him in only his jockstrap. He paid no attention as his black-and-blue behind peeked out from the supporter. Andy was comfortable enough in Eric's presence to be nearly naked, but still kept his face to the floor, unable to look in Eric's eyes.

"It was awful," Andy said quietly, slouching from pain on the cot. "They looked at me like I was a fucking monster. My best friends! I've known these people my whole life and they beat the shit out of me!" His stopped to wipe his face. "And you know the worst part? I let them do it. I didn't stop them."

There was a frightening urgency and anger in Andy's voice. He slowly became more animated, using his rough, cracked hands as emphasis with his raising tone. Eric inched away to give him space.

"Part of me feels like I deserve it." Andy cried harder and aggressively wiped his teary cheeks. "Like, if they hit me hard enough it'll knock the fag right out of me."

Cringing at Andy's choice of words, Eric held his tongue. He knew Andy didn't need a lecture, just support and so Eric sat on the stool with his mouth shut.

The door to the claustrophobic room opened and a short woman popped in. Gray haired and nearly sixty, Nora Hughes wore her uniform proudly and although her face succumbed to weathered wrinkles, her brown eyes and sweet smile drew attention away from them.

"Sorry, honey, no visitors," she said to Eric, matter-of-factly as she flipped through a paper-filled clipboard on her arm.

"It's all right," Andy said. "He's a buddy of mine."

A bright smile came to her face. She focused on Eric and said, "Oh, well, then you need to tell your buddy that he shouldn't play such a rough game of floor hockey in his gym class."

Eric face went blank and he glanced at Andy for guidance, but Andy kept his head bowed to the floor. "Uh…yeah…how 'bout that?" Eric said to the naïve nurse. "We sure can get rough-n-tumble in there, huh?"

Hughes nodded and picked up Andy's paper gown from the floor. "Put this back on, sweetheart," she said, handing it to him. "You're showing all the good Lord's given you back there." She modestly made sure not to look at his exposed rear.

Andy took the gown to please her but didn't cover himself.

"Since you're of age, I gave you some stronger pain meds. Give them a little longer to work and the pain should ease," she said sweetly and looked to Eric once more. "Only a few more minutes, young man. He should rest a bit."

Eric nodded in agreement and Hughes left them alone, shutting the door behind her. Eric stared at Andy and said, "Floor hockey?"

"What was I supposed to say?" Andy said coldly. He took a breath, and switched the direction of the conversation. "How do you do it?" he said, finally looking at Eric's face and demanding an answer. "I've put up with this shit for one morning and I'm ready to drop out of school. How do you do it every day?"

The question surprised Eric because there wasn't an answer. At least, not one he could think of or rattle off the top of his head. Instead, he shrugged, surrendering to it.

Andy grabbed a tissue from the nearby supply stand to wipe his face and nose and winced from the pain it caused in reaching for it.

"Does it hurt?" Eric asked. "Well, does it hurt *bad*?"

"Naw," Andy said, exaggerating his deep, tough-guy voice. For the first time that day he flashed his signature grin and even through the bruises, his trademark dimples found their way to his cheeks. "I'm healing already." His attitude slowly started to change, realizing his pain was hurting Eric just as much as himself.

Eric cleared the lump in his throat and said, "I didn't want to do this to you. I didn't want you to have to deal with any of this."

Andy was quick to point out, "I did this to myself. I wanted the school to know how I feel about you and now that they do—"

"You shouldn't have done it. All this could've been avoided if I would've just kept my big mouth shut," Eric said. His eyes watered and he frantically wiped them, refusing to cry. "I hate seeing what they've done to you."

Andy took a deep breath to ease the hurting and outstretched his hand for Eric. Taking a small step toward Andy, Eric sat beside him and slowly intertwined their fingers together. Andy admired the beauty of the connection and how well they fit together like pieces of the same puzzle. Andy raised their hands to his mouth, kissed Eric's knuckles and gently rubbed them across his face. Andy's day-old stubbly beard tickled Eric's skin. He smiled as Andy looked back to his face.

"I don't regret telling you how I feel or letting the school know," Andy said quietly. "I just don't want to come back."

Eric's shook his head and tightened his fingers around Andy's hand to express his agitation. "But if you leave, they win," he said into Andy's watering blue eyes. "If you leave, everything goes back to normal, whatever the hell that means, and these assholes won't have to worry about opening their minds to change."

"They might just get what they want," Andy said under his breath. "You can't tell me you've never thought about leaving."

"Of course I have," Eric agreed. "I think about it every day, but I'm not giving them the thrill of chasing me out."

Andy smiled subtly, looking at Eric like it was the first time he had ever seen him. It surprised Eric and irritated him a little because he wasn't done being mad.

"Where do you get your strength?" Andy asked.

"I bottle it from Kate and store it for future use. I don't know!" Eric snapped but softened when he saw Andy frown. "The truth is that it mortifies me to think of being known as an Ann Arbor South shit stain. My legacy's not much, but I sure as hell don't want to be known as the scaredy-cat queer who just ran away." Eric's voice was strong and confident. He knew Andy needed to hear something strong and self-assured. "You have to be strong."

"I don't know how to do that," Andy said pitifully. "Ever since Mitch—"

"Come on, Andy," Eric said softly and stood to his feet. "This isn't about Mitch or any lost love or any pain you've suffered and it's not about me. This is about not standing up for who you really are."

"It's not that easy," Andy said, hinting toward a defensive tone. "We can't all be a ball-busting, fight-for-your-rights homo, Eric. At least, *I* can't."

"Because *I'm* holding the flag in the next pride parade? I don't think so!" Eric said and caught his own snappy tone and calmed himself. "I'm not asking you to fight for your rights or be Super Queer. I just want you to have some faith in yourself. If you have no regrets and this is what you want, then you should defend your decision."

Andy shut down and stopped listening. Fighting through the pain, he stood to his feet for no other reason than to turn his back on Eric. "I want you to go," he said firmly, folding his arms and staring at the detailed diagram of an eyeball pinned to the wall.

Even in the midst of the argument, Eric snuck a peek at Andy's bare round behind framed by the straps of the athletic supporter. He cracked a very quick smile and said, "Andy—"

"Get out! I'm going home soon anyway." Andy's voice was loud and hurt.

"But—"

Within seconds of Andy's loud tone, Nurse Hughes peeked her perky face into the room. Her eyes zeroed in on Eric. "Time to go," she instructed.

"But—"

"*Now.*" She opened the door wider.

Eric wanted to slam the door shut with the nurse outside and embrace Andy inside his arms. He wanted to go on and on about how important it was for Andy to be himself and stay strong and not let the abusive bastards get him down.

But he didn't.

He went to the door, took one last glance at Andy's ass, stuck his tongue out at Hughes, and left the tiny recovery room. She escorted him to the main entrance. Eric quickly took his T-shirt off, leaving him in his plain white undershirt, and gave it to the nurse.

"Just so he has something to wear," he said calmly. "Can you get him some shorts?"

Nora Hughes softened and took the shirt. "He'll be taken care of," she assured and gently led Eric out of the First Aid Office.

Standing in the doorway, his face almost touching the glass pane of the now-closed office door, Eric desperately wanted to run and tell Andy everything he knew, everything he had learned, anything to ease the situation.

But what did Eric know anyway? Nothing. Actually, no one knew Andy's pain better than Eric, having lived the same anti-gay misery every second of every day for so many years. But because he had known it personally, Eric knew the best thing Andy needed was time to sort through his thoughts, alone.

Still, it didn't make walking away from Andy McCain any easier.

Chapter Seventeen

The senior parking lot was initially quiet and empty. As her eyes adjusted to the mid-morning sunshine, Kate heard a mild commotion to her left. Neatly nestled between the senior lot and the underclassmen lot were three tennis courts. Happily playing on them, armed with rackets and yellow-green balls, were the remaining members of first period gym class. Justin Drake, Wes Palmer, Matt Murphy and the rest of Andy's attackers were scattered over the courts and playfully engaged in a few games of tennis.

Instantly, Kate blamed Dick. Tennis was never played during the first half of the year since it was an early-spring sport. Dick had sent his goons to the courts to distance them from the gym, the scene of their crime against Andy. The anger quickly moved Kate's small feet.

With her nostrils flared, Kate walked through the empty lot and approached the tall wire meshed fence outlining the courts. Justin was the first to notice the fuming visitor and he proudly strode over to her.

"What's up, *Katherine?*" Justin said. His breath reeked of stale smugness and wintergreen chewing tobacco.

Before Kate could say anything, the remaining jock squad spotted her presence and stood close behind Justin, catcalling and hounding her hotness. With their hands on their waists and legs spread apart, standing firm, they formed a bizarre superhero V-shaped design behind

Justin's lead.

"Couldn't wait to see me later in detention?" Justin asked.

"What the hell are you doing?" Kate asked. She held her head high, refusing to be intimidated by their arrogance or crude outbursts.

Justin smiled through his blackened eye and a few boys chuckled. "Let me make this real easy for you," he said, leaning in closer to the wire fence. His good eye narrowed and focused. "You don't know anything about what happened today."

Kate's face did not flinch. "Give me a break."

"For your own good, babe."

"For my own good?" Kate laughed loudly. "You don't have a whole lot of room to be dishing advice, *babe*. Look at your face. That bruise is the same size as my fist, tough guy!"

Tying hard to ignore the insult, Justin clutched the fence's meshed links and shook hard, rattling it from one end of the court to the other. "If you want us to do a repeat performance on *your* ass," he said, motioning over his shoulder to his backup band of boys. "We can do that."

"You're an—" Kate stopped to calm herself. "You need to get a grip," she continued. "If you're going to go all Ike Turner on each others' asses every time one of you does something the others don't like, you'll be beating the shit out of each other for the rest of your lives."

The boys erupted in loud, dismissive laughter, all of them except Justin. He watched Kate, his breathing heavy, never wavering from their dead stare. Looking closely, Kate saw Justin's eyes glisten so slightly that she wasn't sure if it was the sun reflecting off the shiny fence or something more. Still, there was intensity in his face she couldn't place.

"Are we going to kick her ass or what?" Ben Miller called from the back of the V.

Kate stepped away from the fence, very slowly shaking her head. "I'll go see how *your* friend's doing," she said, her words sharply directed to Justin's bruised face. "And I'll see what kind of damage *you* did to him."

As Kate walked back toward the school doors, the rest of the boys lost interest and returned to their tennis games. But Justin remained clamped to the wire fence, his eyes burning a gaze into Kate's back. His mouth opened a little to speak, but he said nothing.

Instead, Justin returned to his game.

***

The locker room was empty when Nick strolled in. Only the soft stomping of his Doc Marten boots echoed off the musty tiled walls, metal lockers, and wooden benches. It reeked of sweaty boys, moldy showers, and dirty socks. Nick could stand the stench of a greasy boy because he was one a lot of the time, but a ripe old tube sock didn't exactly settle his stomach.

He stood in the doorway, glancing in every direction. Before he could call for anyone, the loud grumble of Dick's raspy voice sliced into the silence.

"Is it done?" Dick said, his voice erupting from his office.

Nick stood around the corner, out of sight.

"Did you get it done good?" Dick asked.

Tilting his head, confused and curious, Nick neatly tucked his arms across his chest and slowly strolled to the doorway of Dick's office. Dick was at the desk, scribbling through papers and paying no attention to the caller. He mistakenly believed Nick to be someone else.

"Depends on what I was sent to do," Nick said sharply into the quiet office.

Startled by the loudness of the voice, Dick abruptly rocked back in his chair and almost fell out of it. He quickly jumped to his feet to avoid hitting the floor. "What the hell're you doing here?" he demanded to know, trying to gracefully regain his balance.

Nick shrugged. "Just thought I'd drop by to see how it turned out for you," he said, his chin held high and arms clenched tight against his chest.

Dick regained his arrogant composure and stood close to Nick. "I don't know what you think you saw today—"

179

"We both know what I saw," Nick interrupted. "Andy got his ass kicked while you watched. I think that was a smile on your face, too."

A creepy grin slithered to Dick's weathered face. "Maybe I didn't make myself clear, Mr. Murphy," he said, his voice low. "Maybe the ball game got a little rough, but it wasn't anything these men can't handle. You saw *nothing* today."

"No, what I saw was a coach who let his team attack one of its own like wild dogs."

Dick's smile changed a little, like he was mildly impressed by Nick's fierce refusal to back down. It wasn't enough to make Dick surrender. Instead, he returned to his wobbly chair, sat down, and put his feet up on the beat-up old desk.

"So what're you going to do, report me?" Dick balked at the absurdity of the notion. "You think anyone'll listen to you?"

"I don't need to report you. I don't really need to do anything."

"Then why are you here?" Dick was impatient.

Nick leaned onto the desktop and said, "You've had championship teams for three years running, with trophies and banners and all the goodies you could want."

Dick's face remained stone cold. "What's your point?"

"But now that you've got your boys fag-bashing the star pitcher and quarterback, how do you think your teams are going to perform this year?" Nick asked. "Andy's already bailed on football and after all this he'll probably bail on baseball too. So much for those state records you wanted to beat. But I guess a team that beats the shit out of each other is just as good—"

"Get out," Dick order, stomping back to his feet.

As Dick moved toward him, Nick stepped out of the office and called over his shoulder, "Nothing I could possibly do could make anything worse for you than what you've already done to yourself."

"GET OUT!" Dick shouted. His eyes were red with rage.

It satisfied Nick to the core and left the locker room. On his way out of the gym, Nick heard Dick furiously smashing up his office.

Chapter Eighteen

After-school detention was held in a small classroom in a secluded corner of the English hallway. Classes ended at 2:10 and detention started promptly at 2:15. Naturally, Kate strutted in ten minutes late on her first assigned day of punishment for the parking lot brawl with Justin Drake. She came into the room sipping on a can of soda and carrying her trusted oversized purse.

When Kate opened the door, Monica Simbeck, the detention instructor, did not greet her sweetly. Sitting at the front of the empty room in an office chair with her slender legs crossed, Simbeck folded her arms as soon as Kate came into the room.

Simbeck was a tiny, thirty-something English instructor. Her short brown hair needed a cut and fell into her small brown eyes. Her jaw was clenched tight, angered by Kate's tardiness.

Taking a quick glance around the room, Kate saw Justin was already there, sitting at a desk in the front of the room with his hands tucked under his arms. He had no reaction to her entrance.

"Guess we're the only sinners worth rehab today," Kate said and looked to Simbeck. "Sorry I'm late." Her unapologetic tone did not convince the instructor.

"That's okay, you can just stay an extra ten minutes longer," Simbeck said, her voice firm. She looked to Justin and added, "You both can."

"No way!" Justin protested. "It's not my fault the princess can't get here on time! I've got football practice!"

"You're both here to learn to get along," Simbeck reminded. "So if one of you is late, the other pays the price too."

"Because *that* makes sense," Kate said and took a seat in the back of the room.

Simbeck took a deep breath and returned to the papers cluttering her desk for a moment. "Do you two know why you're here?" she asked, keeping her head in her grade books.

"Because that bitch attacked me!" Justin quickly replied. "I was just defending myself!"

Cocking her head to one side, Kate narrowed her eyes, zooming in on Justin's lie. "Now I *know* you didn't just call me a bitch," she snapped. "I beat your ass yesterday. Don't think I won't do it again today—"

"STOP IT!" Simbeck snapped. "You will not use that kind of language! It's unacceptable in here and it's unacceptable in life! Do you understand?" She was actually heated, which only brought a smile to Justin's face. He never saw her flustered or heard her voice growl with anger and it entertained him.

"Do I make myself clear?" She spoke slower to emphasize her simple instruction.

Kate finally responded, "We do speak English, so yeah, we get it."

"Don't speak to me like that, Kate, or you'll be spending more than two weeks in here."

Simbeck gathered her papers and packed her book bag. "I'm going to do some work in the teacher's lounge," She said and slung the bag over her shoulder.

"What are we supposed to do?" Justin snapped.

"Stay in this room and try to resolve your differences," she instructed and opened the classroom door. "Or kill each other. I'll be back at three-thirty."

When the classroom door slammed shut, Kate chuckled. "Resolve our differences? Like that'll happen in one afternoon," she said. "Or in this lifetime."

"Maybe we'd get along if you weren't such a crazy *bitch*," Justin hissed with a grin.

"Don't talk to me like I just kicked your mother in the crotch, okay? And don't call me a bitch either," she warned. "You don't know anything about me."

"I know you're psychotic!" Justin laughed. "You attacked me yesterday for no reason!"

"I attacked you because you're an asshole, not because I'm psychotic," Kate corrected just as cool as she pleased.

Justin shrugged with little interest in her response. "Whatever."

Kate shook her head. "Why are you guys so upset with Andy?"

Turning in his seat to really face her for the first time, Justin leaned closer to look into her eyes. Actually taking the time to stare into them, he saw seriousness and sincerity. "How can you ask me that?" he said. "Isn't it obvious?"

Kate folded her arms across her busty chest. "Would I ask if it was obvious?"

Justin doodled nothing in particular on his notebook cover. The ink pen was running out but he paid no attention. The more they talked, the harder he scribbled. "You already know why we're doing what we're doing," he reminded. "Andy's queer."

Immediately, Kate heaved a frustrated sigh. But she took another deep breath, trying to remain calm, and hooked a lock of hair behind her ear. "I was really hoping you'd have something better to say than that. Something like Andy gets better grades or he plays better baseball would make more sense than *that*." She smiled nervously, unable to remain collected. "I mean, come on! He doesn't make fun of the venereal diseases you go out with. So who gives a shit who he loves?"

"Maybe you're just defending him 'cuz you're a carpet-munching dyke!"

"Only with your mom," Kate snapped. "Give me a break! I'm strictly dickly. That's why Eric and I get along so well." She smirked but Justin didn't enjoy her sarcasm.

"It doesn't bother you at all?" he asked, trying to sound surprised.

"Why would it?"

"Because fags are disgusting."

"How do you know?" Kate asked with a wide smile. "Have you thought about it?"

"I'm not gay!" His voice raised and shook ferociously with fear. "Me and the boys don't like the thought of fucking each other!"

Kate giggled. "Then don't think about it."

Justin clenched his fists and turned away from her. The pen tore through the notebook cover and scribbled on the first few pages of paper. He breathed deeply through his flared nostrils, confused that Kate didn't understand him. He tried again, saying, "It makes me and the boys uncomfortable to be around him."

"He used to be one of the boys. Before yesterday you and the boys thought he was the hottest shit around."

"That's before we knew he was queer."

Kate released a tiny scream and ran her hands though her hair. "Do you think he magically woke up yesterday with Madonna songs blasting out of his ass?" she asked. "Did he decide to screw up everything he's ever known just to be with a guy? It doesn't work that way."

Justin stared at her strangely, his head tilted to one side, not recognizing her point.

She continued, "Andy's the same person he's always been. He's still into sports and hanging out with the boys and doing whatever the hell it is you guys do together. He hasn't changed. You just know who he really is now." She calmed herself and spoke with more control.

"But he doesn't *seem* gay. I mean, he doesn't *act* gay," Justin protested.

"News flash, Mr. I-Perpetuate-Every-Stereotype-On-The-Planet, not all gay guys are limp-wristed, flaming drag queens—"

"Like Eric?" Justin quickly added with a wicked grin.

"Watch your mouth," she warned. "That's my best friend you're talking about, not to mention he's the guy *your* best friend's in love with." She sighed and regretfully added, "So whether we like it or not, me and you are sort of like in-laws now, which doesn't exactly get my motor running, believe me. But you need to get over your issues because this is going to happen whether you want it to or not."

Thinking for a moment and nibbling on his lower lip, Justin's eyes narrowed. "He's not supposed to love *guys*!" he said sternly.

"Nobody does anything they're supposed to do," Kate laughed. "He just wants his friends to know who he is. What's wrong with that?"

He paused again and looked back into her eyes. "Because it's just wrong."

Chapter Nineteen

Friday, October 11, 1996

The next morning, Eric took comfort in seeing the familiar, non-threatening faces of his best friends as they gathered together in the parking lot and walked into school together. When Kate picked him up at his house that morning, she got out of her car and hugged him. She did it every morning but there was more to the embrace than usual. It lasted longer and squeezed tighter than the others.

"Are you sure you're okay?" Kate asked, her voice calm and caring. Her concern was always genuine when it needed to be and Eric always appreciated her strength.

"I'm all right," Eric said, smiling at Nick as a way of saying hello. The three of them headed for their lockers.

"Have you talked to Andy?" Nick asked.

"Not since yesterday in the nurse's office," Eric said. "He didn't answer the phone all night."

"It's bullshit what those pricks did to him!" Kate snapped. Her sweet concern was sidetracked by anger. "He needs to get the cops involved if the school's not going to do anything. He needs to get their balls nailed to the wall—"

Eric grew restless and uncomfortable.

Gently, Nick touched Kate's arm to stop her. "Andy doesn't need to do anything," Nick said calmly. "He's not talking to anyone and doesn't want to admit what's going on."

She rolled her eyes, unsatisfied, but calmed herself, knowing he was right. "Did he say anything at the nurse's office?" she asked Eric.

"Not really," Eric said. "He won't open up to me."

"Takes two to tango," she said under her breath, recalling her conversation with Andy about the same issue. But before anyone could respond, she added, "Is he okay?"

"He's beat to hell," Eric said so quietly that his friends had to lean in to hear him add, "He doesn't understand what's happening to him."

"I tried talking to Senor Shithead yesterday but he's *so* not hearing anything I have to say." Kate grew more irritated as she spoke. The very thought of the stubborn Justin Drake and the thick walls he put up to block her words boiled her blood. "He won't talk to me at all now. The silent treatment, like this is third grade—"

"Speak of the devil," Nick interjected, motioning with a nod over Eric's shoulder.

They turned to see Justin and Ryan Roberts at the opposite end of the hallway, walking toward them. Their struts were strong, poised, and dripping with arrogance. Beefy ball-busting arms swung in sync with their tall, toned legs as they marched down the crowded corridor. They seemed directed and determined with a destination in mind as they approached Eric and the others. Justin only briefly locked eyes with Eric; his gaze lasted longest on Kate. For only a moment she saw a possible pleading urgency in them, like he was secretly searching for her help or signaling that danger lurked around the bend. But before Kate could decode any possibly encrypted messages, the glance was gone, overshadowed by Justin's angry scowl, clenched jaw, and the powerfully negative vibe of his brute buddy, Ryan.

And then something incredible and equally alarming happened. For the first time in years, Justin and his ruthless friend walked past Eric without uttering a single cruel word, moaning a hostile grunt, or physically striking him. Instead, the ball players' chiseled chins stayed high in the air and led the way, silently, without a sound. A few long strides later, the jocks were gone.

"What was that?" Eric asked, wide-eyed and wondering. "He didn't say anything to me. He didn't punch me or set my bag on fire. What's going on?"

Although Nick appeared calm with no real visible signs of shock or surprise, he certainly did not understand. "He's never kept his mouth shut," he said. "*Ever.*"

Eric turned to Kate. Her pretty dark pupils were buried behind squinting eyelids and crooked eyebrows. Trying to think, she shook her head slowly. "Don't look at me," she said, never looking up from the floor. "I don't know what that was about."

Eric and Nick didn't move. They just stared at her.

"What did you say to him?" Nick asked.

Kate tossed her hair over her shoulders and held her hands up, empty. "I said a lot of shit," she said, with an unsure laugh. "But none of it sunk in."

"Something's going on," Eric said firmly. His breathing increased to short, exasperated gasps. "Justin's never missed a chance to attack me. He's got something up his sleeve. Maybe they're going after Andy again—" Eric paced the ground nervously, on the verge of panicking.

"Calm down, killer. Your inner drama queen's coming through and its way too early for me to deal with *that* bitch," Kate said, smiling to ease the tension. "Besides, you're probably just overreacting. How 'bout we go to Andy's locker and wait for him. That'll make you feel better."

Eric nodded. "Can we?"

"Of course."

"I can't join you," Nick said. "I have to see Browning before Bio so I'll catch you guys later." He squeezed Eric's shoulder for assurance and jogged off to class.

Eric turned to Kate, his eyes watery and nervous.

Kate smiled to boost his confidence. "Come on," she said, taking his hand. "Let's go before you piss your pants worrying and *really* embarrass me."

***

On their way to Andy's locker, Eric and Kate noticed some stranger-than-usual behavior from their fellow peers. There were stares, snickers, whispers and pointing, but all that was typical whenever Eric walked through a hallway. There was something more in the air, though, something more than just Suzanne Simpson's dreadful perfume.

Always quick to read people in any situation, Eric knew the air reeked of trouble, *calculated* trouble. His classmates, in the restless and hot crowded hallway, watched him, waiting for a reaction. Normally they would continue on their self-involved ways after passing him, but in the anxious energy of the morning, Eric was studied, stared at, and followed.

"What're you looking at?" Kate barked at a few of the gathering students. "Are my tits showing? Take a picture!"

They continued toward Andy's locker. As the students continued circling like hungry vultures, the air thickened with the scent of fresh paint. It wasn't until Kate and Eric reached the locker did they understand why. The second their eyes landed on the red locker door and those surrounding it, everything became clear. Sprayed with dark, drippy black paint were several popular Ann Arbor South vocabulary words:

FAG!

QUEER!

HOMO!

The fresh graffiti spread across several locker doors, bleeding toward the floor.

Eric and Kate stared at the vandalism, initially speechless. Then the words flowed freely.

"What the hell?!" Kate screamed.

"Who did this?!" Eric yelled at the ever-growing crowd of students. His fingers curled tightly into fists. He wasn't sure of what to do with a clenched fist, but they were ready to strike nevertheless.

As Eric had his macho moment, Kate looked beyond the crowd's shoulder and saw Andy approaching from only a short distance away. Kate turned to Eric, grabbed his bony shoulders and pushed him against Andy's locker in an attempt to block the graffiti. She paid no attention to the fresh paint and joined Eric in concealing the door, smearing paint on the back of their shirts.

"What're you—?" Eric began to say, but before he could finish Andy broke through the group and stood only a few feet from his locker. His face was swollen and puffy from the beating the day before but he carried himself nicely, proud, however forced.

Andy was instantly suspicious. Not only was the student gathering eagerly staring at his locker but the exaggerated innocence plastered to Eric and Kate's faces raised his beaten eyebrow.

"What's up?" Andy asked.

"Nothing!" Eric and Kate sang in desperate unison.

Andy saw right through it. "Eric," he said, his voice firm. "Let me in my locker."

Eric didn't budge. His back was pressed hard to the metal door with his arms and hands spread wide to cover every inch he could. At his side was Kate, fluffing her hair and flapping her bulky purse in hopes of concealing any remaining piece of the locker.

"Eric," Andy said again, even harder than before. A chill crept its way up Eric's spine as Andy took a step closer.

Looking to Kate for help and then to the crowd for who knows what, Eric didn't know what to do. Then his conscious crept in and truth was all that came out. He breathed deep to prepare and finally blurted, "IT'S YOUR LOCKER!"

Andy wasn't surprised. He didn't even flinch. Logic and common sense had already prepared him to hear Eric's words. He slowly waved his hand, signaling the caring but interfering Locker Guards to step aside.

"It's just bullshit, Andy," Kate offered, standing firm against the door.

Andy took one final step toward them. With a hand on each of their shoulders, he pried them apart. The separation of their arms gave way to the graffiti. Andy saw it but didn't react right away. He just stared at the door, silent.

Wide-eyed and upset, Eric watched Andy's fixated face gradually ignite with a fiery anger. His cheeks burned red and his nostrils flared with every chest-raising breath. Looking closer, but only briefly, Eric saw Andy's eyes glisten. Tears, maybe, but the hallway chaos was too distracting for him to make a definite judgment.

While his eyes never left the locker door, Andy whispered something too quiet to hear.

"What?" Eric carefully asked.

"Who did this?" Andy repeated, only slightly louder.

"Andy—" Eric stepped toward him but avoided touching him, although he wanted to so badly. Making another hallway spectacle of man-on-man action was the last thing either of them needed. "Don't let it get to you," Eric said, instantly hating himself for the stupid words. Andy hated him for it too. Any possible tears were gone and only anger shot out of his eyes.

"It's what they want," Eric offered. "Don't let them see you lose it."

Without taking his gaze off the graffiti, Andy said again, "Who did this?"

Desperate and lost, Eric turned to Kate. Only in the rarest of moments was she left speechless or unsure of what to do. In the hallway with Eric expecting her to perform in her over-the-top, controlling way, Kate froze.

Eric tried again. "Andy—"

At the same time, without warning, Andy exploded with rage. "WHO DID THIS?!" he screamed and frantically punched the locker. The freshly painted word FAG smeared and bent inward with each blow.

The crowd gasped. Andy's attack surprised them, but the denting force behind his fist shocked them even more. He kept going, screaming and punching and kicking the door.

More drama-hungry students squeezed into the already packed hallway to witness Andy's breakdown. Eric and Kate yelled and pleaded with Andy to stop. They grabbed his arms but he was much too strong, pushing them away at every attempt to stop him.

When he had burned through his energy and beaten the door out of commission, Andy stopped to catch his breath. He turned to see the huge gathering of laughing faces and pointing fingers. His bleeding knuckles stung from the beating, but Andy he was breathing too hard and bravely staring down several dozen students to pay any attention to the pain. His bruised face was puffy, red and unavoidably tear-stained. Looking like a train wreck only added to his embarrassment and shame.

Trying to regain any ounce of control or dignity, Andy wiped his sweaty face with his shirtsleeve and glanced back to Eric. "This is what you wanted me to deal with?" Andy snapped, wiping his forehead again with a shaky hand.

"Andy!" Eric snapped back, trying hard not to be offended, given Andy's emotional state.

Without another word, Andy ran in the opposite direction from his judgmental peers.

Again, Eric hopelessly turned to Kate, looking for guidance.

"Go!" she told him, waving her hand in Andy's direction. "I can take care of these assholes."

Overwhelmed and lost, Eric kept his wide-eyed stare on Kate's determined face. Seeing Eric's uncertainty brought an encouraging smile to her lips.

"Just go," she said confidently. "You'll figure it out."

Eric nodded and ran off.

"Yeah, chase after your boyfriend!" an unknown still-changing male voice yelled from deep within the vicious crowd. The group laughed.

Kate folded her arms and turned to her tormenting classmates. She saw Tara Sanderson and her big-breasted sidekicks Danielle Hemingway and Jennifer Kent at the front of the group. Although Tara wasn't smiling and didn't appear particularly amused or involved, Kate spit her gum at Tara anyway.

"Bitch!" Tara hissed, dodging the flying Bubblicious air bomb.

"What the hell is your problem?!" Kate yelled at no on in particular.

"What's going on here?" a stern and plenty angry voice asked from behind.

Kate swung around to see Principal Spear standing only a few feet away. He had turned the corner from the Math hall and inadvertently stumbled onto the unofficial student gathering. It didn't take him long to zero in on the graffitied eyesore. The hallway fell silent as he examined the dented, profanity-ridden property.

"Who did this?" Spear asked, turning to his students. No one spoke up. He didn't have to think too hard for his next move. "You'll all be held responsible if no one comes forward."

Still no word. Instead, the back of the crowd furthest from the Principal started to fan out and leave to avoid prosecution.

"Nobody move!" Spear shouted. "Now, who wrote—?"

"Dude, they're not going to tell you," Kate interrupted. "And you know they're not going to tell you, so why are you still asking?"

Cocking his head, Spear lowered his gaze to the short spitfire. "I beg your pardon?"

"Oh, sorry, I'll talk slower," she snapped. "They're...not...going to...tell you...*shit!*"

"Watch your mouth," Spear warned. "And answer my question." He took a dominating stomp toward her in hopes of scaring a cringe or some kind of reaction from her.

But Kate's wonderfully wide, painted blue eyes didn't even blink. She calmly folded her arms across her bust and tilted her pretty round face, uninterested in the principal's next move.

Even less surprised than he had anticipated, Spear backed off and lowered his voice to a calmer tone. "Tell me who did this," he said with an almost convincing dose of concern.

"I don't know who did it," Kate said with only a little less attitude. "But even if I did, why would I tell you? You won't do anything about it. You never do."

"Of course I will!" Spear's concern transformed back to defensive warfare.

"You won't punish the precious Jock Squad. They're the ones behind this but they also win the championships, so what's a little fag-bashing going to hurt?" Kate was in her signature over-the-top fashion. Her arms and hands flailed like wet noodles to emphasize her points.

"This isn't *Saved By The Bell* and this shit can't be fixed in thirty minutes like you seem to think, *Mr. Belding*. It wouldn't kill you to open your eyes and see what's going on here."

Spear stood back for a moment, processing everything he had heard. He laughed a little, shocked by Kate's audacity. With her arms folded proudly and her hair neatly flipped over her chipped shoulders, Kate inappropriately oozed arrogance and superiority.

The principal moved closer to her and flashed his own signature condescending power-tripped smile. "I've had it up to my neck with your attitude, young lady," Spear said. "I've been overly patient with your mouth and blatant disrespect for years. I won't have it anymore."

His seriousness made Kate's proud facade fade only a smidge.

"I'm tired of your arrogance. I'm tired of your fighting. Hell, I'm tired of your short skirts! I'm tired of *you*, Miss Crawford." Spear spoke with a firm confidence and power Kate had never heard. "I'm adding a month to your detention—"

"WHOA!" she snapped.

"Would you rather be suspended? Expelled, maybe?" He smiled, already knowing the answer. "And I'm going to call your parents. I won't accept another document with your mother's forged signature. It's time they really know what's going on here. How's that sound, *dude*?"

Kate's eyes widened. "But—" There was actually desperation and panic in her voice.

"Consider the detention a gift. This is your last chance," Spear continued. "Now, if you have any real information to help me handle this situation—" He pointed to Andy's locker. "—I'm ready to hear it. I assure you no one's protected. I'll hold the person accountable, no matter who they are."

Still shocked and unsure, Kate shook her head. She knew names, but couldn't speak.

Spear leaned back and his grin enlarged. "Oh, how the mighty have fallen," he said, beyond pleased. "Maybe you could channel all that energy into trying to get along with others." He walked away. "If you think of anything to help, let me know," he called over his shoulder.

"Now, back to class!"

Kate was left alone in the empty hall, trapped in another one of those rare moments that actually rendered her, *Kate Crawford*, speechless.

***

"Andy, stop!" Eric begged. He had chased the angry ballplayer out of the school hallway, off school property, and onto Caroline Street. It took a lot of death-defying deep breaths and pulled muscles for him to keep a steady pace with the athlete, but he wasn't about to let Andy get away from him. The cement sidewalk went on for miles so he had time to either catch Andy or pass out on the side of the street.

"Stop, *please!*" Eric begged. "I'm losing sight in my right eye!"

Finally, paying attention to Eric's desperate and naturally dramatic pleas, Andy stopped on the sidewalk but kept his back to Eric. They were only a few blocks from Andy's apartment.

Gasping for air, Eric approached Andy but didn't bypass him to see his face. Andy wasn't ready to be seen and Eric knew how to play by his rules. While he waited, Eric dropped to his knees on the grassy patch beside the sidewalk. He breathed deep, trying to calm his racing heart and prayed for feeling to return to his aching legs.

"Well, that's enough to cause a stroke," Eric joked, trying to lighten the mood. "I think I might be having one right now." He looked at the back of Andy's head, wanting a reaction but not really expecting one.

"Why are you here?" Andy asked softly.

Not the reaction Eric wanted. "What do you mean?"

Andy jammed his fists into the back pockets of his jeans. "I'm serious." Andy kept his head away. "Why are you here?"

Eric sat on the lawn, exhausted. "I don't want you to be alone." He hoped to sound caring, not annoyed.

"You don't have to stay." Andy rocked his foot at the ankle on and off the cement.

"Can you look at me when you talk?" Eric asked.

"Why do you want to look at me? All you see is what they see." Andy took a few more steps toward home.

"What do you think they see?" Eric jumped to his feet. His legs burned from the run.

"It's obvious!" Andy balked. "They made it pretty clear on my locker and my *face!*"

"Are you kidding?" Eric walked closer to him. "That's what you think I see?" He gently grabbed Andy's arm and took a large step around to face him. Andy was still crying, his eyes puffy and swollen from the prior gym beating and the current waterworks. Eric squeezed his arm and although Andy tried to avoid Eric's gaze, he couldn't. There was a comfort in Eric's face he needed badly.

"Don't be so dramatic. I don't see you as some graffitied, beat-up gay boy," Eric joked but quickly noticed by the constant flow of Andy's tears that it was no time for lame lines. He rubbed Andy's shaky bicep to apologize.

"Just forget it," Andy said, roughly wiping at his tears with his hands.

"Do you want to know what I see when I look at you?" Eric's voice quivered and tears swelled in his own eyes. Andy looked at his face and nodded. Eric thought for a only a moment and began, "There's the obvious. You've got this whole butchy, rock-hard-body-and-smooth-skin thing working for you and lord knows that's easy on the eyes." He laughed a little with embarrassment and added, "But that's not the real reason I'm here."

"What is?" Andy tried to sound impatient but only succeeded at desperate.

Eric smiled and softly said, "The way you look at me."

Andy cried harder.

"When you looked at me for the first time, I became a whole person, but not in a you-complete-me kind of way, like that damn *Jerry McGuire* everybody's talking about," Eric said. "My heart almost beat out of my chest that day in the pool when you really looked at me and I saw that you could see me." He laughed again and paid no attention to the tears on his cheeks.

Andy gasped for air and unsuccessfully tried to keep his own face dry. "Really?" was all Andy could utter between cries.

Eric nodded. "Don't you know what you've done for me?" he said. "You've made me trust someone besides Kate. You opened my eyes and made me realize that I don't have to be mad or scared all the time. Not everyone's an asshole out to beat my ass."

"How can I teach you anything when I don't even know how to live my own life?" Andy said. "I mean, look at me, I'm a *mess*."

"Maybe," Eric agreed with a grin. "But I'm still here. No one's going to chase me away."

A look of realization brightened Andy's face. Through the tearstains and bruises, his eyes shined bright and his lips curled into a tiny smile. Eric was right. All the endured abuse had a larger purpose. He had gotten the fireball rolling for a reason: to be with Eric, fully and unashamed. During the gym attack and spray painted insults, Andy had forgotten what it was all about. Standing on the sidewalk with beautiful Eric in front of him, he was wonderfully reminded.

"You're right," Andy said quietly. "I'm sorry I've been pushing you away. I sure as hell don't want to screw up what we've started."

"I know."

"I've gone through too much to get us here."

"I know, Andy."

"And I need you now, to help me through this," Andy added.

Eric tenderly took Andy's hand and tightly intertwined their fingers. It was a bold and brave move for him. Not only were they two boys standing affectionately close on the busiest street in town with cars zooming by, but Eric wasn't one for public displays of affection. He had never found himself in a romantic predicament before with a potential need for a display, but an uncontrollable urge made him take Andy's hand.

"Come on," Eric said. "Let's ditch the rest of the day. I'll pretend I'm a gentleman and walk you home."

Andy didn't say another word. He smiled, winked at his *boyfriend*, and squeezed Eric's fingers as they kept walking.

Chapter Twenty

After sixth period Spanish, his last class of the day, Justin Drake went to his locker to load up on plenty of homework and magazines to keep his mind occupied during detention, anything to keep him from interacting with the relentlessly talkative Kate Crawford.

As Justin dug through the mound of garbage at the bottom of his locker, searching for a working pen, Tara Sanderson strolled up beside him. She leaned against the wall of lockers and crossed her tanned arms.

"Hi, J," she said. Her voice was sweet but there was something in it he couldn't place.

"Hey, Tara," Justin groaned. He pulled a pen with a chewed-up cap from the pile of trash and stuffed it into his open book bag. He stood up, slammed the locker door shut and looked at her. Tara was smiling but there was also something in her grin that meant more.

"What's going on?" she asked.

"What do you want?" Justin asked, dropping his History book into the bag.

Tara shrugged a little. A curly lock of her white blonde hair fell into her face and she flipped it over her ear. "I just wanted to know how you're doing," she said.

Justin's patience expired as he sensed her point surfacing.

Tara's smile dropped and her face hardened when she asked, "How's Andy?"

Immediately, Justin's fists clenched and he took a deep breath, preparing for battle. "What's your problem?" he snapped. He towered over her and breathed heavy fire on her face. "You want to say something to me?"

Tara was not intimidated and didn't even flinch. She casually took a step back to distance herself from her fuming friend, but she was not surrendering and Justin knew it. "I know what's been going on," she said.

"Yeah, you and everyone else in this goddamn town. So what?" Justin shook with a defensive edge that almost frightened Tara. His attitude changed so fast from one extreme to the other, leaving Tara amazed by the wicked Jekyll to Hyde transformation. But Tara was seasoned with many years in reading him and knew his reactions well.

"Justin," she said, calm and careful. "This is Andy we're talking about."

"So?" Justin wasn't focused enough to think clearly.

Disappointment came to Tara's face and she paused for a moment to gather her thoughts. "Do you remember the summer we were nine and we went to my Dad's house in Detroit?"

"What?" Justin said, confused by the relevance of her question.

"Come on, you remember," she urged. "We built that tree house in the backyard. I was going to be the Tree Queen and you and Andy were going to be my slave boys? God, even at nine I was a bossy little bitch, huh?"

Justin softened only a little and cracked a very small smile he tried to hide. "What's your point?" he asked, forcing himself to stay strong.

Tara laughed at the memory and, in seeing Justin was caving, she continued, "Do you remember what happened?"

Realizing Tara meant no harm and she was, after all, one of his oldest friends, Justin's defensive tone retreated and he calmed himself. "Of course I remember," he said.

"Good," Tara said, satisfied. She took a step closer to him and kindly put her hand on his arm. Her voice lowered and she said, "I don't

know about the gay thing, Justin. I don't know anything about it. All I
know is that this is the guy who broke his arm trying to catch you when
you fell out of that tree."

Justin briefly fell silent, thinking, searching her face for more help.

Tara glanced at her watch. "I have to go," she said and backed away
from him.

"It's not that simple," Justin said.

"If you need to make it easier, just picture yourself falling out of a
tree again," she said. "I think everyone knows he'd still be there to
catch you."

***

As Eric and Andy skipped their classes, Kate trudged on through the
day only to have detention awaiting her at the day's end. She was
already in Monica Simbeck's classroom by the time Justin arrived. His
face was hard, staring only at the floor as he walked in, never once
glancing at Kate's face or even in her direction. He bypassed Simbeck,
who sat quietly at her desk, and B-lined straight for his own seat at the
front of the room. He sat many chairs away from Kate, who stationed
herself comfortably in back. She watched Justin tear through his book
bag and pull out a notebook, pen and textbook. Without even looking
at the page numbers or chapters, Justin flipped the book open and
frantically started writing in his notebook.

As in the previous detention session, Simbeck gathered her papers
and left the two troublemakers to fend for themselves and resolve their
differences while she headed for the teacher's lounge. Avoiding the
constant bickering between the detained students motivated her to
clear the room faster each day.

Once Simbeck was gone and the echo of the slamming door faded,
the room fell so terribly still that Justin's heavy breathing suffocated
the air. Kate paid little attention to his hot breath, though, since she had
more important matters on her mind and many questions to ask.

But she hesitated, unsure of how to begin. There was an unsettling
tension between her and the burly footballer that distracted her

200

concentration. Even sitting diagonally back from him without a full-on view of his face, she could see a hint of the black eye she had given him. How was she supposed to have a calm, serious conversation with the guy she attacked?

There were so many questions and so much more she wanted to say. So after a deep yoga-trained breath to calm herself, Kate rose from her seat and slowly approached Justin's desk. He was pressing his pen hard into his notebook, a safe, non-violent way to release his aggressive, pent up energy. She was sure to keep a watchful eye on his hands, though, just in case he had any sudden urges to use that pen as a stabbing weapon as she scooted a desk close to his. She sat directly in front of him, sliding gracefully into the seat without a sound.

Still, he didn't look at her. All his energy shot through the ink pen onto the empty pages of the notebook. Glancing between the open Algebra textbook and paper, Justin wrote word after word. It was illegible and Kate wasn't sure if he was actually doing homework or just copying words from the book to avoid her face.

"I don't want to fight," she finally said into the silence. Her voice was calm and quiet but its disturbance of the stillness startled them both. "And I don't know what's going on with you guys but…why did you do that?"

"Do what?" he asked. The immediate denial and attempted innocence in his voice was painfully forced. His pen swirled faster and harder on the page while he refused to look into her waiting, accusatory eyes.

Kate made a strong effort to keep herself composed. Her hands shook so badly that nibbling on her glossy fingernails was difficult but she still managed to mangle the manicure. Justin's blatant avoidance of her face frustrated her more because she wanted the truth spoken to her face and it complicated reading him.

"Are you proud of yourself?" she asked. "Beating him up? Spray-painting his locker?"

Finally, Justin's eyes rose from the scratched notebook and met with hers. There was a deep longing inside them. Her eyes were swelling with tears, so she couldn't clearly see if it was anger or regret subtly shining through his when he very quietly said, "It wasn't me."

Justin's response surprised but didn't satisfy Kate. "Am I supposed to believe that?" she asked.

"Believe whatever you want." His smugness was strained.

Hooking a lock of hair behind her ear, Kate exhaled a low sigh. "Then who was it?"

"Just some of the guys." Justin shrugged. He dropped his pen and folded his arms across his chest, faking boredom.

"Who?" Kate insisted.

He was annoyed, but certainly not shocked by the persistence. "Why does it matter?"

"I want to know whose ass I need to kick!" she snapped.

Rolling his eyes, Justin rocked on the creaky back of the desk chair. He grabbed the ink pen again and drummed it in no particular rhythm against the edge of the desktop.

Kate clenched her teeth but managed to speak through them. "Was it worth it? Did you guys get a good laugh?" As soon as she spoke the words, she dreaded the answer.

With a tiny, possibly faked smirk, Justin replied, "Sure. Everybody did."

"Not everybody," Kate was quick to point out.

"Oh, sorry, Andy and that other fag didn't think it was funny." His attitude and tone was worsening and gaining a fiery, defensive momentum. "Big surprise."

"No, I didn't think it was funny either and I was ripped a new asshole by Spear, of all people, so your shit's trickling down on me and that sucks!" Kate's mood mirrored the aggressive shine of Justin's. "I just don't get why you guys are doing this."

He squirmed in his chair, uninterested. He tossed off his cap and ran his fingers through his black hair, roughly scratching his scalp. "We're not going to talk about this again, are we?"

"We wouldn't have to if you'd just answer my question!" Her fingernails cut into the palms of her hands as they curled into fists. "Why're you guys being such pricks?"

Justin took a deep breath and began, "When I was growing up, my parents taught me that being queer is wrong. Me and the guys just live our lives the way we were raised and we believe it. *I* believe it."

"Now, see, that's cool with me. I'm totally fine with the fact that your parents are complete morons for teaching you fools that." Kate grew hotter by the second. "But open your mind. People aren't friends with each other because they're exactly alike. How boring is that? It's the differences that make them interesting. But by interesting I don't mean busting up a friend's face or going all graffiti on his locker—"

"We're just expressing our beliefs."

"Screw your beliefs! What if someone wrote *Redneck Asshole* or *Two Inch Dick* on your locker? How would you feel?" She stared at him coldly, demanding an answer. He just sat there, silent but fuming, teetering in his chair. "And don't act like you can't hear me."

With his face an angry shade of red, Justin slammed his hands down on the top of the desk and furiously replied, "I don't have a two-inch dick! That's bullshit!"

Kate released a tiny frustrated scream. "You just proved my point! The stuff on Andy's locker is bullshit too!"

"No, it's not. He is gay." Justin nearly choked on the word.

"That doesn't mean he's as bad as the shit on that locker."

Turning away, Justin shrugged his shoulders. For the first time, Kate noticed he was absentmindedly chewing on his lower lip. She cocked her head, unsure if the gesture was due to nervousness or contemplation. Did she actually make a point that sunk in? She hoped so with a little spark of excitement. It was short lived, though, since the lip nibbling lasted only a few moments before Justin said, "They were just kidding when they wrote it." His voice was softer, less aggravated.

"I doubt that." Kate pulled her hair into a ponytail to keep it away from her face. "Why can't you guys just accept Andy's little difference and get over it?"

"Because it's not a little difference. It's not like he told us he listens to country music or eats liver or something—"

Kate's face scrunched into an odd expression and Justin reacted to it with a small smile he tried to hide. "Yeah, okay, those are really good unrelated examples," she said, her voice saturated with sarcasm.

"What about…okay…what if he liked a girl you didn't think was hot or he wanted to buy an ugly car that wasn't cool enough? Sure, you'd bitch about it and give him shit but you wouldn't actually care because whatever's good enough for him is good enough for you just because he's your friend."

Slowly, Justin folded his arms across his chest and hesitated on responding. He twiddled his thumbs, tapped his feet, and shook his legs. Finally, without looking at her, he said, "He doesn't like girls so that wouldn't happen."

"You know what I mean, Justin."

Quickly, he looked up at the sound of his own name, as if it was the first time he had ever heard it. The reaction was sudden and surprised her and she knew why: Justin was finally starting to take her serious and listen to her words. Just as sudden, there was a different look in his dark eyes. They glistened faintly with a soft beam of light she didn't recognize but didn't shy away from. He stared at her for a long time, as if battling many ideas in his head and not knowing a single way to express any of them.

Gently and without demand, Kate said, "You can't beat the gay out of him. You can't yell at it or smash it with your fists or cover it with spray paint. It's here to stay. This is who he is." Her eyes watered again and she didn't hide it. Quietly, she added, "He's your best friend. Why can't you accept the way he is because it's good enough for him?"

Justin's face was blank. His eyebrow twitched with such a fast awakening flash that Kate would've missed it if she weren't staring at him so intensely. Justin leaned his arms onto the desk and opened his mouth, but nothing came out, not even one of his signature belches. In an attempt to force his thoughts out, Justin moved his head in a few different directions, but still no words. Kate looked back into his awakening eyes and saw a hunger for knowledge and a thirst for more explanation. But a fierce stubbornness and opposing lifelong education kept him quiet and confused.

Without forcing the issue further, Kate leaned back. The classroom regained its silence but was strangely comfortable. There had been no vocal confirmation that her words had sunk into his stubborn skull, but she didn't need it. She was calm, satisfied, and went back to her own desk. Justin didn't look back at her for the remainder of detention. Instead, he silently channeled his uncertain energy into his homework.

As Justin tore through his notebook, Kate let her hair down.

***

Spending the day hiding out at his apartment with Eric and skipping school kept the disastrous repercussions of Andy's all-around-town coming-out fiasco out of his face, but it didn't get his homework done. An hour after school let out for the day and with the majority of the students gone, Andy returned to the library to research his English midterm. Eric headed back to his own house, knowing Andy needed time alone to catch his breath.

The topic of Andy's paper was an examination on the cultural significance of a great writer or book either classic or contemporary. Although Andy had not yet chosen a topic or even narrowed one down, just being in the quiet, Innards-absent library was a nice change of pace, a safe zone from the judgmental eyes and abusive hands of his former friends and classmates.

After an hour flipping through old editions on Shakespeare, Poe, Dickens, and a dozen others, Andy's head hurt, bursting with too much information. He grabbed a copy of Anne Frank's diary, a Shakespeare anthology, and *Helter Skelter*, figuring one of them would spark his interest. When he approached the tall, shiny wooden checkout desk, Leslie Rose, the candy-conscious librarian, was sitting quietly at the computer, scanning books and checking for damage. She glanced at him briefly as he placed his reading choices on the countertop.

"How are you today, Andrew?" she asked. Her soft, monotone voice made it hard for Andy to determine if she was actually interested.

"I've been better," he said, laughing a little and wincing from the pain it caused his bruised face.

Rose did not look up from the computer as she registered his selections. "Everything happens for a reason," she said softly.

"What?" Andy asked, unsure of whether he heard her correctly.

Without speaking, Rose handed the books back to him. The care and comfort in the chubby smile gracing her face was enough for Andy. He dropped the books into his backpack.

"Thanks," Andy said politely but with little excitement.

Rose looked at him and he smiled, but the vibrant glamour to his signature McCain grin had faded, losing its light to the black and blue haze of his bruises. Rose's eyes narrowed, searching for the shimmering smile she and so many others had grown to adore. Studying his face closely, her eyes widened a bit when they recognized the smile was still there, faintly, buried under the pain.

"Those are fine choices," she said sweetly. "Shakespeare's always a good one."

"I guess," he said, shrugging. "I don't really know yet."

"He was wonderfully talented and very wise."

Andy nodded again, unsure if leaving was appropriate or rude.

"Simply the thing I am shall make me live," Rose added.

"What?" Andy asked, surprisingly anxious for her to repeat herself.

"In his play *All's Well That Ends Well*," Rose said, her voice soft and graceful in the still library air. "Shakespeare said, 'Simply the thing I am shall make me live.' I think it's fitting for you, Andrew. Remember that who you are, what's in your heart, is all that matters, not what others think or say—" She held her hands up to his face, motioning to his painfully bruised flesh. "—or what they do."

The kind words touched Andy so quickly and so deeply that he nearly dizzied himself repeating them like lightning in his mind. But maybe it wasn't the words. Maybe it was the quiet, understanding help from the librarian that really made his heart soar.

He opened his mouth to speak, but didn't know what to say. Rose smiled warmly at him again and gently nodded, peacefully letting him know that no words were needed.

"You know where to find me if you ever need any help," she said, nestling back into her comfy desk chair. "On Shakespeare that is," she added and winked at him.

Andy held his backpack, as if finding comfort in knowing her books were inside it. "Thank you," he said. His crackling voice startled himself but only brightened Rose's smile.

He went to the main library door and opened it. When Andy turned back to the librarian, Rose had already returned to her computer and the mound of returned books next to her desk. Andy smiled again, happy and at peace. He turned again and headed for his locker.

Chapter Twenty-One

Much to his surprise, when Andy turned the hallway corner, with the Shakespeare anthology back in his hands, searching for Rose's quote, he saw Justin kneeling in front of his locker. Beside his former friend was an array of uncapped cleaning supplies, mounds of dirty paper towels, and a bucket of soapy water labeled JANITOR on the side in fading black marker. Andy glanced at Justin's hands. He was wearing rubber gloves and holding a coarse scrub brush. Justin was removing the graffiti from Andy's badly dented locker, most of which he had already erased.

Justin heard Andy's tennis shoes approach but he didn't look up from his hard scrubbing. Even after Andy had reached him, standing only a few feet away, Justin still didn't look at him. Instead, Justin put more muscle into eliminating QUEER from the bent metal door.

Andy broke the silence with a simple and cautious, "Hey."

Justin scrubbed harder and said "Hey" in no special way.

Andy glanced down the hall, at the ceiling, behind him, around, everywhere, searching for something to say. "Is this your punishment?" he asked, unsure of where it came from, and he hastily stuffed the book back into his bag.

"What?" Justin asked, keeping his eyes on the locker.

"Is Spear making you clean up your mess?"

Justin kept cleaning. "It wasn't me."

The answer didn't satisfy Andy. "Come on, J, I don't need anymore shit—"

"It wasn't me!" Justin's voice bounced off the walls.

The strong reaction made Andy cautiously step back. He believed Justin, recognizing the shouted jumbled mess from his friend's mouth as the truth. "Then who was it?" Andy asked.

Dropping the sloppy scrub brush to the floor, Justin finally looked up to Andy's face. Andy saw anger and a surprising hint of hurt in Justin's eyes. Andy knew the anger well, but had never seen hurt present itself over the years.

"Cut the bullshit," Justin snapped. He took a deep breath to calm himself, another move Andy had never seen. "Why didn't you tell me?"

Andy shook his head. "I was scared of how you'd take it," he said. "I guess I was right."

"I don't like it, that's for sure, but I should've heard it from you, not through all this."

"I know—"

"No, you don't." Justin was firm and focused. "I felt so stupid finding out in the hall with everybody else. Now they all say, 'Did you know?' 'Oh my god, that fag's your friend?!' 'Did he ever suck your dick?' What a way for me to find out, Andy!"

Surprised by Justin's seriousness, Andy wasn't sure what to say. He kept his jaw closed tight and his arms close to his chest.

"I can handle those assholes," Justin continued. "I can't handle you lying to me."

"What would you've done if I had told you?" Andy asked, truly interested in the answer.

Justin shrugged. "I don't know."

"Oh, well, why didn't I come to you sooner?!"

"Don't be a jerk," Justin quickly said. "All right, fine, I probably would've freaked—"

"Exactly! You don't know what it's like for me," Andy explained. "This is the hardest thing I've ever had to go through. I don't need you or any of the other guys giving me shit about something I hardly know anything about and it's my *life!*"

"But I don't know *anything* about it! Nothing!" Justin snapped. "I don't know how it works or what's going on with you or how you can like *guys!*"

"You want to know how it works?"

"Yes!" Justin demanded, although nervous to hear the reply.

Quietly but with a surfacing sense of pride, Andy said, "Eric loves me."

Justin's steely expression didn't change. He stood still, waiting for more.

"Whether you can accept that or even understand it, he loves me," Andy added. "I've never gotten that from anyone. Not from my parents, not from you or the guys or anyone who's actually known who I am."

Justin's strong, stone-cold gaze softened with a disappointed frown. "I've never known the real you," he said slowly, as if understanding it for the first time. "Whose fault is that? I've known you my whole life and you've never let me get to know you."

"Why would I have opened up to you of all people?" Andy said with a laugh. "You're not exactly the gay-friendliest guy on the planet."

"That doesn't matter. I might give fags a lot of shit, but so what?" Justin said without guilt. "I'm not just some fag-basher and you're not just some fag. You're my best friend and I should've heard it from you, not through all this bullshit. You could've told me."

"Come on, you didn't have any idea?"

"NO!"

"Why do you think I haven't been around the past few weeks? Why did I give up football this year?" Andy asked. "Haven't you ever wondered why I live alone or why I never talk to my parents?"

"You said it's because they run their house like Nazi Germany and you didn't want anything to do with it."

"Yeah, but you knew they kicked me out and you never asked questions—"

"Andy—"

"Haven't you noticed I never join in on the gay bashing?" Andy asked. He was on a roll. "How often do you hear the word *fag* come out of my mouth?"

"I just thought you weren't a raging dick like everyone else!" Justin snapped, firmly holding his own. "Sure, you've always been quiet and nicer than the rest of us, but why the hell would that make me think you're gay? You have met me before, right? You know I don't think like that. I'm not *that* much of an asshole." He thought a moment and added, "Well, maybe I am, but not to you."

The surprising comment put Andy at ease. He nodded, sighed, and said, "I know."

"How long has this been going on, anyway?" Justin asked.

Andy didn't want to answer, but he did. "Six weeks."

"Six weeks?!" Justin echoed. "You've been gay for *six weeks*?!"

"No, I've always been gay," Andy carefully corrected. "I've just been seeing Eric since school started."

Justin's eyebrows crinkled inward as he thought long and hard about his next question. "Well, is Eric your...you know...*first* or whatever?" With each spoken word, Justin eased up and became a little more comfortable and curious. "Or is this, like, a phase or something?"

"It's not a phase," Andy said so firm that it made Justin cringe.

Uncomfortable in the seriousness, Justin casually shrugged and said, "What's so great about this guy anyway? What does he have that you couldn't get from Tara? I mean, she was *hot*, man!"

The relaxed tone and silly interest in Justin's voice comforted Andy.

"You really want to know?" Andy asked.

Justin nodded.

Andy responded honestly and without humor. "There's no bullshit with him," he said. "He doesn't care if I'm popular or a State fan or shitty at Math and he supports my dream to be a Detroit Tiger, no matter how unrealistic it might be. If it's good enough for me, it's good enough for him *just because*." His face lit up at the thought of Eric and he continued, "And I know his friend Kate's a pain in the ass, but she and their friend Nick accept me no questions asked. They're friends to the core, Justin. We're not like that with each other or any of the guys."

"So what? We're guys!" Justin said. "We don't need some chick or some fag thrown into the mix—" He bit his tongue.

Andy rolled his eyes and shrugged. It was his classic way of forgiving Justin's trademarked foot-in-mouth goofs. "That *chick* and that *fag* have taught me a lot," Andy said calmly. "I'm just not who you thought I was, not completely anyway."

Justin didn't speak. He just nodded, as if anticipating the remark.

Andy added, "I didn't fuck up my future for no reason—"

"How'd you do that?" Justin asked, raising his head, his eyebrows creased.

"Come on, man, like any college recruiter's going to want the Queer Pitcher for his team now!" Andy balked at Justin's assumed foolishness.

"Shut up!" Justin snapped, only half-joking. "The recruiters were here last season and you already got your full ride to State."

"They'll take it away from me after all this."

Justin was annoyed. "Give me a break!"

"Who knows what you guys'll tell them when they're back this season to check on me."

"We're not going to—"

"Justin!" Andy's simple interruption was harsh, hurt and begging for honesty.

Justin paused and squeezed his hands out of the tight rubber gloves. He tossed them into the bucket and wiped his hands on his jeans. "You're going to be a Tiger someday, man," he said, gathering up the dirty towels and cleaning supplies. Concentrating on the cleaners provided a good outlet to avoid eye contact. His voice was calm and genuinely honest, a welcomed change from his patented everyday aggressive tone. "Everyone's known since we were kids that you'll be hitting them out of Tiger Stadium someday."

"What's your point?" Andy asked impatiently, fighting off tears.

Justin looked back to Andy's face and said, "I won't let anyone screw it up for you."

In an instant, Andy was reminded that the foul-mouthed badass was, after all, his best friend and perhaps the gay roadblock was not the end of a shared sixteen-year friendship. Through his words, Justin obviously still considered Andy a friend, one he wouldn't hesitate to defend. Maybe after the horrendous events of the previous days, Andy and Justin could find common ground and move forward.

"All right, I have to ask or I'll go crazy," Justin said, swallowing an unfamiliar lump in his throat; he didn't get them, ever, since he never felt guilty or scared, but lately his throat was congested with a wide variety. He tried to pay no attention. Instead, his next words came out in a heated rush, "So is Eric, like, your best friend now?"

It took a few seconds, but it finally clicked for Andy and the odd question made sense coming from such the overly self-centered young man. "Are you jealous?" Andy asked, never thinking he'd ever ask ultra-arrogant *Justin Drake* such a question. Nevertheless, it certainly brought a pleased grin to Andy's face.

"NO!" The quiver in Justin's voice embarrassed them both. "Well—" he paused to find the words. "It's just that he's a guy and you're a guy and you're together, so I don't really know how that's any different than what you and I've had going on for all these years."

"Are you asking me to be your boyfriend?" Andy's joke wasn't appreciated. Justin instinctively clenched his fingers into fists and flared his nostrils. "Sorry!" Andy said quickly, tossing his hands up to surrender. "Bad joke."

"I'm trying here, man, buy you have to meet me half way," Justin said, breathing deeply to bring himself down from the adrenaline rush.

Andy nodded and thought for a moment. "He's something different. He's not my best friend," he said calmly. "You are and you have been my whole life, so it's not like Eric's replacing you. Yeah, he's a guy but it's on a different level."

Justin shrugged, unclear by Andy's meaning.

Andy tried a different approach. "When you were dating Ashley Fitzgerald, was she my replacement?" he asked. "Did you like her more than me?"

"No! It's not the same thing!" Justin said, laughing at the silliness but quickly realizing Andy's point. "Oh—"

In seeing the light finally flick on in Justin's eye, Andy nodded. "See?"

"All right, so I'm a dumbass. So what?" Justin snapped. "I guess I got a lot to learn. It's just that I don't know shit about any of this gay stuff, you know?"

"You're not the only one," Andy said, his voice low, sad.

Justin ran his hands through his hair. "You know what? I'd really like it if we could get the hell out of here and do something to forget about all this bullshit for a while," he said, all smiles as he spent a few moments thinking. "How 'bout some ball at Bush Park?"

Andy's blood raced. Justin's simple invitation was a start, an outstretched hand, a beginning. "You sure?" Andy asked, cautiously. "You don't have to—"

"Do you want to or not?" Justin's head hurt from too much talk. "One on one?"

With a deep breath full of relief and a sense of safety, Andy agreed, "Sure."

Justin nodded, grabbing the bucket and cleaning supplies.

"You think you can take me?" Andy asked.

"As long as you keep your hands off my ass," Justin joked.

"Very funny!" Andy's laugh was loud, nervous, and embarrassed.

"Hey, you know Eric's girl Kate?" Justin asked, attempting to be nonchalant while loading the last of the cleaning supplies into a blue plastic organizer.

"Of course!" Andy laughed, astounded by Justin's impossible suggestion that anyone would not know Kate Crawford. "What about her?"

Again, organizing the cleansers as his scapegoat, Justin said, "Think she'd go out with me?"

Andy made a goofy face and laughed. "J, she beat the shit out of you."

"That's just a technicality," Justin said, laughing at his own absurdity. He grabbed the bucket filled with dirty water and wet towels in one hand and the supply organizer in the other.

"Well...I don't know..." Andy couldn't keep a straight face. He laughed continuously as they finally headed for the senior parking lot. "I mean, she's about as predictable as a tornado, so it's possible she might give you the time of day—" He laughed again before adding,

"But it's also possible she'll just shove the time up your ass."

Setting the bucket down for only a second, Justin playfully punched Andy's arm, causing Andy to flinch a little from the already slow-healing bruises decorating his arms. Justin made an apologetic face, scrunching with regret. Andy shrugged and they continued on their way.

As they walked through the last stretch of hallway before the senior lot, the air was comfortably still, although there were many words waiting to be said and so many unanswered questions left to explore. But there was no rush or urgency to do it all at once.

To Andy's continuing surprise, Justin was the first to break the silence. "So, this is the last thing I'm going to say," he said awkwardly, switching the handles of the bucket and the organizer between hands.

"What is it?" Andy asked.

"I know I give Eric a lot of shit," Justin began but paused between words, searching to gather his thoughts. "But I don't even know him."

Andy nodded. "Yeah—?"

"Well, my point is—" Another pause. "It's just that, well, I don't know how it works, liking guys or whatever—"

"Spit it out, man," Andy said.

Another deep breath.

Another pause.

"Well, I guess since you're my best friend and he's good enough for you—" Justin said and quietly added, "—then he's good enough for me."

Andy's breath escaped his lungs. His mouth moved without sound, "What?"

"I'll try to cut him some slack," Justin added and quickly walked away, frantically avoiding any further discussion. The janitor's bucket and supplies banged against Justin's rushing legs, the dirty water spilled on his shoes as he hustled to the janitor's closet at the end of the hall to return the borrowed items.

In the few moments waiting for Justin to return, Andy didn't move.

Or speak.

Or *breathe*.

He was overwhelmed with pride.

Chapter Twenty-Two

Bush Park was incredible, buried deep within thick walls of trees and seasonally juicy raspberry bushes. The shallow Shiawassee River babbled around the basketball and tennis courts. The easiest way into the park was through St. John's back parking lot. The private Catholic school was known not for their academics, but for its killer county fair held on the property every fall.

The best-known way into the park was through a dirt trail leading from the sidewalk on Leroy Street, over the old corroded cement bridge onto the grown-over sand pits of the volleyball courts. In the good old days, the bridge doubled as the hot spot to beat an enemy's ass for middle schoolers looking for trouble. Cops caught on, though, and started patrolling the area regularly.

In the late autumn evening, as the cool winter weather crept its way in, Andy and Justin parked in St. John's back lot. Justin left his windows open and blared the radio while they took to the court. Why hip-hop sounded so much better barreling through a bass-bumping pickup truck, he didn't know. It just did and he wasn't the only one who thought so.

Justin and Andy were only on the court a few minutes, without enough time to start a game, when they heard the all-too familiar beats of several obnoxious car stereos roar into St. John's lot.

Andy's heart raced as the pimped-out fiery red Mustang of spoiled Wes Palmer and Matt Murphy's cobalt blue Trans-Am drove up. Seconds later, the deep beats of another former friend annoyed the air as David Johnson arrived in his canary yellow Camero. Behind him was the equally arrogant but often quiet follower Jeremy Flint in a sleek black Jeep.

As the self-righteous young men gathered in the lot and headed for the basketball court, Andy turned to Justin. "What the hell are they doing here?" he asked, nearly panic-stricken.

Justin shrugged. "I don't know," he said. "I haven't talked to them all day."

Andy watched the small gang strut toward him. They seemed to move in slow motion and their angry muscled arms and fists tightened with each move. The proud swagger lasted long enough for each of them to exchange disgusted stares with Andy. The sheer anger in their eyes rattled Andy's bones, but he stood tall, strong, refusing to show any sign of weakness.

They stopped only a few feet from Andy and Justin. In Justin's absence, Wes Palmer stood in front as the Innards' leader. His handsome face was proud and natural, as if he had been waiting to occupy Justin's leadership spot for quite some time.

"Way to go, J!" Wes cheered. A large smile slithered onto his face.

"What?" Justin asked. He was impatient but not overly annoyed.

"You got this fag right where we want him."

"Yeah, with no witnesses," Matt Murphy happily added.

"No witnesses for what?" Justin asked. He was confused.

Andy wasn't. "To beat my ass," Andy said, not as a question. His heart raced.

The sparkly Cheshire cat grin on Wes's face grew larger.

Andy stared at Justin. "Is that why you brought me here?" Andy asked, wanting to vomit. "To get me alone and kick my ass?" Clenched any tighter, Andy's fists would have burst through the skin.

"No way, dude," Justin said firmly. He took a big step toward Wes. Their chests bumped and bounced them both back a half step. Wes's sour hot breath blew onto Justin's face. "We're here to play ball, man,"

Justin said, his own breath heaving back at Wes. "So if you guys want to play, let's do it. If not, take off."

Wes's slimy smile lingered. "Let me get this straight, oops, no offense, fag—" Wes said and winked at Andy before turning back to Justin. "You're *not* here to beat his ass?"

"Like I said, we're here to play ball," Justin fiercly repeated.

"Wait a minute!" David Johnson said, nearly panicking. "Are you one too?!" He stepped back, terrified.

"One what?" Justin asked.

"A FAG!" David shrieked. The boys' mouths dropped open and they joined David in a cautious step away from Justin and Andy.

With fire burning his knuckles, Justin concentrated on keeping his fists tucked at his side instead of burying them in David's stomach. "I'm not gay," Justin said as calmly as he could.

"Bullshit!" David said without thinking. "Why else would you be hanging with that fag unless you're a fudge packer too?!" David spoke fast, his nasally voice shaky, loaded with fear.

With his holier-than-thou friends standing ahead of him, Justin shook his head, surprised by what complete idiots they were. Thinking two seconds longer, Justin recalled his own behavior the past few days. He was an idiot too and once looked at Andy through the same disgusted eyes as David, Wes, Matt and all of Ann Arbor South. Justin's stomach churned at the thought of it. The sickness took him by surprise because he had never felt guilt before and it didn't taste so great.

"Don't call him a fag," Justin said, unsure of where the words came from. "And I already told you dicks I'm here to play ball with my friend. He's the same now as he's always been."

"Bullshit!" David barked again.

"Chill out, Dave." Justin turned to Andy and slapped his arm. "Come on, dude, let's go," he said and headed back to the court, anxious to start a game.

Andy cracked a tiny grin, pleased by Justin's remarkable unforeseen stance. A few days earlier, Andy never would have even imagined Justin thinking on his own, let alone standing up to the crew he had been thick as thieves with since their days in diapers. Andy followed Justin to the pavement, proud of the man his friend was becoming.

"I thought we were friends, man!" Wes Palmer yelled.

Justin tossed the ball to Andy, turned around, and said, "I am your friend, Wes."

"How can you hang with him after he jumped me in the gym?" Wes whined. "You have to be a fag too because there's no way you'd betray me like that!"

Justin laughed a little and walked back toward Wes. "You're calling me gay? You're the fucking drama queen!" He kept smiling. "You deserved that shit in the gym and you know it. And I'm not betraying you. Give me a break. I'm here because Andy's my boy. If you think real hard you'd remember that he was your friend too a few days ago."

"That's before he went homo!" Matt Murphy shouted.

"Wake up!" Justin laughed again with frustration. "He's the same guy he's always been!"

A silence swept over the boys as Justin's words sunk in. They exchanged confused, uncertain, baffled looks. Finally, David Johnson looked over Justin's shoulder to Andy.

"You've always been a fag?" David asked.

Andy rolled his eyes and said, "I didn't flip a switch if that's what you think."

"You have!" David panicked. "You've always been a faggot! You've probably been checking us out too! I've been in the shower with you, man!"

Justin took another firm step toward the gang. There was something in the move, though. Andy saw it. The other boys saw it too and it surprised everyone, even Justin himself. He moved toward Andy's potential attackers out of instinct to protect his friend.

"Shut up, Dave!" Justin ordered. His white knuckles ached.

"Fuck you, J!" David shouted. "You've probably been checking out my dick too!"

Justin laughed and softened a bit, realizing punching David wasn't worth the energy. His fists loosened and he said, "Even if I was the gayest guy on the planet, I still wouldn't want to look at your dick."

The boys fell silent again, although Jeremy Flint chuckled quietly at Justin's remark. He was quick to ditch the grin and laughter when Wes and David shot him an awful glare.

"Don't you guys get it? He's the same!" Justin was past frustration and bored with repeating himself. "He's the same guy from the team who took us to the finals two years in a row and he's the same guy who's had every one of your backs since kindergarten!"

"So what? Are we supposed to open our arms, drop our pants, and bend over for him now?" Wes snapped with a loud laugh. "That's not going to happen!"

"We're not letting that fag back into our group!" David added.

"Oh, hell no, Dave! What would people think?" Justin mocked.

Jeremy Flint stepped to the head of the small group. "Why should we have anything to do with him?" he asked, his voice calm and interested. "You want us to get over it and accept him, but he lied to us and he's different. Why should we forgive him?"

Justin breathed quietly for only a moment and said, "Because he's our friend." The words came quickly. "Why isn't what he wants good enough for us just because he's our boy?"

Jeremy had no vocal response, only a gapping pie hole, as did motor mouth David Johnson and aggressive Matt Murphy. Fearless leader Wes Palmer folded his arms with arrogance oozing out of his pores. They exchanged their patented dopey, unknowing, ignorant stares with each other and in their silence a smile came to Andy's dimpled face.

"You guys need to chill out and get over it," Justin instructed and turned his back on them. "And get the hell out of here if you're not going to play ball."

The boys didn't protest or speak. They filtered back into their pimped rides and sped off. Jeremy Flint was the last to leave. He fidgeted in his seat with the window down, keeping his eyes fixated on Justin and Andy. Jeremy's face was pained and he tried hard to speak, opening his mouth a few times to no avail. Instead, he revved the engine, blared the horn, and sped away.

Noticeably shocked with a low-hanging jaw, Andy didn't move while Justin returned to the basketball court. He stared at Justin closely, unsure of what he expected. Maybe he wanted further explanation of Justin's miraculous attitude change that only happened in the movies or maybe Andy was just making a memory of the moment when his best friend became more to him than he ever imagined.

Instantly awkward and uncomfortable from the staring, Justin avoided Andy's face and rapidly dribbled the ball.

"J, what—" Andy couldn't finish. He didn't know what to say.

"Look, are we going to do this Oprah shit all day or are we going to play?" Justin said, shooting the ball to the hoop. It swooshed through the net.

Andy smiled, pleased that the emotionally frigid Justin Drake had returned and they didn't have to go any further with words.

They just had to enjoy the court.

Chapter Twenty-Three

Monday, October 15, 1996

"So, let me get this straight," Kate said. "Justin actually told off his goonie sidekicks in Andy's defense? Did I hear that right?"

"Yep," Eric replied. They walked with Nick from the senior lot through the main school doors three days after Justin's miraculous transformation. The weekend had been full of too much thought. Eric, of course, had filled Kate and Nick in via telephone. As soon as Andy told Eric what had happened at Bush Park, Eric instantly called Kate. Kate, in turn, told Nick. Even after two full days and a third morning, they still weren't finished analyzing every angle. It was fresh and lingered on their minds.

"I still can't believe Justin Drake, of all people on the planet, did that!" Kate said.

"Andy said he came around," Eric said. "They even hung out this weekend."

"No way! How? Why?"

"I guess Justin was inspired." Eric laughed.

"By who?"

"You, dumbass. He was asking a lot about you. It sounds like he might fancy you a little."

"That's so sweet," Nick chimed in. "Looks like West Side Story can have a happy ending after all." He and Eric laughed louder.

"Oh please!" Kate balked. "If I set myself on fire, Justin would light a cigarette off my burning body before he'd ever listen to a word I said."

"Maybe not."

"I'm fed up. Talking to Jockstrap Justin's like talking to my little niece, Julia. Sure, she talks a lot but it's mostly in this goo-goo-ga-ga language I don't understand." She hooked her hair behind her ears and added, "Only Justin calls me a bitch a lot more than Julia does."

"Well, Aunt of the Year, don't get too blue," Eric said. "I'm just suggesting you might've gotten through to him."

As Kate, Eric, and Nick walked through the main hall, past Spear's office, Tara Sanderson stopped them. She looked beautiful as always, her white-blonde hair meticulously curled into shiny little ringlets, giving way to her pretty, wide dark eyes intricately painted with a shimmering pink eye shadow.

"Good morning," she said to no one but Eric.

"Do you guys smell skank?" Kate snapped. "Or is that dollar store douche?"

Tara looked at Kate only briefly and said nothing. Kate wasn't worth the aggravation of a fight so early in the morning, so Tara refocused her attention on Eric. "Can we talk?" she asked, her voice was sweet and controlled.

"Hell no!" Kate said.

Nick nudged her and said, "Stop."

"Why?" Eric asked Tara.

"It'll just take a sec," Tara said, smiling.

Feeling fearless and refreshed, Eric shrugged and agreed, "Sure."

"What?!" Kate was pissed. She instinctively blocked Eric, sliding in between her best friend and the venomous blonde creature. Tara giggled at the reaction and fluffed her curls, springing them in every direction.

"Don't have a pre-menopausal breakdown, Kate," Tara said. "I just want to talk to your boy for two seconds." She slung her hand on her hip and tapped her high-heeled toe.

"It's okay," Eric said, bypassing Kate's roadblock and moving closer to Tara.

"You can't trust this skanky bitch!" Kate protested.

Eric gently touched Kate's arm, not only in an attempt to get her to back off, but also to let her know she was his girl and a simple conversation wouldn't change that.

"It's fine, Kate," Eric said firmly. "I'll just be a minute." He glanced to Nick.

"It's cool," Nick said, and stepped up to Kate. He held her shoulders, preparing to prevent her predictable violent outburst.

Eric smiled, touched by Kate's overprotection and turned to Tara. "What's up?" he asked.

Tara took several steps away from Kate and Nick to give her and Eric privacy. "I know we don't really know each other," she began. "But I've been watching what's been happening the last few weeks and, well, I just want to know how Andy's doing."

"Why don't you ask him?" Eric asked, firm but not rude.

"I tried, but he's not exactly an open book with his feelings," Tara replied and saw her remark bring a very tiny smirk to Eric's face. "But you know all about that, huh?"

Eric shrugged. "I've noticed," he said. "But I'm not an expert on spilling my guts either."

"Must make it interesting between you two."

"It has its moments," Eric said, slightly impatient. "What do you want?"

Tara nodded at his edginess. "Look, Eric, I've been a real bitch to you over the years," she said, unapologetically. "Me and my girls, we're all bitches. Okay, some of us are even cunts, but don't tell them I told you that that because we supposedly hate that word, probably because it perfectly describes us—"

Eric managed to laugh. "Wish I could argue with you," he said. "But, well, I can't!"

"Oh, I know! We're *total* snobs!" she said, giggling. "Anything that's different, especially with the guys, we don't want to deal with it. I'm not proud of that. I'm just being honest. We grow up thinking the guys have to be the piggish brutes of the football field and the girls have to be the prissy little cheerleaders. So when one of the pigs falls for another pig and not a prissy princess, our whole world turns upside down."

"It's not like we wanted this to happen. We didn't want to go against anything—"

"Let me finish," Tara said. "I'm not making excuses for anybody or saying you chose to turn this place on its ass." She paused to think and calmly added, "It's bullshit that we think like that, any of us. Stupidity isn't an excuse for what's happened to Andy, the fighting, the spray paint. I mean, what the hell is *that*?"

Eric laughed again.

"My point is that I'm sorry for what's happened to you guys," Tara said. "I'll get the girls to back off and I'll see what I can do about the guys, too."

"Well, that's cool but...why?" Eric was confused. "Why do you care?"

Tara took a breath. "Because he holds a special place in my heart," she said softly and smiled at a mindfull of memories.

Eric wasn't threatened but overly curious. "Because you dated him?"

"Yeah, for a little while. Seems like a hundred years ago, though."

"Just out of curiosity and he'll be pissed if he finds out I asked you this," Eric said, reddening from embarrassment. "Did you ever have any idea, about the gay thing?"

"Oh, please, honey, I've known for years."

Eric's eyes widened. "No way!"

Tara nodded. "It doesn't take a genius to figure it out, at least not for anyone close to him who can actually put two and two together," she said. "The guys never figured it out because it's just *sooo* inconceivable to them that anyone in their crowd could be gay! OHMYGOD!"

Eric laughed.

"Those creeps are led around by their dicks, not their under-developed brains so their minds don't stray from the vagina. Trust me,

I've been fighting off Wes Palmer for years, who in this case I can confirm has an under-developed dick to match his under-developed brain, so I know what raging assholes they can be."

Eric laughed again, partly because Tara was so funny, but also because his perception of her changed. Maybe she wasn't the raging cunt, er, *bitch* he thought she was for so many years.

"How'd you know? About Andy, I mean," he asked, truly intrigued.

She shrugged and said, "We've known each other forever and we used to have these long talks about anything and everything. There was always this comfortable vibe between us. It wasn't awkward or forced. It was awesome but then I realized I had the same relationship with him that I have with Jennifer or Patty or Alison, like, a great *friendship*. There was never any real horniness to my relationship with Andy, which I thought was weird because all the other guys around here are controlled by their dicks. Andy was always a gentleman."

Again, she and Eric exchanged laughs. Kate stewed on the sidelines, hearing only giggles and not the actual conversation. Nick kept her contained at a safe distance.

"Don't get me wrong. Andy never gave me any real hints that he was gay and we weren't together very long so I guess I just assumed and put it all together." She adjusted her purse strap and added, "I know I shouldn't assume because it's not like he fits some kind of homo mold or anything."

"Did you ever say anything to him about it?" Eric asked.

"That's none of my business," Tara answered quickly. "If he wanted me to know, he would've told me. He was probably denying it to himself or trying to bury it or whatever. I don't know how it works. All I know is that it wasn't my place to say anything."

"Not that it's any of my business, but did you and Andy ever fool around?" Eric asked.

She wasn't offended. Her face remained warm and inviting as she replied, "Are you sure you want me to tell you?"

His answer was quick and short of breath. "No."

Taking a step closer, Tara spoke loud enough for only Eric to hear. "He was always a gentleman," she repeated. "Always nice and quiet and one of the only guys who's ever treated me with respect. He has this way of making anyone feel alive." She smiled and added, "But I think you already know that."

Eric was pleased to hear Andy regarded so highly and he certainly understood how Tara felt since he too knew the power of Andy's attention and respect. Still, Eric frowned a little at Tara's words. He seemed to hear the answer he hadn't hoped for.

"Not to say I didn't want to," Tara continued. "But the answer's no."

The sun shined back on Eric's face and it lit up.

"Besides, forget about my slutty reputation, we weren't together long enough to have dirty boy-girl relations," she said with a giggle. "Plus, like I said, I already had a feeling about the gay thing so I didn't want to make him do anything he didn't want to, not just for him but for me too. I didn't want to fall for some hot gay guy!"

"Can you do me a favor?" Eric asked. "The next time you see Andy, tell him what you told me."

Tara laughed dismissively. "Why?"

"He could really use some reassurance right now that he's not alone or doomed with the gay plague or something."

She frowned at her brief lack of compassion. "I'm sorry."

"He doesn't want to hear you're sorry," Eric said, smiling to lighten the air. "He wants to know he still has friends who aren't out to beat his ass."

"Sure," Tara said, nodding proudly. "I'll tell him in third period. We have Super Crotch McCarthy together. Do you really think it'll help?"

"Oh, yeah. It's been such a rough couple of days. He could use a boost."

Tara pressed her lips together to refresh her frosty pink lip-gloss. She tilted her head and looked at Eric in a way he'd never seen before, as an equal, a human being, a friend. "I'm sorry it's been so shitty for you," she said sweetly. "High school, I mean. I'm sorry for everything you've gone through.

"You already said that," Eric reminded. "You don't have to apologize."

"Yes, I do because I'm an asshole and I'm actually admitting it for once," she said and added under her breath, "Just don't tell anybody or I'll kill you."

Eric laughed. "I'd like to say you're secret's safe with me."

"Everyone already knows I'm an asshole," Tara said. "It's a hard burden to carry, but I've perfected it after seventeen years. You've perfected your own thing too, Eric. The I-don't-give-a-shit attitude works for you, especially since we all know the crazy bullshit you have to put up with. It's amazing how you never let anything bother you."

"Well, I don't know about that." Eric stared at his feet. "Maybe it seems that way."

"Then you're holding the same secret a lot of us hold," Tara said and leaned in closer to him. "We all have to put on a front. Don't let them see you sweat or else they win, right?" There was a hard, forced strength to her voice, like she knew all too well what she spoke of. Maybe living the prestigious, envied Innards highlife wasn't so glamorous after all.

Eric met her eyes and smiled. "Right," he said, pleased he was now trusted to share her anxiety-ridden secret of being an always-on-top troubled popular girl.

"The moral of the story, Mr. Anderson—" Tara was quick to draw attention away from her own problems. "—is that Justin and his crew are raging twats. Don't let them get you down."

Eric laughed again. The razor sharp wit and crude language spewing from her mouth vividly reminded him of another short, pretty lady in his life. "You know, you and Kate might actually get along if you gave it a chance," he said. "You've both got a flare for the dramatic."

"Oh please! I don't want anything to do with *that* bitch," Tara snapped with a grin. She glanced at her watch. "I have to go. I'll catch you later, okay?"

"Thanks, Tara," Eric said. There was a brief, awkward silence between them. He inched toward her, as she did to him, both of them unsure if a hug was going too far.

"Come here!" Tara said and wrapped her arms around his shoulders. "Feel free to share that hot-ass baseballer with me anytime, okay? I think a threesome is a great compromise."

"I don't play well with others," Eric teased.

"That's okay. I'm a true dominatrix at heart. I'll beat you both into submission."

Chapter Twenty-Four

Heading for the dreaded but slowly progressive torture of detention, Kate hurried toward instructor Monica Simbeck's classroom. Kate was running late, having spent more time than usual in the restroom primping and checking her look for reasons she couldn't pinpoint. Still, something urged her to flip her hair and reapply the shimmering lip-gloss once more before joining Justin in the Spear-assigned confinement of detention.

On her way, zigzagging through the hustle of the noisy, crowded hallways, Kate ran into a fellow classmate. Their shoulders bumped and the blow stumbled her into a row of lockers. Very briefly disoriented but uncharacteristically calm, Kate focused on the classmate. She was not surprised to find Justin Drake as her unintentional attacker.

Justin was dazed, staring mostly at the floor or walls instead of her face and he glanced at her only briefly to ensure she was unharmed from the minor hallway collision. When he saw she was, in fact, all right, Justin turned away, avoiding her eyes.

"Your week's just been packed to the brim with brawls, huh?" she said, scratching the tiny sting of pain on her left shoulder, which hit the lockers hardest.

Justin shrugged and said, "Shit happens." The icy tingle to his words and uncaring voice were strained and his restless, pacing feet gave way to an unhidden nervousness.

Although she could read his on-edge reaction well, Kate was still annoyed he wouldn't give her something more, something real. Even though she heard rumors of him rekindling his friendship with Andy, she had yet to see any change.

"Does your heart pump battery acid? I mean, do you feel *anything*?" she asked, quickly jumping into the perpetual Kate vs. Justin fighting ring. "How about seeing your best friend bleed? Does that affect you at all?"

"I don't want to talk about this." He tried to walk away but Kate tightly clenched his arm, pulling him back in her direction.

"Don't start your shit with me today!" she demanded. "I thought you were coming around, especially after your ball-busting vigilante stance at Bush Park. What's going on?"

"I don't know." He shrugged with uncertainty. "It's hard to explain."

"Oh, please try because I've *got* to hear this!" Kate sarcastically begged.

Still unsure, Justin paced the floor. Standing together in the hall, he and Kate seemed to go unnoticed by their fellow students. For once, it seemed no one anticipated their drama or it was simply old, uninteresting news. The hall remained busy and crowded and Justin and Kate found a slight peace in the disinterest. They could finally coexist among their classmates without an ensued fight or verbal bashing. Blending into the crowd seemed to ease the tension.

Kate took a breather and relaxed. "Look, there aren't any of your dopey friends around. No one's going to hear anything you say," she said, her voice calm and unthreatening. "Just be honest with me for once."

Justin stepped back and thought for a moment. He didn't shy away or dismiss her direct tone. In fact, it seemed to comfort him and relax his tense shoulders. Without paying attention to the unconcerned surrounding students, Justin quietly said, "I saw him cry."

Kate's eyebrows bent inward, trying to detect sarcasm or an

inevitable vindictive motive. She found neither. Justin was sincere and it scared the living shit out of her.

"You saw who cry?" she asked, cringing, waiting for his smart mouth to return.

"Andy," Justin said calmly. "The day we kicked his ass in the gym, I saw him cry."

Still cautious, Kate readjusted her bag and flipped her hair. "What'd you expect?" she asked. "You beat the shit out of him. He's not exactly going to burst into song with *That's What Friends Are For*."

Justin scratched an itch on his muscular shoulder and nibbled on his lower lip. He glanced at Kate's pretty face every few moments to let her know he was thinking, organizing his thoughts. She appreciated the honesty, but waiting for him to speak bored her to tears. She tapped her well-dressed toe and exaggeratedly drummed her fingers against her folded arms.

Finally, Justin broke his silence and said, "I saw my dad cry once." His voice trembled so slightly that only a trained ear would've detected it.

Kate heard it loud and clear and she cautiously asked, "What?"

"At my grandfather's funeral, it's the only time I ever saw my dad cry," Justin said, fidgeting with the zipper on his backpack. He zipped it open, then closed it, then opened it again and dug his bitten fingernails into its teeth. "It was scary as hell because he's the strongest person I've ever known and I put so much trust in him that when he broke down and cried, it made me feel—" He took a deep breath before quietly adding, "—*helpless*. I mean, how do you help the person who's always helped you? Where do you find strength when the person who's always given it to you falls apart? That's how I felt seeing Andy cry."

Kate's mouth dropped open like an old broken drawbridge. Justin's deep confession wasn't exactly the venomous response she'd dreadfully anticipated. He was actually sincere, honest, and showing human emotion! Kate was beside herself.

"I don't know if you're close to your dad," Justin continued. "But I know you're close to Eric and you've seen him cry because everyone knows I've given him enough reasons to—" He stopped himself and looked hard at Kate's face. His eyes pled for forgiveness from the endless pain he'd inflicted over the years. His fingers fiddled faster with the bag's zipper. "I guess what I'm saying is that now I know how you feel whenever you see Eric cry and, well, it's shitty."

Somehow recognizing it as an apology, Kate closed her eyes, strangely touched. "Thank you," she said softly. "I'm very close to my father too so I know how it feels when someone you love needs help you don't know how to give."

"It's *shitty!*" Justin said loudly with an uneasy smile. The seriousness made him uncomfortable and he kept zipping the backpack.

Kate nodded and said, "It's like poetry rolling off your tongue."

Justin softened and said, "I've never known a life without Andy. He's been my boy since we were two and my parents always taught me that family and friends are the most important things in life—"

"Hmm, maybe they're *not* the monstrous morons I thought they were," Kate said sweetly.

Justin laughed. "Thanks for kicking my ass, too."

"Why, because even you can make bruises look good?" Her voice was light and upbeat.

"It woke me up," Justin said. His nervous zipping continued, gaining momentum. "And I meant to tell you that, you know, our fight in the parking lot and me hitting you—" The zipper tore open and shut, open and shut. "You know, I didn't mean to do it."

"I did!" Kate cheered. "But thank you."

The speedy zipping and unzipping annoyed Kate and against her better judgment, she reached out her hand and put it on Justin's shaky fingers to stop the nervous reaction. Immediately, she noticed something different. Over the years, Kate had hit Justin many times and enjoyed most of the slaps, but she had never casually touched him with an open hand. She knew his skin to be like ice. Perhaps she imagined it, like he needed a cold, clammy touch to match his icy, hollow heart. Not now.

With her hand gently on his knuckles, Kate found something different in the touch. There was a faint glow to Justin's hand, warm and tender. She remembered his skin rough, scaly, razor sharp. Now her fingertips slid over his flesh, finding it smooth and graceful. The unexpected comfort she found there frightened her, so much so that the uncertain fear superseded her curiosity. Once upon a time she would've clawed samples of his skin tissue under her nails.

So why was she admiring how lovely his skin tone accented her own?

Kate snatched her hand away.

Justin noticed her odd, questioning reaction and said, "Are you okay?"

Before Kate could respond, Principal Spear swaggered over to them, a chubby smile stuck to his face. "How's detention going, kids?" He asked, his condescending tone intending to pick a fight. He wanted a rise out of them, another reason to remind them they were waging a war with no chance of winning it.

Kate and Justin didn't react with their usual, disrespectful verbal bombs, though. Instead, they exchanged brief, cordial glances with each other and then with the principal.

"It's going good, Mr. Spear," Kate said, taking only a slightly longer look at Justin.

"Yeah," Justin agreed, indulging himself in Kate's gaze. "I think it's helping."

"Yeah...*maybe*," Kate added quietly.

And maybe Justin Drake wasn't such an asshole after all.

Chapter Twenty-Five

Eric knocked once on door 33 before turning the handle and walking inside. It took many visits to Andy's apartment before he felt comfortable walking in like he owned the place. Andy didn't mind and told Eric to treat the apartment like his own home. Still, Eric was polite and knocked each time. Besides, it tickled the butterflies in his stomach each time he walked toward door 33. The anticipation of knocking on it and walking into superstar Andy McCain's apartment was part of the fun.

The fluttering of the flies was in full force as Eric knocked and entered. The air was excited, vibrant, and almost colorful with a vibe so positive even the apartment walls beamed brighter than sunshine. The newfound bliss circling the surroundings even made the smelly cleats in the corner without shoelaces less intense. Ankle-biter Buddha was in full swing, barking loudly at Eric's arrival and scurrying over to get his fuzzy head scratched.

Andy stood near the large, still-cracked picture window, barefoot and wearing a tight tank top and jeans. His face once again gleamed with the dimpled cuteness and shimmering white smile that had reeled Eric in from the beginning. The smile made Eric's heart skip, as did the beefy biceps protruding from the shirt and the bubbly behind popping through the jeans.

Blushing, Eric's mouth curled into a smile so wide his cheeks ached. He covered the grin with his hand and giggled a little from embarrassment.

"I just got off the phone with Kate," Eric said. Telling insignificant, mindless stories always helped him cure his embarrassment in extremely awkward situations. "You'll never believe what just happened to her!"

There was no time to explain. The very instant Eric blushed, Andy strutted toward the door and the cute boy holding its handle. His hands grabbed Eric's waist and powerfully pulled him closer. Eric playfully screamed as Andy tightly embraced their bodies together and kissed him, passionately locking their lips and intertwining their tongues in a quick, hot, heated rush.

Eric gasped for air. "What's that for?" he asked, his ribs aching from laughter and shock.

Andy shrugged. "No reason," he said. His strong hands slowly crept under the bottom of Eric's T-shirt, caressing the smooth, soft bare skin of Eric's lower back. His fingers pressed deep into Eric's flesh and somehow managed to merge their waists even closer. Their faces locked within a few inches of each other, their noses lightly touching.

"Did Tara talk to you?" Eric asked, taking in Andy's warm, sweet breath.

Andy's dimples deepened. "She was very nice."

"You know, I thought she was a rampant super-bitch, but it turns out there's actually a heart under that flaming demon exterior," Eric said with a laugh. "She told me I'm a lucky guy because I'm dating you."

"Can't argue with that," Andy said, kissing Eric's forehead. "She said something about being pissed she'd never get to sleep with me, but if she had to lose me to a guy, it's cool that it's you. She was rambling so I didn't really get it all, but it was sweet."

"It's kind of like when a compliment comes out of Kate's mouth. You don't know if you can enjoy it because it's sincere—" Eric laughed before adding, "—or if she's just distracting you before she goes all Praying Mantis on your ass and eats your face."

Andy smiled brightly. He was happy, his eyes gleaming in the sunlight filtering through the wide-open apartment window. There were no more tightly drawn blinds to hide behind. The glass pane was still cracked from Eric's fit of textbook rage, but it served as a nice reminder of their difficult journey.

"How was gym today, by the way?" Eric asked.

Andy shrugged, but the simple gesture had a positive flow to it, like the question was welcomed. "Okay," Andy replied. "Some of the guys are still pissed at me, but a few of them are coming around, which is all I can ask for right now. Justin's really come around a lot, too. He's trying hard and it's nice having my best friend back. Remind me to thank Kate next time I see her. She really had an impact on him."

"I know!" Eric agreed, laughing loudly and making Andy jump. "She told me he apologized to her, well, not exactly in those words, but it's what he meant."

Andy's eyes widened. "He's never apologized for anything in his life."

"That's not the weirdest part," Eric added. "She says he looks at her different now."

"What do you mean?"

Eric calmed himself and said, "She says he looks at her the way you look at me."

Andy's eyes lowered with determination and he whispered, "I guess love's in the air."

The confession left Eric breathless. Inching toward Eric's open mouth, Andy kissed him again, softer. His tongue grazed Eric's lips with on the way in. Eric didn't fight it. He expected it with a dreamy, hot desire he couldn't control and hoped he never learned how.

"It's going to be a lot better," Andy said, leaning out of the kiss.

There was a confidence in Andy's voice that Eric hadn't heard in a while. Seeing Andy's head held high as he spoke made Eric realize how much he missed that confidence and really loved it. Eric could feel Andy's hands tremble against his skin but knew it wasn't from fear or anger, but joy jolting through his fingertips.

Andy added, "I just have that feeling, you know?"

"I think so too," Eric agreed. "But there's always going to be—"

"Don't say it," Andy interrupted. "I know there's always going to be people giving us shit and the fighting's never going to be over, but let's worry about that later. Right now I'm just glad you're here and you're mine."

An excited chill tickled Eric's body, decorating his skin with goose bumps that Andy read like brail with his strong hands. Andy licked his hungry lips and nibbled on Eric's neck, gently using his teeth on his way to Eric's silky earlobe. His hands caressed their way down Eric's back, teasing past the waist of Eric's jeans and into the elastic band of his underwear. He playfully tickled the very top of Eric's behind, but respectfully went no further.

Backing away to breathe, Andy said, "I was wrong, you know?"

"About what?" Eric asked, yearning for more kissing

"Playing ball isn't going to make me who I am," Andy whispered. "You are."

Not a single sound came out of Eric's gapping mouth.

"You're going to define me," Andy said. "Baseball's just going to be an awesome extra."

Panting and trying to catch his breath, Eric quietly said, "You know what?"

"What?" Andy asked.

"I think you just hit another home run."

Andy's dimples gave way to his pearly whites and he playfully added, "Who's using the lame-ass lines now, babe?"

"Shut up!" Eric snapped, mortified with embarrassment.

"Hey, wait a minute," Andy said and leaned back, his eyes narrow. "You're not going to make me take you to the prom, are you?"

Eric laughed loudly at first. The very idea was just so outrageous, but when he thought a moment longer, his eyes lit up and twinkled brightly, full of thought.

Epilogue

Three weeks before graduation, on May 10, 1997, Eric Anderson and Andy McCain caused yet another stir within the walls of Ann Arbor South: they took each other to the senior prom. They had only a minor fight with Principal Spear before the prom committee approved their registration as a same-sex couple. Eric had another "You're failing to protect me and now you're discriminating against me" talk with Spear. Not until Eric threatened to go to the local newspaper did the principal's attitude change dramatically.

Plus, Spear softened by the end of the school year since the school was once again an athletic champion. Andy stayed strong in his own skin during the spring of 1997 and played his heart out for the Ann Arbor South Tigers. It was his best baseball season ever, due largely in part to his positive attitude. He channeled any lingering tension between himself and his teammate friends into breaking the state-held high school home-run record. Andy was alive and no one could steal his thunder. He won the championship for the school, thus making Principal Spear much easier to please come prom time.

The night of the party, Andy and Eric looked absolutely dashing in their black tuxedoes. Eric's blood-red bowtie and cumber bun complimented the sleek all-black style to Andy's penguin suit, making for a very striking couple. Andy spent a week's worth of tips from The

Crow's Nest and even his first two lawn mowing jobs of the spring season on a limousine and dinner at Eric's favorite Italian restaurant for a pre-prom celebration.

Perhaps the most interesting thing about prom night was how uneventful and drama-free it actually was. Eric had bravely confessed his feelings for the Ann Arbor South superstar to his parents by prom time and they were expectantly supportive. His mother even had the boys over to the house to take pictures in her pretty spring flower garden prior to the event. It was awkward for Andy to be accepted unconditionally by parental figures, but Eric held his hand through the painless photos and pinched cheeks.

The actual event itself ran relatively smooth. There were still angry homophobes against Eric and Andy arriving together and a few Jesus freaks spewed bible verses their way, but by then most of Andy's numbskull friends had come around and re-embraced their buddy and helped him ward off any protesters. So Andy spent most of the evening ignoring the anti-Andys and anti-Erics and danced like a supreme fool with Justin Drake, Jeremy Flint, and the others. Only a few refused to rekindle any friendship. Wes Palmer and Matt Murphy led the small group of haters. By then, though, Andy had become so comfortable with himself that it made no difference. Winning the last baseball championship of their high school careers helped reestablish Andy's macho man credibility among the guys too. Whatever the reason, if Wes and any of the others wouldn't come around, Andy couldn't force it and didn't want to. He only wanted to surround himself with people who made him flourish.

As Andy and his reunited cohorts enjoyed the night, Eric Anderson couldn't have imagined his senior prom without his best friend by his side. Kate Crawford was breathtaking. Her low-cut, backless red dress turned heads and dropped jaws throughout the Ann Arbor South gymnasium, which was converted to mirror the glamorous and gothic underworld of *The Phantom of the Opera*.

Their third Musketeer, Nick Murphy, also joined Eric and Kate at the party. Nick arrived stag and dressed in an all-white tuxedo with a deep green tie. They looked amazing and had three rolls of film taken to prove it as they spent most of the night sitting at a reserved table, drinking secretly spiked punch courtesy of Justin Drake's flask, and giggling not-so-quietly about the tragic fashion mishaps of their peers. Eric, Kate and Nick had considerable laughs at the expense of Andy and the other dancing clowns. There was only so much chicken dancing and Michael Jackson impressions they could take before spiked punch came spraying from their mouths.

As prom came to a close, Andy McCain separated from his buddies and took Eric's eager hand and proudly led his date to the dance floor. Andy specially requested *You Are So Beautiful* from the DJ. It was their last dance together as high school seniors and their first as *boyfriends*. Seeing the two young men hand in hand made many of their classmates snicker and point fingers, but Eric and Andy were oblivious to anything other than their own eyes. During the dance, in Andy McCain's arms, Eric had never felt so special, important, and wanted.

Joining them on the dance floor was a unique new couple and the reluctant underdog winners of the Prom King and Queen titles: Justin Drake and Kate Crawford. The victory no doubt came as a thankful joke from their peers for the scandalous butt-kicking drama they had entertained the school with throughout the year.

It was a night of celebration and goodbyes; one last hurrah before everyone parted ways for college and beyond. Kate was off to fashion design school in New York City. Andy and Justin had their sports scholarships locked into State and their request to share a dorm room was promptly approved. It would be a temporary location, though, since they both planned to pledge the same fraternity as soon as possible.

Although Eric did not envy Nick's cross-country journey to stuffy law school in southern California, he very much wanted to follow Kate to New York to pursue his photography as they had planned since kindergarten. In the end, though, Eric traded Manhattan for Michigan and decided to attend State with Andy. Kate bitched, of course, but understood and ultimately accepted his choice. Plus, State had a design program she could fall back on if New York proved too small to contain her.

***

Graduation commenced on May 30, 1997, Eric's eighteenth birthday. They were all there, sharing the day together. Kate switched seats with Cathy Anders just so she could sit next to Eric during the ceremony. They held hands and actually shed a few tears. Eric's tears were loaded with relief. Just the thought of spreading his wings the second the ceremony was over made his smile ache. It also helped getting through the drawn-out ceremony easier because just a quick glance over their shoulders, they could clearly see Andy and Justin. Kate wouldn't admit it just yet, but it was nice having Justin Drake in her sight and, of course, Eric couldn't take his eyes off the McCain boy.

After everything Andy went through over the course of his senior year—leaving the football team, confessing his love for Eric, the vicious way word spread around town, the fistfights—there were two very special unexpected guests at the graduation ceremony in his honor: his parents. They weren't ready for an introduction to Eric, but they went to support their son on his special day. Andy was touched by their appearance, yet cautious and unsure of a future with them. Still, it made the day promising and complete.

***

On the night of graduation, after all the pictures and parties, Andy took Eric back to his apartment. Walking into the stillness of the tiny home, with Buddha snoring lightly on the mattress, their ears were ringing. They had been non-stop for days with final exams, celebrating and saying goodbyes that their minds weren't ready to sit on a sofa in pure, uninterrupted silence. After a few moments, they adjusted nicely and the ringing subsided. They left the lights off, too. It was calmer and more relaxing to be out of the light.

"I can't believe it's over," Andy said. His deep voice broke the silent air and startled Eric. They laughed and Eric dropped his jacket over the back of the couch.

"Thank god!" Eric said. "I never thought this day would come."

"Oh, come on, this year wasn't so bad," Andy said, playfully pinching Eric's shoulder.

"Well, I guess," Eric teased. "I did meet this great guy."

Andy played along. "Anyone I know?"

"No. Just some random man-whore—"

"Thanks a lot!" Andy faked anger. "But wouldn't I have to put out to be a man-whore?"

Eric nodded. "You're right, you'd have to be a lot sluttier."

Through the darkness of the apartment, Andy took Eric's hand and led him to the front of the sofa. They laid together, their arms and legs intertwining in a beautifully cuddled mess. Andy's hand crept up the back of Eric's shirt and caressed Eric's soft flesh. Andy knew it drove Eric wild. As his heart rate increased, Eric twirled his right index finger through Andy's short hair. Andy loved Eric's touch and it relaxed him. Eric knew it well and gently played with Andy's right earlobe and cheek with his hand.

"It was all worth it," Andy whispered. "All the bullshit we went through to be together was worth it. I just want you to know that."

"I know," Eric said softly. "I don't regret anything either. Everything happens for a reason and that's why we're here right now, together, because we're supposed to be."

Andy glanced across the room at the VCR buried beneath the television. The white clock blinked with the time. 11:56. It was not yet midnight and a smile came to Andy's face.

"Since it's still technically your birthday and you should get everything you want," he said. "I was thinking...maybe...you'd want to make me sluttier." Andy blushed at the not-so-cryptic come-on and his smile was so wide he had to turn his embarrassed face away.

Eric gently tugged on Andy's ears to redirect his gaze back around. Moonlight filtered through the open blinds of the living room window and gave just enough light to showcase Andy's handsome face. Andy stared long and saw a strong determination in Eric's eyes.

In a soft, anxious hush, Eric added, "I'd love to," and kissed him.

Printed in the United States
49818LVS00003B/307-396

9 781424 112692